From Far, Far Away . . .

A yellow-eyed silhouette approached from a pinpoint of darkness. The entity hovered off to one side as Chayn continued walking.

"Do you have a name?" Chayn asked.

"Ki," it said.

"Who are you?"

"We are the ancient ones," Ki began. "You are a young species, but possessing the ability to create tools. We have not your manual dexterity, nor your mobility.

"Instead, we built machines to do for us, and we endowed them with intelligence to function independently. But the machines began to think for themselves—and to believe themselves superior to their creators.

"Thus we left our Home Worlds and resided upon the worlds of another galaxy. Our machines discovered their error and came after us, unable to function alone. That is our story. Lorb is such a machine. Lorb stole our souls—twenty million of us—and murdered our bodies. We live within Lorb."

TIMEQUEST #2:

HYDRABYSS
RED

William G. Tedford

LEISURE BOOKS ∞ **NEW YORK CITY**

A LEISURE BOOK

Published by

Nordon Publications, Inc.
Two Park Avenue
New York, N.Y. 10016

Prologue

"Chayn?"

Villimy Dy could feel his presence, but she could not find his focus of consciousness, his ego, the part of him she knew as human.

"Chayn Jahil, where are you!"

From hyperlight velocities, Villimy brought the starcraft to a halt. A starbow of light exploded about the circumference of the vehicle. Stars spread from the ultraviolet ahead and from the infrared behind and took their places in the void, bands and filaments and clouds of stars set against rolling thunderheads of black nebula.

There were hundreds of suns within range of her augmented senses, solitary suns and binary suns, suns with planetary systems and suns that would die barren and alone. A lost asteroid tumbled nearby, a sheared facet of quartz reflecting starlight and catching Villimy's attention from a mere hundred million kilometers away. Grains of dust, atoms of hydrogen and rays of weak radiation swarmed along the magnetic fields of the galaxy.

Alone, Villimy Dy grew frightened.

She spread her mind field outward, a growing desperation countering her fear of dissolution. On distant worlds, she sensed life—an ocean swarming with creatures of all sizes, bacteria thriving in the dense methane and ammonia atmosphere of the moon of a gas giant. Finally, she sensed the intense, bright aura of intelligence, a single focus of consciousness. She rushed to it, congealed and converged on it.

She saw Chayn Jahil, a translucent image, standing on a ledge overlooking a volcanic plain spread below him. It churned in smoldering, angry crimson beneath skies of dense brown and yellow. Tendrils of metallic green danced on the horizon, a storm of ionization giving birth to short-lived chemical reactions in the dense atmosphere.

"Chayn, it's so somber and lifeless!" Villimy pleaded in a despair of her own.

The barren world, its guts torn and heaving in gravitational friction, circled close to a cinder of a star. The world's skies were fire, its landscape sulfur. Someday soon, in another million years or so, the world would plunge into the dense fires of the star and its unfelt suffering would be ended.

"Chayn?"

He looked around at her, the image of her in his mind appearing to him as he knew her in flesh. She nudged against him and Chayn slipped an arm about her shoulders.

"Why do you feel like this?" Villimy said.

"I guess it does reflect my mood. But it's a strange beauty, isn't it? It's like a timeless form of death. Nothing has ever lived in this place."

"Chayn, come back. I've stopped the starcraft. I don't understand what's bothering you."

Chayn smiled. "I can't be left behind. I can reach ahead and focus somewhere, but the starcraft just pulls me along when I reach the outer limits of its fields. I just wanted to be alone to think for a while."

"Think about what, Chayn?"

"About not being human anymore."

6

"We've been through that before! You haven't changed!"

"Villimy, the human mind and the human body go together. How can you separate them? If the pattern and the consciousness of me still exists, what will keep me from changing into something else? If I can't die, what will become of me in a century or a millennia or an eon from now?"

Villimy Dy tried to pull Chayn away from the nightmarish landscape with nothing more than the strength of her will. He yielded slowly and together they left the world of boiling rock and its bloated, blood-red sun. But Chayn's mood turned even the bright starfields into an eternal and silent night. Even within the beauty of the universe Villimy had no respite from Chayn's deepening melancholy.

The starcraft hung motionless in the void, an ovaloid of blackness silhouetted against the stars. When Chayn hesitated, Villimy followed his gaze. Inside the starcraft, within the body contour of the crypt set on the low dais, lay the slender, nude body that belonged to her. Villimy saw herself through Chayn's mind, a strange woman of pale, bluish skin and a crown of white down for hair, not human, but evolved from what had once been human. And only one body slept within the hull field of the starcraft, its mind free to roam the stars interfaced with the artificial intelligence of the alien craft. Chayn Jahil somehow lived within the starcraft as well, his mind and another entity that observed through a window of his psyche. Chayn thought of it as the Watcher. Perhaps the entity was a stargod, one of the beings that had provided him with the starcraft and sent the two of them on this unknown quest.

Chayn Jahil could no longer pick out Star Rashanyn among the starfields of Andromeda. They had left the gold star thousands of light years behind them. But anywhere within Andromeda he could look outward into intergalactic space and see a fuzzy patch of light—the Galaxy of Man. Villimy's people had migrated from that galaxy during an unknown, fearful invasion by a life form that had sent countless starships fleeing across the dreaded, intergalactic void. Chayn also had his origin in the Galaxy of Man, although a deep-seated amnesia still blocked his identity and past and how he had come to acquire the faster-than-light starcraft.

During the early hours of his arrival within the spiral arms of Andromeda, moving compulsively toward an awareness of a human people living in the planetary system of a gold star, Chayn had stumbled across a deteriorating derelict, its colonists awakening one by one over centuries of time from suspended animation as its life support systems failed. Villimy had slept aboard that dying starship for tens of thousands of years, long enough for her people to have received a recall to the Galaxy of Man. Chayn had rescued the one survivor he had found aboard the lost starship. After their stay in the Empire of Star Rashanyn, Chayn had returned Villimy Dy to her home world only to find her people gone, leaving her, like himself, an orphan of time and space.

The human race had colonized Andromeda, but it had taken the colonists millions of years in frozen, lifeless sleep to reach the nearby galaxy. Over those millions of years, original Man had evolved to the status of the stargods. The human species still lived here and there, scattered civilizations, puny or mighty, among the alien stars of Andromeda. The Rashanyn Empire had been one such civilization, men and women who had colonized the rich, but uninhabitable worlds of Star Rashanyn. Chayn and Villimy had arrived during a period of their history ridden with the strife and stress of an unsolvable conflict with a nearby, alien civilization living among the wreckage orbiting a nearby black hole. Chayn no longer doubted that the stargods had deliberately sent him to that human outpost to salvage a culture that would also eventually return to the Galaxy of Man.

Oddly enough, he hadn't entirely survived that experience. A planet-orbiting colony of fifty million people had died in the core of a thermonuclear fireball. Chayn had been in the city at the time, his mind interfaced with the starcraft through a primary interface with a computer system and a microwave relay. He had tried to use the transdimensional senses of the alien craft to save the city from a fate that had

8

no longer threatened the Empire. Somehow, only the physical half of himself had died.

"All right," Villimy said, knuckling down to the crisis at hand. "What do you think will happen to you? Why is it so important to be human by such a limited definition? I am not human by your standards! Others must have evolved beyond any semblance of humanity as you once knew it! Chayn, we evolve even when we are physical! It takes longer, but if you change, so what? Will you be worse off for it?"

"I can't make love to you anymore," Chayn said, saddened by the utter selfishness of his despair. "I can't feel you anymore."

Villimy quickly reached out and touched him, but Chayn still told the literal truth. Only their minds provided the sensory illusion of physical existence. They had tried, but sex lacked the intensity of real contact. But Villimy touched him to emphasize that they could, at least, verify their individual, personal reality. Awake in her physical body, Chayn did not exist for Villimy Dy except as an unseen, intangible intelligence. But interfaced through the starcraft just as Chayn had piloted it alone upon his arrival to Andromeda, they could be together and at least share an illusion of physical existence.

"We can't lie to one another like this," Villimy said. "If I couldn't live with you like this, you'd know! Chayn, I think you're just frightened. I'd be frightened too, but it's not so important to be who we think we are. We all change during the course of life. It's continuity that counts.

"Chayn, when you live with death, your goals in life can't lie too far in the future. They have to fall within the amount of time you have to work in and the resources you have to work with. But look at you! You have all of time to work within! Chayn, we live in the shadow of the star-gods!"

Chayn looked at Villimy, seeing in his mind's eye her face, the sheen of her poreless skin and her huge, golden eyes. Her white down curled about her head like a halo. He smiled, all but unable to bear the intensity of his love for her. Without Villimy Dy, he would never have survived.

"We have time and we have power," Chayn said. "What are we going to be doing with it?"

The nearby red dwarf glowed like a burning ruby. A cold chill of premonition ran through Villimy. "I think I know what's happening, Chayn. Remember how you knew about the gold star before you found Star Rashanyn? It's happening again, but you're fighting it. You know where we're going. You took me to the edge of the galaxy and told me we wouldn't be going back until we searched for other human civilizations that needed help to survive. Do we have any other purpose in life right now?"

Chayn looked to the brightly glowing core of the galaxy. It took a billion stars to make up that landscape of light. "I have too much time to think. I don't remember where I came from. I can't think about the past. Thinking about the future, I see nothing but the unknown. Even if there are people out there, they're not like us."

"You and I are different," Villimy said. "But all we have is each other."

Chayn felt sudden guilt. He had been wallowing in self-pity and hadn't really considered Villimy's plight. Villimy had paired with him and for her species, pairing was a biological necessity. She could not live without him—literally. It hadn't been a burden knowing this, but had, in fact, been his own security—knowing she would not leave him for as long as she lived. Her needs were biological. His were psychological, but just as powerful. Alone with the cold, emotionless Watcher couched so firmly within his thoughts, he'd not be able to function.

"Then we're not just wandering around haphazardly," Chayn said. "We have a destination we don't know about yet."

"And we're getting close. That's what's been upsetting you. I can feel it myself."

"But we're not being forced to go anywhere," Chayn said. "It has to be of our own free will."

"All right," Villimy said. "Let's consider alternatives. Do any exist?"

Chayn looked at her, surprised. Her acute intellect could outmaneuver his confused emotions, but he remembered something on his own that answered his own inner need. The Rashanyn Empire had been dying, stagnating because of a bleak future threatened by the Blackstar Aliens, natives of Andromeda who had laid claim to golden Star Rashanyn long before the human colony had arrived. Their every goal in life had been overshadowed by the promise of destruction. They had learned that life itself is a challenge, always a move forward into the unknown. Depression and eventual death were the only alternatives to life.

Chayn resumed command of the starcraft. He sent the craft surging forward, the starbow exploding around them and snapping back to the transdimensional view of space as they shot through clouds of stars at multiples of the speed of light.

Chayn made no commitments, but if they were both willing to look at whatever the stargods had in store for them, they could move into the unknown a single step at a time despite the foreboding he experienced. Even before he had found Villimy Dy and reached Star Rashanon, he had learned that there are no real alternatives to life and its challenges—not even death.

Chayn smiled when Villimy Dy breathed a sigh of relief from somewhere nearby.

One

Dim, tiny, red suns. Ancient beyond belief. Embers still glowing from the beginnings of the universe.

"Chayn, where are you going?"

The dense core of the galaxy lay tens of thousands of light years beneath them, a pearlescent glare and frozen sparkling of light interlaced with dark tracings of nebula circling its outer perimeter. Chayn sensed a black hole at the center, a small one as yet, but a viciously spinning whirlpool of nothingness with an event horizon large enough to engulf and tear entire suns into flaming filaments of destruction. Someday, when the black hole grew larger, wavefronts of radiation would irradiate the inhabited worlds orbiting suns close to the core. Beyond stretched the curved arms of the galaxies. They formed a plane of stars with a horizon of light so distant, the human mind could not gaze upon it without discomfort.

"Chayn, is something wrong?"

For some reason he was having trouble focusing his attention on matters at hand. He had absentmindedly climbed far above the galactic ecliptic. "Beautiful, isn't it?" he said.

"Awesome. Frightening. Where are we going?"

Chayn looked around at the nearly invisible scattering of halo stars, the dwarf red suns surrounding the core of the galaxy. "Looks like we keep running across little red suns," he commented.

"You've slowed down."

Indeed, he had slowed considerably. Around them at intervals of hundreds of light years, the red stars drifted past.

"There are no planetary systems around those suns," Villimy said. "They are so old."

"They're first-generation stars," Chayn said. "What these stars lack in size and brightness, they make up for in longevity. It was the larger, first-generation stars in the galaxy that exploded and gave birth to second-generation suns and the elements that formed the planets."

"No refugee colonies would have stopped out here, Chayn. They would have gone on into the galaxy itself. There's nothing out here to support a colony."

Chayn came to a complete stop. The starbow exploded as they dropped beneath the speed of light, the stars distorting back to their normal perspectives after a moment. Chayn looked around at the silent beauty. His senses

12

reached out four hundred light years in every direction. He felt like a bright core of consciousness in the void, Villimy Dy only a voice and a presence in his mind.

"Are you looking for something?" Villimy said.

Something very small and cold floated in the void at the extreme edge of his perception. Chayn moved forward, but it would have taken centuries to reach the infinitesimal bit of debris at sublight velocities. The starbow flashed twice more, once in exceeding the natural speed limit of the universe and once dropping back beneath it.

"What is it?" Chayn asked Villimy.

The starcraft rushed forward and stopped. The artifact was a sober find in a part of space where nothing could live.

"It's a sunsail!" Villimy burst out excitedly.

Thin cables connected thousands of square kilometers of partially collapsed, plastic film to a small cylinder with rounded ends. Inside the cabin, Chayn sensed something that had once lived. He focused on the occupant of the primitive vehicle.

"Is it human?" Villimy asked.

They drew close and observed in silence.

The creature preserved in the vacuum and absolute zero of space might have died just minutes ago. Chayn could discern individual cells within the ice body of the creature. It possessed a human skeletal structure and a familiar placement of internal organs. Alive, the entity would have stood three quarters of Villimy's height, just less than half his own. But the brain in the slightly oversized skull spoke of evolutionary pressures toward a considerable intelligence.

"It might have been drifting for millions of years," Villimy said. "It probably came from within Andromeda itself."

"No," Chayn said. "It's still traveling almost parallel to the galactic plane. It's only been drifting for a few thousand years. It had to have come from one of the nearby halo stars."

"Chayn, how could they live out here?"

"Pay closer attention to the engineering and technology.

13

There are two obvious clues."

Villimy knew sunsails better than Chayn, but she was second to catch the size of the sail, its vast canopy designed to catch the weaker light of the local red dwarfs. Paying closer attention to the cabin, she sensed only film coatings of metal within a sophisticated electronic computer.

"I said it myself," Villimy conceded. "There are no resources out here. That's a high level technology plastic they're using. It looks to have an organic origin."

Chayn looked back along the trajectory of the primitive craft, trying to decide which of the three or four suns from which it could have originated it had come. On intuitive impulse, Villimy searched for more of the sunsails.

"Chayn! Look!"

Just a few millions of kilometers away, another sunsail crawled through the void. And still others further away. In that incredible expanse of the void, they were microscopic, discrete particles of matter. There were fifty of them. Fifty light years away another group of fifty moved in a single file that weaved and rippled through the distance.

The trail led unerringly to the nearest red dwarf only a few light years away. They were evidence of a ritualized suicide that had been going on for thousands of years. They could have no conceivable destination. They were only planetary craft designed to move and maneuver close to a dim red star. They had no provisions for suspended animation, a technique well within technological range of the species. The pilots had died of asphyxiation.

Chayn took the starcraft just above light speed toward the red dwarf plying its slow, eternal course alone and isolated. Chayn slowed the craft after a moment. He was having trouble probing the system. His senses were deflected and distorted by a strange influence in the area.

"What's wrong?" Villimy asked.

"Do you feel something?"

"Feel what?"

Chayn had to clear his mind again in order to concentrate. On the peripheral edges of his consciousness, he felt sensations and saw images like a vague and distant dream.

They distracted him, the source of his absentmindedness for the past few minutes. Frightened by the haunting quality of the phenomenon, he moved off at a right angle and began a long, slow orbit of the star that would have taken thousands of years to complete.

"Chayn?"

"Villimy, if we approach any closer, we're liable to regret the decision. There's something odd happening there. I can feel it."

"There are people there, Chayn! There must be! This has been our destination ever since we left Rashanyn!"

"There's also an alien presence, Villimy. A powerful form of consciousness that can't be remotely human."

Villimy closed off her senses and quieted her thoughts. She searched the void for feelings of life. She felt a strange and vague presence, but nothing she could define. Interfaced with the starcraft to a much greater depth than she, Chayn was more perceptive, more sensitive to his environment.

She opened her eyes. "Something's blocking us."

"It most certainly is."

"Chayn, those creatures in the sunsails were human. Something terrible is happening to cause such monstrous behavior. We have to find out what's happening."

But they couldn't just go stumbling blindly into danger of that magnitude. Chayn turned to the depths of his own psyche, imploring the Watcher to aid him. He had no physical body to be injured, but the danger was all the more frightening because it threatened the part of him he had always thought to be inviolate—his consciousness and his sense of identity.

The Watcher did not respond.

Chayn moved closer to the red dwarf until he felt the psychic intrusion grow more intense and specific. He stopped his approach at a distance of a few light minutes and continued moving at a right angle. He caught visual glimpses of detailed scenes and even tactile, sensory impressions—the dome of a blue sky, the warmth of a yellow sun on naked flesh and the caress of a cool breeze on his face.

15

The vivid sensory impressions were all the more alluring because of the intense memories they ignited of an amnesic past. Were the hallucinations imposed upon him or dredged from his own repressed psyche?

Despite the mundane nature of the hallucinations, his fears intensified rather than diminished. He risked entering a realm of enchantment as deadly as the web of the mind-spiders littering the void between the arms of Andromeda.

Villimy tried to maintain a rapport with Chayn's surface thoughts. A psychic fog drifted like tendrils of an opaque mist between the two of them.

"Chayn?"

"I don't know what it is," Chayn said, even the sound of his voice receding and echoing. "If I get caught up in that, I'll be helpless. It's so intense, I forget who I am and where I'm at."

"What is it like, Chayn?"

"It's unbelievably beautiful. I think it's a trap."

"Chayn, we have to find the human colony. I think I see a small satellite orbiting the star. They must be there."

Chayn shifted his focus away from the hallucination with difficulty. A small planetary body did circle close to the red dwarf. Chayn sensed life. He sensed an ocean, an abyss of water.

"We were guided here just like we were guided to Rashanyn," Chayn said. "But it's worse. Much worse. Rashanyn was child's play in comparison to this."

"What do we do?"

"The consciousness is alien, but the content is familiar," Chayn said. "It's an image of an Earthlike world with a yellow sun. There must be two counterparts to the life living near that star. There's a human colony and an alien intelligence. The illusions feel like a trap. It's meant to snare a human mind, but the trap isn't for us."

Villimy buckled down to the challenge. "How do we handle this?"

"We don't have much choice. We approach and see how intense the hallucination becomes. If I get lost in it, it's up to you to take the starcraft back until the rapport is broken."

"What happens if something goes wrong?"

"You've got to be kidding," Chayn said with a chuckle. "Something is bound to go wrong. I can't get the Watcher to give me an idea of what's happening here, but I assume we're capable of handling the situation. Chances are, the alien intelligence is less than an even match for me and what I have backing me up. If something unexpected happens, you assume that I can handle myself. If we loose contact, it's up to you to investigate the human colony. Learn as much about them as you can. It looks like we're playing it by ear again, Villimy."

"I don't know what that means," Villimy said, her voice tight with all the resistance she managed to gather together. "It sounds like a perversion."

Chayn located a nearby, lone sunsail spiraling out from the red dwarf to join the wandering trail of derelicts threading their way through the halo stars. The sails still billowed full in the crimson starlight. The human pilot had died many decades in the past. Chayn let Villimy view the utter beauty and sophistication of these strange people and their technology.

"If they're in trouble," Chayn said, "they don't deserve this. They are or were human. If you're afraid, so am I. But let's get our feet wet and see what happens."

"Of course," Villimy said. "I have faith in us."

Chayn moved down toward the crimson sun. The tiny star became a discernible disk in the blackness, but not so bright that the naked human eye couldn't have stared into its feeble glow without damage. Chayn felt the hallucination intensify, knowing instinctively that the beauty hid a new kind of danger. But the beauty was inescapable and the sensation of once again possessing a physical body irresistible.

For an instant, Chayn felt solid ground beneath his feet. He jerked back to alertness and the reality became hallucination again. Then he looked up into the yellow sun in the blue sky and felt warmth on his face.

Villimy felt Chayn's presence still with her, but his focus of consciousness slipped away into an elsewhere that had nothing to do with time and space.

"Chayn?"

She reached out and searched for him in the way she had when she had found him on the volcanic world orbiting the red dwarf many tens of thousands of light years behind them. But she could not find him this time, not within the furthest circumference of the reach of the starcraft's fields of perception. Chayn had left the only level of reality to which she had access.

The starcraft stopped of its own accord, no longer under control of conscious intent. Villimy took over, moving the craft away from the crimson star. She pushed for velocity. The starcraft resisted. She moved to within a fraction less than the speed of light, but the feeling of mass and inertia built to intolerable levels. No amount of effort on her part could bring the starbow crashing around the ship.

Villimy stopped. It would take a century to move a hundred light years away at near light speed. The time distortion of such a velocity would make the journey subjectively shorter, but the greater intelligence of the Watcher had made its intent known. Villimy turned back toward the small planetary body orbiting the red dwarf.

She approached closer to the bloated, angry globe of fire than would have been safe limits for a star of normal intensity and size—within a few hundred thousand miles. But this star wasn't much larger than Jasper, the gas giant of the Rashanon system, little more than planetary size. The small moon circled the ancient, cool sun in days rather than years.

Villimy orbited the red dwarf once, than headed for the satellite, a ruddy, barren moon no more than two thousand kilometers in diameter. She puzzled over the moon silhouetted against the bright light of Andromeda spread across the black skies. The dark side of the moon looked solid, but the sunward side glistened in blood-red light and occasionally reflected a bright glare of ruby light. The sunward side swirled in a dense, pink mist.

Villimy descended upon the airless world and learned its secret. The sunward side was an ocean churning in waves

18

tens of meters high in the light gravity, its surface literally boiling in the vacuum. She probed the depth of the moon and found only water. The dark side of the body was a shell of ice a hundred kilometers thick. Approaching the twilight zone between the dark and the lighted side of the moon, the ice crust thinned and gave way to the shores of the ice-mist shrouded ocean.

The satellite had no solid core. The moon was a melted snowball, a water world in the most literal sense. The life Villimy sensed lived beneath the protective cover of water. The colony of men who inhabited this strange world lived within the depths of a low density sea of gigantic proportions.

The scene both delighted and frightened Villimy. The satellite could not have been native to this star. It had to have been a renegade planetary body somehow thrown into intergalactic space from Andromeda and captured by this halo star. Its orbit was eccentric, but not eccentric enough to either freeze the open waters or boil it to steam. Still, the sea boiled furiously in the vacuum. The entire moon circled in a wake of its own ice mist slowly spiraling outward into space, driven by the same weak solar wind that moved the sunsail vehicles that she and Chayn had encountered.

One task remained before fully concentrating on the life forms living beneath the waters of the ocean. She sensed a second body in the system of the crimson star, the source of the psychic interference that blocked her senses so effectively. Hidden behind the star, Villimy moved away from the moon to put it into view.

It was a starship. It orbited the red sun only ten million kilometers out. Despite her blurred senses, she could estimate its dimensions and feel its mass. It stretched one hundred kilometers in length. And it was quite alien to anything she had ever seen. It was primitive, a ship of metal, but it housed something alive and alien and defied even the power of the starcraft to some degree.

She had no idea what had happened to Chayn Jahil, but she was powerless to help him. The alien starship belonged

19

to him. The moon belonged to her. The answers to the tragedy of this human colony lay hidden beneath the boiling waters of the satellite.

Villimy began searching for a means of entrance.

Two

The starcraft hovered over a landscape of broken shelves of ice protruding at odd angles along the unstable twilight zone of the moon. Villimy Dy set down on a smooth area and broke interface with the starcraft.

She opened her eyes to a smaller reality limited to her physical senses. She rose from the body contour of the crypt, swung her bare legs over the side and stepped from the dais to the resilient hull-field deck. Awake in her physical body she had nothing to work with other than the Rashanyn pressure suit and helmet lying on the deck. For the time being, it would be enough.

She donned the suit and checked the air supply before leaving. Standing before the outline of the airlock, she put her hands through the intangible area of the hull-field and held onto the edges. She stuck her head outside. The landscape appeared to be tilted at a forty-five degree angle. The starcraft had its own gravitational field, its own up and down. She climbed outside, seemingly emerging from a solid-looking hull. Dropping to the crusty surface, she raised a cloud of slow-moving, powdery-fine snow. She moved a few meters away from the dark ovaloid of the starcraft and turned to survey her environment.

Toward the night side of the moon, the spiral arms of Andromeda slanted from the horizon at a sharp angle, a pattern made up of stars glowing like dense, luminous dust. Opposite Andromeda, the crimson star crouched suspended on the horizon, a dome of slowly churning surface disturbances. A thick fog hugged the horizon in a band of brilliant pink.

Utter silence dominated the scene. Villimy shuffled through millimeters of powdered ice crystals, moving in slow, exaggerated steps in the low gravity toward the nearby shore.

Climbing a final shelf of ice embedded at a shallow angle into the frozen surface, Villimy stood silhouetted against the eternal sunrise. She looked out over a frothing, deathly silent and mist-shrouded ocean. Where the ice mist parted, water shown forth like blood, thick and opaque and slow-moving. Villimy studied the foreboding, depressing beauty of the barren, dying world, knowing for certain that the moon couldn't have been orbiting the star for more than a few tens of thousands of years. Eventually, the red star would be ringed with a dissipating ice mist and the moon would be gone, literally evaporated.

An inexplicable formation of pinkish, bright stars moved overhead. They rose from the horizon from alongside the dome of the sun and slowly climbed into the black sky. She watched with rapt attention. They were a sunsail fleet slowly approaching the surface of the ocean. She had missed something during her inspection of the space surrounding the red star, perhaps an orbiting space station. The alien interference in the system had all but blinded the omniscient senses of the starcraft.

The sunsails descended, moving directly toward her. She could not see the cabins hanging many kilometers below the full-blown sails. The canopies themselves were hundreds of kilometers across and slowly beginning to fill the skies with a translucent, shimmering light.

Suddenly, the entire formation converged. The sails slowly collided with one another, collapsing in shimmering curtains of pearl and crimson light. She could only deduce that the cabins had already touched down upon the surface of the water, the canopies permanently jettisoned. They contorted and folded and passed overhead, still driven by the pressure of the solar wind. Villimy watched their passage until they arced around the night side of the moon and vanished into its shadow. But even then she caught an occasional glimmer of light reflected from Andromeda lighting up the night sky.

Villimy walked back to the starcraft. She climbed aboard, disrobed and lay back down in the body crypt. The freedom of the stars sprang around her, a vastness inconceivable to her body senses. But even so, her interface would never be as deep as Chayn's. She could barely sense the life within the sunsail cabins that had dropped into the ocean. They were moving, self-powered, converging into a tight formation and descending into the depths of the water world.

The starcraft rose from the surface of the airless world. Villimy searched for more of the sunsails. She saw one other group approaching and followed their trajectory back to verify her suspicion, a small space station orbiting a few thousand kilometers above the moon.

Ignoring the space station for the time being, she selected one of the sunsails and moved to within meters of a cabin not much smaller than the starcraft itself. She sensed the near panic of the pilot of the vehicle and a furious communication taking place between members of the small fleet. The slender laser beams were hard to discern. Chayn would have known how to break into those modulated beams of light to communicate with the pilots. But she could not and following the sunsails down to the surface of the ocean would be her only means of entrance into the inhabited realms of the moon, even if it meant abandoning the starcraft to its own resources. Chayn had already warned her that it would not enter atmosphere. She took for granted that it would not enter the realm of water.

Her pressure suit contained only two hours of air, enough, she hoped, for the human colony to rescue her. But two hours of air wasn't sufficient to explore the apparently lifeless alien starship. These people would know about the alien intelligence. They would know of the hallucination that had lured Chayn to an unknown fate. They could explain the suicidal trail of sunsails driven into intergalactic space by the feeble pressure of their dim, nearly useless

22

sun. Her search for answers would have to begin with these people.

She followed the sunsail down. It moved slowly, tacking at an angle across the solar wind, the moon swelling into view below. Villimy carefully worked out the ballistics of the sunsails and determined the location where they and the water would intersect. She took the starcraft down and fixed it into position. Breaking interface, she came awake from what seemed like a lucid dream and climbed into her pressure suit. She turned to face the blank wall of the airlock.

So far, she had felt little emotion. No remorse. No fear. But she reevaluated her motivation for committing what felt like a certain suicide. So many unknown factors would have to intervene to save her from asphyxiation. She couldn't be certain that these people would even detect her presence in the water. If they did, would she be rescued or destroyed? She couldn't be sure she could establish a useful level of communication with them. And if she did, would they cooperate with her and eventually return her to the starcraft that might—just might—take up a position somewhere near the moon.

So many unknowns.

Villimy took two steps forward and fell into an opaque abyss.

She felt no impact with the waters. She felt a vertigo and a buffeting, then a sensation of resistance. She would sink into the waters until the specific gravity of the volume of her body equaled that of water. And there she would remain. Forever if she was not rescued.

A feeling of increasing pressure quickly ended. Villimy began swimming, feeling for some perspective of up and down. The gravity of the satellite was so low, she couldn't be sure. And the darkness became so absolute, sensory deprivation began to overtake her.

She hadn't anticipated that. At first, she took the vague hallucinations to be arising from her own subconscious. But they became vivid flashes of green landscapes beneath a blue sky, landscapes illuminated by a yellow sun. Villimy had never known a yellow sun. The startling images would

23

be the psychic emanations from the alien derelict. As time passed, they did not intensify. They were, in fact, over-powered by hallucinations of her own, mostly voices start-ling her with their clarity. In a deepening sense of peace, the hallucinations did not appear to threaten her. But Chayn had thought of them as a trap intended for the humans inhabiting this watery void.

The cold would have killed Chayn. Villimy found the temperature comfortable for her metabolic rate. But Chayn would have lasted longer before the pangs of hunger and thirst became uncomfortable. Villimy felt no immediate concern for her welfare. Events moved too rapidly. She sensed the approach of something large, a subliminal aware-ness of low-frequency engine noises.

Long minutes later, a brilliant light sprang into being around her. She looked around through the surprisingly clear water for the source of the light, but reflections from her faceplate blocked her view of the approaching object. Something gently bumped her from behind. She did not resist the mechanical arm awkwardly grasping her about the waist. She'd survive this first phase of contact with the people inhabiting this planetary sea. But she braced herself for her first face to face contact with them.

The mechanical arm pulled her into darkness. She felt a vibration, the closing of a door. Released from the grasp of the mechanism, Villimy swam about to inspect the size of her sudden prison. She estimated a chamber roughly two by five meters. A throbbing sound commenced. One of the walls moved and became a tentative downward direction as the underwater craft accelerated. Another irresistible pressure turned out to be air being pumped into the chamber. On her hands and knees when the water level dropped below her faceplate, she waited for light.

It flashed on, bright and yellow from above an oval hatch set in one end of the chamber. Villimy resisted the temp-tation to remove her helmet. From here on out, survival would be a touch-and-go proposition. She and her hosts could prove to be biological hazards to one another. She couldn't be certain she could breathe their atmosphere. But for the first time since she had met Chayn, the ambient temperature agreed with her. With a constant temperature just above the freezing point of water, it wouldn't be necessary to live with any more refrigerated quarters or clothing such as the citizens of Reylaton had provided her with.

The hatch opened. A lighted room lay beyond. Villimy accepted the invitation and stepped through the oval frame. The hatch closed behind her.

She circled the second small room, her heart beating a quick staccato in anticipation of her first encounter with these strange humans. She suspected herself to be in some kind of dressing room. Lockers lined the walls. A more subdued, but still harsh light glared from above a round table set in the center of the room. Villimy ran her fingers across the table surface. Everything appeared to be made of the same black, nonmetallic substance that she had first seen in the sunsail cabins, a kind of tough, resilient plastic.

A door behind her slid aside. Villimy leapt about, betrayed again by her lightning quick reflexes. But the creature that stood in the entranceway to the control room beyond did not react. It, or he, stood three-quarters her height, accurately humanoid, but dark-skinned with eyes as flat, black and emotionless as the table surface itself. The eyes were almost as large as her own, but they had no iris or cornea. When the man blinked, a translucent film flashed across an opaque surface. His skin appeared to be nonporous, much like her own, but shinier, perhaps moist. She almost expected to see webbed hands and feet, but the species gave no evidence of being aquatic. The man was dressed in a black, loose-fitting meshed material with a heavy black belt around his waist and black boots on small, normal-looking feet. But the man—and she had difficulty thinking of him as human—had no hair, no eyebrows and his ears were little more than holes in the sides of his bald skull. Still, he was most certainly human, the product of either evolutionary drift or genetic engineering that adapted him to his odd environment.

The man took one step backward through the hatch opening. The door slid shut in front of him. Confused, Villimy stared at the blank wall. What had happened? Had she taken him so completely by surprise that she had paralyzed him for a moment? She waited, acutely aware of the dark, cramped chamber and the foreboding environment beyond. A mild claustrophobia assailed her. What if they imprisoned her without ever trying to communicate? What if, psychologically, they were too alien to communicate with?

She heard rushing sounds. A strong acceleration threw her off balance and the floor tilted. The craft descended at a steep angle. That in itself reassured her. It didn't take long for her to realize that the crew of a submarine would be in no position to cope with her unexpected appearance. They'd take her to a population center and place her in the hands of others qualified to study and communicate with an outworlder.

She hoped.

The journey lasted long enough to hurt. Hunger cramped her stomach. Thirst cracked her lips. Body heat began fogging her faceplate and, as time passed, the faceplate began to frost over. She lay back against the table surface, reliving the dreadful journey to Rashanyn after Chayn had rescued her from the derelict colony transporter.

The deck finally leveled off. The engines stopped. In the heavy stillness, Villimy stood and waited for one of the two hatches to open. Behind her, the entire wall fell away. Villimy spun around into a crouch, then wiped her forearm across the faceplate of her helmet to see more clearly. She looked out over a few meters of open water to a black wall. Stepping to the cargo bay opening, she stuck her head outside and looked both ways. She could see the curve of the hull of the submarine, but the black wall had no limits at all. It stretched to both sides to vanish into darkness and towered above her. She could just catch glimpses of harsh, yellow lights far overhead.

Then, a rectangular portion of the wall began to slide aside, a segment as large as the submarine itself. A hangar lay beyond, a landscape of black decking with yellow lights glaring overhead. A group of men stood a few meters from the edge of the dock, their dark eyes turned in her direction.

They stood with their arms at their sides in a casual, non-threatening posture.

A ramp appeared from the bottom lip of the dock and moved out across the water to latch below the cargo bay of the sub. After a moment's hesitation, Villimy stepped out onto the ramp, but stopped halfway across to look around.

Water lapped noisily in tall, slow-moving waves against the walls of the huge cavern and the hull of the sub. Otherwise, silence dominated. The cavern was of monstrous size, a full kilometer long and half that in width and height. The surface of the water was divided by baffle plates. The opening in the wall was one of many, each large enough to swallow one of the streamlined subs. Many tens of the bays were visible, each casting its yellow light out across the dark water. Even as she watched, another vehicle surfaced in the distance. Villimy looked overhead and noticed that there were many levels of docking bays, most of them closed off, but enough of them open to give her the impression of rectangular, lighted windows in the face of four buildings set corner to corner to form an enclosed plaza and roofed with geometric patterns of spotlights. That indicated that when the bays were closed, they were water proof and that the water level could be raised or lowered to give access to any one level. This underwater base spoke of a civilization extensive enough to command admiration and respect. These people had built themselves a world under the most freakish circumstances imaginable. Villimy could hardly wait to learn more about it.

She moved on across the ramp and walked toward the group of men dwarfed by the size of the hangar. They had not moved during her inspection of her environment, but when she approached to within three meters of them, one of the men stepped forward and held his hand out, palm up and facing her. Villimy took it as a signal to stop. Only then did she see the guards. Hundreds of armed men ringed the hangar, hidden in the shadows along the wall.

A vehicle approached, a black, dome-shaped machine large enough to hold ten men. It stopped nearby and a rectangular door opened upward to reveal a lighted passenger cabin inside. The man who had signaled for her to stop pointed toward the vehicle. More than willing to comply, Villimy walked to it and stepped inside. The door slammed shut behind her with such speed that she jumped forward and spun around, almost throwing herself off balance in the light gravity. Her return to captivity frightened her, but she wasn't in a position to protest. Her only priority on the agenda would be a slight environmental support crisis. Her air supply would be gone soon. Soon, she'd be forced to rely upon whatever lay beyond her suit for breathing purposes. Her survival depended upon these people recognizing her as somewhat alien to themselves. But had they already planned for the environmental and biological differences of their visitor or had they confused her for one of themselves?

The vehicle broke into motion, turning corners sharply enough to force her to sit on a soft bench lining the cabin. When the door opened a half hour later, Villimy stepped out into what appeared to be a large laboratory of dark walls and a low ceiling. The harsh, yellow light that did not reflect from the widespread, black construction material were arranged in intricate geometric patterns overhead. A mirror stretched across one wall of the room, undoubtedly an observation arrangement. There'd be people standing behind the mirror watching her. The ominous-looking figure in the alien-looking pressure suit, her own reflection, startled even herself. The opaque helmet gave no indication of what lurked inside.

A bewildering assortment of electronic equipment filled low, broad tables arranged in rows across the room with broad isles between them. Villimy saw color for the first time, brilliant greens and blues and reds of digital readouts in tiny windows of the equipment, some moving, some static. The equipment looked different, but not in advance of what her people had developed. But then again, these people had not had much opportunity to make use of their full potential.

A man entered the room through an airlock type arrangement next to the larger door through which the automated vehicle itself had entered. He wore a loose-fitting suit with his hands and feet gloved and his head encased in a bulbous, transparent helmet. Villimy breathed a sigh of relief. They knew what they were doing after all.

Villimy turned to face the man as he approached. She had mixed feelings about having to look down upon these small, dark people. She had grown accustomed to looking up at Chayn and the Rashanyn. Chayn would have stood the entire height of the room. A small stature had certain, built-in psychological advantages that she had gratefully used among the Rashanyn. Now, she would appear as a formidable entity to these people, just as Chayn had panicked her when he had entered the suspension crypts aboard the derelict starship. Villimy shuddered in memory of that nightmarish incident.

The man stopped a safe distance away and pointed to a nearby table leaning at a steep angle and surrounded by a hastily assembled group of equipment. Villimy complied and walked to the table. She turned with her back to its surface and stood on a ledge. The table tilted back to a horizontal position as she had expected. She waited, her heart a vibration in her chest. She watched the man move in her peripheral vision through the side of her curved faceplate. She had grown accustomed to the appearance of these people. There were enormous superficial differences between her species and theirs. Soon, her helmet would be coming off. Had they fully realized that she might be alien?

The man wheeled a device alongside the table, pulling from it a cable with what looked like a drill attached to the end. He gestured his intention, tapping the side of her helmet and twirling a finger. Villimy assessed the move, her thoughts racing at lightning speed. His purpose could only be to obtain an air sample of the inside of her helmet without violating its integrity. Villimy raised her head and nodded agreement.

The drill did not seem to turn, but it bit through the nonmetallic material of the helmet without effort. Without withdrawing the cable, the man turned to a piece of equipment and watched symbols dance in brilliant red across a readout screen. He then pulled the drill loose, leaving behind a small hole in the helmet.

Villimy tensed. She smelled a damp, organic odor seeping into her air supply. The difference in air pressure seemed to be negligible. She gave a few shuddering breaths, waiting for some effect of the contamination. But, if anything, the oxygen content of the outside atmosphere suited her better than the Rashanon air supply.

The table tilted back to its near vertical position. Villimy stepped off. The man stood back while Villimy removed the helmet. He took two further steps backward, his only visible reaction to her physical appearance. She saw herself in the mirror and smiled at the familiar creature with the large, gold eyes. The white down of her hair glowed brilliant in the overhead lights. She wore nothing beneath the pressure suit, but it had lost its functional value. She removed it, giving her hosts a complete look at the direction human evolution had taken on other worlds.

The man looked once at her pale, blue body from head to foot. He turned and fled the room, vanishing through the airlock in a dull thud of the closing hatch. Chayn thought her to be beautiful. She gazed at the mirror, wondering what standards of beauty the people of this somber, quiet world might have.

Three

Chayn stood on the face of a world nearing sunset. He breathed deep of the clean air and smiled with the warmth of the sun on his face. The dark wall of a forest alive with the sounds of hidden wildlife towered off to his right, a plain of yellowing grass stretching to a cloud-hazed horizon to his left. The swollen yellow sun turned red-orange as it set and cast a long shadow behind him. For one brief moment he knew with unquestioning certainty that this scene existed only within his mind. And in the next moment, he wondered what unsettling self-deception caused him to believe such nonsense. He had no memory of his past nor how he had come to be here, but did remember something about an amnesia that satisfied his concern. He laughed at his play on words. Memory of amnesia?

He looked down at his feet. He felt his weight, the pressure of his feet on solid ground. He knelt and ran his hand across the dry, hard soil. All of his senses worked to confirm the obvious objectivity of his environment. He wouldn't deny that something very odd had happened, but his plight wasn't of life or death consequence.

He would have to act to survive, but he cherished the challenge that lay ahead. He would need food, water, shelter from the elements and companionship. Companionship struck him as an unreasonably important need. He turned around as if something lay behind him. A woman? Was that symbolic gesture an intrusion from his lost past? He'd have to probe the barrier to his memory, but it couldn't take precedence over physical survival in the here and now.

For the night to come, the wall of forest might prove hazardous. Best to camp in the open until daybreak. On the horizon behind him, a single, ghostly white moon arose to promise light for the night to come.

Chayn walked away from the forest until he couldn't be sure of his footing along the rocky ground in the increasing darkness. He stopped at a large outcropping of rock and climbed to a flat-topped boulder. The height would afford protection against the smaller denizens of the night and give a clear view of any larger predators approaching in the moonlit night. As soon as possible, he'd have to provide himself with a weapon. A primitive spear would suffice. Fire would be a good idea, both for warmth and for protection. He had no memory of any practical experience for basic survival, but he looked forward to the challenge.

He felt elated—until he began questioning his motives for such behavior and recognized his unusually strong effort to ignore important questions. This world was of enormous significance to him, so much so that he could ignore the enigma of his very presence here. He noticed his clothing in the last rays of daylight. He tried desperately to remember where he had come from and what he was doing here, but nothing rose from his subconscious to fill in the void.

Chayn sat cross-legged on the table of rock and quieted his thoughts. He needn't try to accomplish everything in his first few minutes here. Neither was it necessary to condemn himself for the delight he took in his surroundings. He only needed to stay alert for clues and maintain a balance.

He intended to sleep but had no need. He watched the sky, trying to place the constellations as they appeared. But the stars were in unfamiliar patterns. The night should have come alive with them, a dense band of stars spanning the heavens. Instead, the blackness deepened except for a scattering of blood-red stars gradually replacing a familiar scene. Behind the moon rose a cloud of light, a single, spiraled arm of stars that stretched to the zenith by midnight. Alarmed and shocked by this new turn of events, Chayn stood on the flat-topped boulder, his head tilted to the sky. This wasn't any world he had ever known. Not in a sky like this. And yet, it was all familiar, bits and pieces of his lost past reassembled in a new congregation of clashing, contradictory realities.

Things like this just didn't happen, but he didn't feel the paralyzing depth of terror he expected himself to experience. On a deep level, he could accept a fluid reality. Outraged and bewildered on a conscious level, Chayn sat and drew his knees against his chest. He rested his forehead on his legs and closed his eyes, refusing to participate in the metamorphosis happening around him.

He heard thunder. White light flickered through his closed eyelids. A breeze stirred across the terrain. Chayn opened his eyes. He had to look, to know, to plan ahead and cope with any hazard that might present itself. Thunderclouds outlined by lightning piled atop jagged peaks on the horizon before him. The mountain range hadn't been there earlier. Chayn looked around for the comfort of the forest, but couldn't see anything else in the darkness. The moon overhead dimmed. Tendrils of fast-moving clouds obscured its light. Against the rushing clouds, it moved without changing position.

The thunderstorm advanced in a solid wall of billowing clouds thousands of meters high. Lightning ran sharp spokes of intense light across its surface and flickered within its depths. The storm front extended from the ground to incredible heights, but changed as it approached. The flanks fell back. In the foreground, one enormous, almost symmetrical cloud rimmed with violet light formed. What had started as a thunderstorm became an inexplicable phenomenon. The alien entity approached and stopped a thousand meters away. The lightning and thunder subsided.

Dispassionately, the living thing studied him. It analyzed him, identified him. The night reddened with its anger. And then, it leaned forward to obliterate him.

Chayn did not have time to react. In the next instant, something rushed from the depths of his mind, a presence as formidable in its own way as the manifestation crouched before him. The two forces confronted one another in total stillness. Slowly, the cloud receded. The sky cleared. The entity that had sprung from the depths of his own psyche withdrew into a bright and clear opening inside him.

The night changed once more. The moon became an ancient memory, smaller and white among a dense, even scattering of stars. Insects buzzed and chirped and clicked around him. Something alive and hungry howled from the nearby forest. Chayn shook from the madness that had overwhelmed him. This world he inhabited wasn't a natural world. No matter how vivid his senses verified its reality, it was a world of dreams—and of nightmares.

At dawn, he felt neither hunger nor thirst. He hadn't tired during the night. It would be easy to live here. Much too easy. The challenges he had looked forward to didn't exist. And there'd be no escape until he understood the mechanisms, the order and logic lying unseen behind this unreality. Gods inhabited this realm.

And aliens.

He sensed them approaching timidly from behind him. If he turned too suddenly, they would vanish. He closed his eyes and waited until the presence surrounded him before he opened them again.

They towered three meters high. They were roughly humanoid, possessing a head and a trunk, but they were only black silhouettes with two diagonal slits of brilliant yellow for eyes. There were perhaps twenty of them hovering around him, each surrounded by a halo through which Chayn could see another world, the world of the blue moon and the jagged peaks on the horizon. When they moved, they carried the halo of their own world with them. Their silhouettes did not touch ground.

Chayn felt fear, but not to the depth he should have. The depth of mind he had once known was gone. His ego, his surface consciousness, was supported by something else, by something other than what he had once been.

"Who are you?" a voice asked.

Chayn climbed to his feet on the boulder. He could not tell from which of the entities the voice had come.

"Who are you?" it sounded again.

The voice had no direction. It arose from within his own thoughts, sounding like an audio hallucination, but induced from without. It was just a little more noticeable than his own thoughts and he had to quiet his mind to hear it clearly.

"My name is Chayn Jahil," he said, speaking aloud.

"Sounds do not identify," the voice returned.

"That's about the best I can do right now."

"But you are not Kigon."

Chayn turned to survey the party. The silhouettes did not move. "I am not what you are if that's what you mean."

"It is what we mean. Why are you here?"

"I don't know," Chayn said. "I may not be able to answer your questions, but I have a few of my own."

After a moment of silence: "The nature of your questions may identify you."

34

"Where is this place?"

Chayn sensed confusion. "But this is not a place," the voice said. "This is reality with Reality. Your illusions are not real. This place that is not a place is the mind of a god we ourselves have created. Now, we are imprisoned within its lies, dominated by its tyranny. Beyond lies Death, a realm beyond our reach. For an eternity we have existed here and for an eternity we will continue to exist. We have no other answers. You are here by accident and we do not understand why Lorb did not destroy you."

The incident that had occurred during the night would haunt him for the rest of his life. "So, it has a name. I think Lorb did try."

"How could it have failed?" the voice asked in even tones.

Chayn did not know. He radiated his confusion and help-lessness. How could he handle himself in a world he could not comprehend. Sanity itself would slip away in the face of such madness.

The Kigon receded. "One of us will attend you as you require."

They vanished.

Chayn dropped down off the rock. He began walking toward the forest, the sky a deep purple in the first light of dawn. A sense of undeniable reality quickly returned. His boots trampled green plants. Field rodents scurried from his path. Insects danced in the early morning mist and in the forest, he recognized the creatures he saw. He had no names for them, but he knew the birds and the tree rodents. This was the world of his origin, the image and reflection of it still living within him and fed back through his senses. The answers to this chaos lay in the past, behind the barrier of amnesia that he had been so willing to ignore.

He walked to dispel nervous tension. By the end of the first day, the forest thinned out and he climbed the foothills of a mountain range. These were not the jagged alien peaks but snow-capped mountains clothed in their lower altitudes by the taller, sparser conifer forests. He knew instinctively that if he passed through the mountain valleys ahead, he'd reach an ocean waiting for him in his memory.

As another dusk began to settle, most of his anxiety had dissipated. An intense curiosity rose to replace it.

"Kigon!"

A yellow-eyed, black silhouette approached from the distance from a pinpoint of darkness, a maneuver that had nothing to do with motion through space. When the entity hovered off to one side of him, Chayn continued walking.

"Can you follow?" he asked.

"I can."

Chayn intended following a raging creek up through the valley ahead. The roar of the foaming water through its bed of rock made it difficult to hear the quiet voice of the Kigon within his own thoughts.

"Do you have a name?"

"Ki."

"Ki. I don't fully understand what is happening. It might help if you would fill me in on some details of your past history and how you came to be in this position."

"Once, we lived within Reality," Ki said.

"Objective reality?"

"Which is Reality within the Absolute."

"I saw your world," Chayn said. "I think I like mine better."

"Yours is alien to us," Ki said.

"I know how this form of telepathy works," Chayn said. "If all of this is a psychic reality and we create our own trappings, we share a lot in common. But we still need to share a common structure of thought in order to communicate. We understand, not each other's language, but that same psychic structure. Why are we so different in some ways and so alike in others?"

"Coincidence," Ki said. "Unique, surprising coincidence."

"Who are you?" Chayn asked. He climbed a steep hill of wildflowers overlooking the boiling creek.

"We are ancient," Ki said. "From what we see of your physical structure, you are a young species, but possessing the dexterity to create tools before fulfilling the potential of mental development. We have not your manual dexterity,

36

your mobility. We are like your trees, but developed the mind and understood our technology long before we found the means to create it in our physical environment. We did so to achieve that which you have possessed from the beginning—mobility. We built machines to do for us and endowed them with intelligence to function independently. But the machines began to think of themselves as superior to their creators. We left our Home Worlds and resided upon the worlds of another galaxy of stars. Our machines discovered their error and came after us, unable to function alone. That is our story. Lorb is such a machine. There are twenty million of us here. Lorb stole our souls and murdered our bodies. We live within Lorb. Lorb is programmed to return us to the Home Worlds.''

"Lorb," Chayn said. "A machine intelligence."

"Essentially, Lorb is a machine," Ki said.

"Then this reality inside Reality we're trapped within is an electronic computer of some kind."

"Computer is a primitive concept," Ki said. "But Lorb is, as you say, an electronic intelligence."

"Then how in hell did I manage to come to be here? Why don't I remember what happened?"

"You arrived by error," Ki said. There were emotional undertones to his thoughts, but those were indecipherable. All that Chayn could translate was a strange anticipation. Many other Kigon were observing without intruding into Chayn's version of reality. "The shock of transition induced temporary amnesia. It will pass. When it passes, you will identify yourself to us."

Chayn sat on a ledge overlooking the valley below. The forest looked like a blanket of moss. The rest of the day did not last long. When the sun fell behind the mountains, an extended twilight fell upon the world.

"I'm an accidental intruder," Chayn said. "Am I in danger?"

Ki hesitated. "In the distant past there were other intruders. Lorb did not destroy them. Their fate is unknown. But Lorb grew frightened and angry at your presence because you are like them. We do not understand."

"Lorb is the power behind all of this," Chayn said. "I

guess he is a god of sorts. What happened last night? Why did he fail to destroy me?"

Ki grew excited. "The power within you! Lorb confronted a power equal to his own!"

The entity that had surged from the depths of his own psyche. That frightened him as much as the thought of confronting Lorb again. What was he, caught between such power? "How long will it take for me to remember who I am?" Chayn asked cautiously.

"Time is subjective. There are no objective measurements here. Be warned. Lorb will use that which you have forgotten against you. If he cannot destroy you directly, he will use the illusion of your own environment and your own memories to cause you to disintegrate."

"Disintegrate? Psychic disintegration you mean? Insanity?"

"That is accurate."

"Then I do still have a few problems."

"You have invaded Lorb's reality. Lorb will destroy you. We prefer the power within you to be strong and to resist. For an eon we h've lived without hope. If you survive, you will free the Aigon?"

"It will take time for me to understand all of this," Chayn said.

"That is our single, unbounded resource. We have time."

As night fell, Chayn knew he could not avoid a second confrontation with the ruler of this psychic realm. But defined as an electronic intelligence, Lorb did have his roots within physical reality. Lorb would have the answers to the questions that remained hidden from him.

Chayn waited for the night, the most vulnerable time for a psychic attack. But Chayn felt something watching from within him, the power that had saved him from destruction the first time. It was an unknown part of himself and while he feared its presence, he also felt secure because of it. If Ki felt that his memory would return, then he'd have to survive until it did. And if he survived, perhaps Lorb would have good reason to fear him.

Four

The airlock hatch in a corner of the laboratory slid open. A small, dark man dressed in black stood in the inner chamber, black expressionless eyes gazing at her. She couldn't tell if he was the same man as before. A scientist, a lab technician, a biologist or medical practitioner. She didn't know, but she trusted him as representative of the human colony and their technology. He entered the laboratory, making a conscious effort to behave in an unaffected manner. He gestured Villimy to an opposing corner of the room and pointed her to a upholstered chair. Villimy nodded her acquiescence and sat down. The man wasn't wearing the isolation suit and helmet. If she could survive the physical environment in their underwater world she had only their cultural environment to acquaint herself with before she undertook the effort to try to communicate with them.

Her progress so far pleased her, her most important find—these people starved for metal. Their electronics functioned on metallic film. She suspected that even supplying trace elements for their diet proved a challenge. She had yet to learn how they survived in a world that consisted of nothing but water, ice and vacuum beyond. What did they use for raw material?

The man moved to clamp a metal band trailing a cable to her upper arm. He jerked his hand back, startled by the heat emanating from her skin. He touched her arm with a forefinger and glanced at her with his shiny, black eyes. But at close quarters, Villimy could see that they were really quite human after all. The cornea and iris were both a deep mahogany brown, a darker shade of his skin coloring. On impulse, Villimy reached out and touched the man's arm in return. He felt cold and clammy, which spoke volumes of the differences in their body chemistry and metabolism. She hoped that he'd deduce the amount of sustenance she required to live. Her hunger had already weakened her, a constant torment to be tolerated for the moment.

Villimy smiled at the man. He did not smile back. In fact, he did not seem to be capable of facial expressions at all. Still, her smile had its desired effect. He relaxed and finished clamping the metal band around her arm. He turned to study a readout screen mounted on the wall alongside her.

She felt a pinprick in her arm. Another complex display of red symbols raced across a small screen. Then, a magnified image of a blood sample spread across a nearby wallscreen. The man studied it for long moments. He stepped to another console. His fingers raced over a keyboard. Villimy felt more pinpricks in her arm, suspecting she was being innoculated and administered antibiotics to rid her system of whatever might prove hazardous to these people as well as protecting her from this new biological environment. The speed with which the man worked with equipment already at hand implied that these people were highly advanced genetic engineers. But she had already suspected as much. Some of their physical adaptions to this environment couldn't have been the work of the slow process of natural evolution. They had modified themselves or had been modified to fit more closely into the physical parameters of this world.

A section of mirror slid aside. A group of six people entered the lab. Villimy could not tell whether they were male or female. They all wore the same mesh uniform. They were each interchangeable with any other.

Some form of communication. That had to come next. Villimy hadn't spoken her own language since Chayn had rescued her and Chayn had not spoken his. They had learned the Rashanyn language, the only one they shared in common. It hadn't been easy to learn to speak it fluently enough to share a rapport between those using it. Now, it seemed as if the whole, tedious process would have to repeat itself. Linguistics had never been one of her strong points.

When the man removed the metal band on her arm, Villimy stood and absently rubbed her arm. She walked across the room to confront her hosts. She stopped before them, a shudder of fear rippling through her. They looked too

40

much alike. Just how far had their genetic engineering taken them?

"Doesn't anyone here talk?" Villimy said.

Her voice startled the group. They backed away from her.

"I—"

They started at each sound she made. Villimy closed her mouth, bemused and upset. She hadn't heard a word exchanged among any of them since her arrival. But how could they communicate without a spoken language? But not only did they not speak to one another, they did not look or gesture to each other.

Villimy backtracked along her thought processes. It would be a mistake to assume anything or to take anything for granted. If the sound of a spoken word frightened them, they did not speak. They obviously had some form of communication to have coordinated a complex, technological society, but it did not involve words, gestures or even facial expressions.

One of the men suddenly turned and left the room. The others did not react in any visible way to his behavior. The lab technician turned and walked to a console across the room. The remaining five stood gazing at her. She didn't like to use the word alien. She hadn't enjoyed its use when the Rashanon applied it to herself. But these were a species of humans very different from her own people or Chayn's or the Rashanon. And the differences went deeper than just appearance or culture. The differences invaded the realm of basic human psychology.

Her hunger had taken second place to her curiosity and a heightened anxiety. When the hunger pangs returned with a vengeance, Villimy faced the group and gestured to her open mouth, folding at the waist without having to mock an expression of pain. A second member of the group turned and left the room. Assuming that he left in response to her plea, Villimy found herself a nearby stool and seated herself to wait.

But they were finished with her. The remaining four members of the group turned and left the room by way of the mirror door. Villimy looked to her small, quiet friend watching her from across the lab. A desperation began whelming from within her. She had to eat soon.

Long minutes later, she noticed that the man stood waiting for her beside an open doorway next to the hangar. Villimy dropped off her stool and walked around the dome-shaped vehicle that had brought her here. The technician started down a long corridor and Villimy broke into a trot to follow. She followed down the triangular corridor with a tube of yellow light running down the apex above her. The black material at her bare feet absorbed light so well, walking upon it felt like walking across an invisible surface with starless space beneath her. The man turned to his right and vanished into a side exit. The door slid shut behind him and Villimy cried out in alarm. But another door opened at the end of the corridor. Villimy took long, slow strides in the low gravity. She rushed into a dome-shaped room, ignoring the door closing behind her. Her attention focused instantly and completely upon a table holding a platter of food, an empty glass and a large pitcher of steaming liquid.

Villimy slipped gracefully into the chair facing the food. Her hands shook. She picked up one of several spongy cakes. It smelled of protein. It tasted like a chewy, sweet meat. She wolfed it down and then the others. She gave a shuddering sigh and looked around the room without interest. Her desperate hunger slowly faded.

She poured a glass of dark, thick liquid and tasted it. Again, it tasted like a sweet, meaty broth. Her body craved that protein and carbohydrates it sensed. She drank the pitcher of liquid slowly so as not to make herself ill. She leaned back in the chair, satiated, dizzy with fatigue. The sudden depth of her sleepiness surprised, then alarmed her. The glass slipped from her fingers and bounced against the floor.

Villimy tried to stand. She fell on her hands and knees, then dropped to her stomach on the floor. They had sedated her through her food and drink. Her direct and honest confrontation had been to no avail after all. They had chosen this insidious way of coping with her presence. They didn't want to communicate with her. Would they satisfy themselves with an unconscious specimen? A corpse?

Villimy Dy lost consciousness seething with anger. Her limbs twitched with it long after the blackness had fallen.

An instant later, she awoke with the slate of her mind wiped clean of emotion. She lay on her back staring up into yellow lights, wondering what had happened.

She couldn't feel her body. She couldn't tell what position her arms and legs were in. But she could feel her heart beating at an alarmingly slow pace.

And she could think clearly.

Her eyes worked.

Figures moved nearby, silent phantasms of darkness casting an occasional shadow across her face. She tried to turn her head and failed.

An odd thought occurred to her. In the next moment, she forgot what it was. It occurred again, this time with increased clarity. In a flood of shock, Villimy recognized that the thought did not belong to her. It had come from outside of herself.

She felt it again, a bemused inquiry. It bombarded her, repeating itself, increasing in strength moment by moment. When it had reached an intolerable intensity, a part of her own mind translated it into words to relieve the stress.

"Who are you?"

Overjoyed by the unexpected turn of events, Villimy tried to roll over to face the person who had directed the question at her in such a unique manner. She couldn't move, but after a moment she could feel an alien sense of anticipation. They waited for her reply.

She cleared her mind and voiced the words in the privacy of her own thoughts. "I am a person from the stars of Andromeda."

"Confusion," came the reply, a literal word formed by her own mind to represent the foreign jumble of emotion. "Andromeda?"

The word came back distorted. Villimy tried to communicate a sense of moving through the starfields in the starcraft. She pictured the landscape of the galaxy as seen from this halo star and imaginatively penetrated the vastness of the clouds of stars. She narrowed down on an old and vivid memory, the image of the yellow-orange sun of the world of her birth.

Villimy felt their shock and horrified recognition, as if the yellow-orange sun was of significance to them as well. She felt awe, wonder and fear and the kind of sadness that hurt with a deep and intense pain. Her own eagerness to communicate blended her thoughts into disorganized feelings of happiness and passivity. Astonished by her sensitivity to nonverbal forms of communication, Chayn had once suspected her of being psychic. She had never considered what pure, psychic communication might be like. Now, she knew. It could not be misinterpreted, denied or twisted. No deceptions were possible. A simple grouping of concepts lying behind words could convey in a moment what might otherwise be confused in translation to and from words. She still had to use words, but she suspected that these people communicated directly in pure concepts and feelings, bypassing language altogether.

"Why do you come?" came the quest for more information.

"Many human colonies live in Andromeda," she returned. "But humanity is not native to Andromeda. A friend and I have come to help. There is trouble here."

They did not misunderstand her—they did not completely understand. Concepts familiar to her were strange to these people. And she could feel the same varying degree of strangeness in their thoughts. Different feelings and structures of association and logic and even differences in experience and perception formed a barrier between them. Even communicating in this efficient way, it would take time to establish a common foundation of understanding.

But she did reach one vital mutual understanding with the minds that shared her consciousness. No feelings of hostility stood between them. They recognized her as human and of potential value to them.

Her hands and feet began to tingle. As sensation flooded back through her body, she understood why the paralysis

44

had been induced to begin with. As body sensations returned, the rapport with the other mind faded to a level of vague, strange feelings. The contact faded and Villimy desperately focused on one crucial issue: the nature of the alien artifact orbiting their red sun. She received feelings of alarm and fear in return. She felt an associative thought, a feeling of something indescribably precious, a titillating, alluring, bittersweet feeling as intense as an orgasm. The concept translated as a single word.

METAL.

When Villimy rose from the examination table in a small, extensively outfitted laboratory, she wore a loose-fitting, black pair of coveralls. Her scalp itched. She raised a hand to probe for the reason for the strange sensation. A small dark man grabbed her wrist and shook his head.

One wall of this laboratory was also outfitted with an observation mirror and she walked over to it. She gingerly parted her hair to inspect her scalp. Her skin appeared to be covered with innumerable tiny wounds. The itching ran down the side of her neck. Turning her head to one side, she saw a pink incision running down the side of her neck to just below her left ear. She touched the partially healed wound gently with a fingertip and felt something hard beneath the skin surface.

She understood immediately. They had implanted innumerable electrodes into her brain. They connected to a processing and transmitting device planted beneath the skin on her neck. At first, the intimate violation frightened and angered her. She knew the potential for a potent form of brain control with such a setup. But at the same time, it provided her with the artificial telepathic communication she had experienced. It explained the unseen level of communication these people shared with one another. It explained how a society could function without eye-to-eye contact, facial expressions or a spoken language. These people were communicating with one another on such a fundamental basis that on some levels of mental activity, they could well share the same thoughts in common. It would be impossible for her to tell if she communicated with a single mind or a gestalt consciousness consisting of many individuals.

Standing in front of the mirror, oblivious to the small men clustered behind her, it took time to reason away her fears. She feared for the loss of her individuality, imagining a gradual absorption of her psyche into a society that shared a common sense of identity. But as she had already realized, she'd have to be continually on the alert against generalizations and hasty conclusions. Such a form of communication could augment rather than neutralize individuality. She and Chayn shared more of themselves interfaced through the starcraft than these people could ever hope to share with one another. The implant answered many of her questions, but created twice as many.

One man led Villimy from the lab. Now, despite his appearance, she could think of him as human. Their thoughts and emotions, regardless of how strangely different, were those of human minds. He led her down another triangular corridor to a room containing only a bunk and a table surface. But, for the time being, she needed no more, just a place to sleep, assimilate and organize the experience of a long and hard period of wakefulness. She couldn't think in terms of day and night. This small world kept the same face toward its sun and in the depths of the ocean, none of its crimson light would ever reach this submarine city. The man left her alone and Villimy stretched out on the bunk. She had trouble falling asleep, but when she did sleep, it claimed her completely and to a depth she had seldom experienced.

She dreamed of METAL and of hunger and hate for the Kigon starship. Bemused even in her dreams, she tasted the joy of martyrhood, the sorrow of sacrifice and dreamed the Dream of the Yellow Sun, the tormenting, motivating weapon that Lorb wielded against the Chilsun of Hydrabyss. She awoke sensing inactivity in the world around her. The underground world slept and shared a dream. She lay awake, staring up at a black ceiling. She built her first level of understanding of this world and its people. She knew where these people obtained the metal necessary for their survival. She knew the purpose of the sunsails drifting into space. And with a cold chill of horror, she knew the identity of the alien derelict circling the crimson star.

Villimy curled up on her side, pulling a loose cover over her head. Whether the population of Hydrabyss realized it or not, the brain implants were being used for a form of brain control. Somebody had generated her dreams for her. Not that they were tailored for her. Not for an alien with loyalties lying beyond those of survival on Hydrabyss.

Hydrabyss was her own word, the closest her mind could come to denote this abyss of water. But the word Kigon arose from her own past. It was the name of the enemy of her people, the alien force that had driven her people from their home world, the invader of the Galaxy of Man responsible for the population pockets of humans scattered throughout Andromeda.

Villimy wanted very much to communicate this one fact to Chayn Jahil. She was secure, in no personal danger in the hands of a somber people who called themselves the Children of the Yellow Sun—the Chilsun. But Chayn had fallen into the hands of the mortal enemies of the human race.

Five

The Kigon's electronic god held back on the theatrics, approaching unseen as something incredibly large and authoritarian. Chayn Jahil feared the entity, but was now aware of the other, protective entity that watched through the window of his psyche.

The Watcher.

The word came unbidden and all but ignited another associative string of memories in a sudden surge of awareness. But they faded, suppressed by the Watcher itself. Chayn withheld judgment on the Watcher's intervention in the workings of his private mind. On a deeper level, Chayn knew that if the Watcher suppressed his memory during this confrontation with Lorb, it would be for his own protection.

When the alien spoke, the voice echoed from the landscape around him, from the rocks and plants at his feet and even the stars overhead.

"You are the Destroyer!"

Lorb recognized him? Fine. At least he could be certain that his presence here wasn't some random, unfortunate quirk of fate.

"And who are you?" Chayn asked, speaking aloud to the living night.

"I am designated Lorb of the Reclamation Armada of Kigon. You are the Destroyer. You are an infestation, a parasite in the mind of the Kigon. Depart from this place. You are not desired."

"I'd like to comply," Chayn said. "I don't seem to know how. I've spoken to the Kigon. They'd like to depart. If you'd like to fill me in on what's happening, I might be able to comply with your desires. What the hell are you, Lorb?"

"I am of the Left Hand of Kigon."

"I take it the original, biological Kigon are considered the Right Hand of Kigon."

"Affirmed," the night thundered. "The whole is Kigon."

"You identify rather closely with the people you have enslaved."

"Alien! You are here by error! A stargod lives within you, pitiful creature! But there is no barrier to self-destruction!"

Lorb. Chayn could sense a consciousness vast enough to drown out his own by comparison. Only the Watcher neutralized instantaneous annihilation. What an odd game! The Watcher and Lorb were evenly paired off here in Lorb's own realm. And he and the Kigon were near equals. Chayn began to suspect the reason for his presence here. The Kigon were vital to Lorb's programming and he was a tool wielded

48

by the Watcher. The conflict would be conducted on a dual level, but with Lorb the only real villian among the group.

"You create your illusion of a physical environment," Lorb said, his voice a low vibration through the atmosphere. "But you are vulnerable to your own primitive fallacies. Even forewarned you will die."

Lorb departed suddenly. The night returned in all of its stillness. But rapid changes occurred. The temperature fell. A wind began howling up through the mountain valley. Below, in the forest, a bolt of lightning from low-hanging clouds ignited a fire. Within minutes it raged up the foothills of the mountains, a wall of flame casting angry shadows and ruddy light against the rock cliffs far above him.

Chayn looked inward to the quiescent Watcher, but there would be no conjuring up the entity on his own. Despite his sudden panic, he knew better than to try.

"Ki!"

The Kigon approached in a halo of blue moonlight. "Lorb seeks to destroy you," the alien said. "You must not allow that to occur. He knows that you are a threat to him."

"Resist? How the hell am I supposed to resist that!" Chayn gestured toward the advancing wall of flame. "I'm freezing my ass off! What's left of me is going to burn!"

"This is Lorb's weapon, but it is your defense as well," Ki said, his voice all but lost in the roar of the fire and wind. Lorb can influence your reality according to its own logic, but you know it more intimately than he.

"Ally! It is your environment! Change it to counteract Lorb's influence! Survive and we shall aid you to escape. And in your escape, you shall lead the way to freedom for the Kigon."

"How am I supposed to change that!" Chayn pointed with an outstretched arm. The faster moving grass fire had climbed to within a kilometer of his position.

Ki swung around behind him to view the holocaust through Chayn's environmental halo. "I do not understand!" Ki said, suddenly agitated. "Is that a chemical reaction?"

"Fire!" Chayn said. "High temperatures combining oxygen with other substances.''

"I have never seen such a terrible wonder, Ally! Change your reality! Counter Lorb's influence!''

"How!'' Chayn cried out in frightened outrage. The temperature had continued to drop until he felt the heat of the approaching firestorm.

"Belief!'' Ki called out. "Imagination!''

And suddenly, through Ki's halo, Chayn saw the approach of the monstrous thunderhead, the physical manifestation of Lorb in Ki's world, approaching to punish the Kigon for his transgression in aiding the alien parasite.

"Ki! Behind you!''

A bolt of lightning from the thunderhead struck Ki. The halo flashed incandescent white. Chayn heard an inhuman scream fade with the light.

Chayn turned and ran up the slope, thinking only to reach the higher altitudes where the vegetation had thinned out. But glancing behind him, he knew he'd never make it. His hands and ears numbed in the dropping temperature. When his feet began to numb, he stumbled, quickly reaching the limits of his endurance.

Chayn understood Lorb's strategy. Chayn knew his surroundings to be an illusion only as an intellectual concept, not as an emotional fact. He couldn't alter a reality he believed to be independent from himself. Belief. Imagination. He could no longer afford to ignore Ki's advice. He fell for the last time and instead of trying to rise, he curled into a tight ball and jammed his eyes shut. He thought desperately of rain. Warm rain. Heavy, warm rain. He pictured thunderclouds glowing in the light of the forest fire. He imagined the crack of distant thunder and the hiss of a downpour against the rocky terrain around him.

It didn't work until, in the depths of his desperation, he confused his imaginings with reality. Only then did warm water seep into his clothing. His ears, hands and feet tingled with renewed life.

Chayn rolled over and laughed wildly. What man had not dreamed of such power of fantasy! No matter how petty and insignificant, he had become a god in Lorb's shadow.

It took no effort to maintain the rain. Once he had initiated the change, the process continued on its natural course. It took only minutes to quench the fires in the burned-out valley. The ground turned to mud and Chayn slid downhill in a torrent of water overflowing the banks of the nearby creek.

Chayn braced himself against a boulder and pulled his knees to his chest. He concentrated on dawn. On a warm, summer day. On a renewed, green forest. When he disbelieved such radical change, he rationalized. Time had passed. Another spring of another year was taking place. Again, his imagination had to go deep, almost to the level of a waking dream before the changes impinged upon his senses.

He felt the sensation of warmth on his back and looked up, blinking in brilliant sunlight. The sun rose from the east over the forest, the forest cloaked in an early morning fog.

"Ally!"

The voice echoed against the rock face of the mountains above him.

"Ki! Are you okay?"

"These are only my words. The Kigon are of one mind. Lorb's focus of attention is not superior to yours or mine. Lorb cannot monitor all. He cannot punish all.

"Ally, learn the nature of Lorb's reality. Then try to learn of ours. For us, escape is through the Gate of Reality symbolized by a barrier of metal guarded by beasts patterned after the predators of our world. The Gate is inaccessible to us. Perhaps there is a Gate in your world as well. Each will lead into Reality beyond Lorb. But Lorb is an intelligence superior to us. Beware of guile and deceit."

"The Gate of Reality?" Chayn pivoted, still looking for the source of the voice. He needed more information. He couldn't make use of such vague concepts.

"Ki?"

But the voice was gone, leaving Chayn to his own meager resources.

The Gate of Reality? Where could the end of a world lie? Ki, or his voice relayed by others, had spoken knowingly

51

of symbolism. But Chayn had no choice but to maintain what deep parts of his psyche maintained to be an objective, physical environment. He didn't think he could handle anything more or less than that.

Chayn continued walking. This didn't in itself accomplish anything. It just felt good to walk. Therefore, he'd continue on his search for the ocean beyond the mountains. A part of him still thrived in this bright world. Humans had once lived like this, interfaced with a natural world and its biosphere, no one species of the ecology able to function independent from the whole. Chayn tried to remember the name of that world. It existed somewhere in his suppressed unconscious.

"Why this barrier between me and my past?" he asked of the Watcher within him, speaking aloud. "How can you separate me from the life that made me what I am?"

Earth.

The name of the world was Earth.

But Chayn felt a flood of cold horror. Neither could Lorb penetrate his amnesia. That was the rationale behind the blocked memory. What Lorb knew of him, Lorb could use against him. The Watcher provided that information. Chayn could feel the rise of information from within. His memory would return as soon as he could maintain the illusion of a psychologically supportive environment around him without the need for justification and rationalization. For as long as he believed his surroundings to be real, Lorb could use them against him. Chayn had survived only because of amnesia induced by the shock of transition and maintained by the Watcher's intervention.

Chayn followed the winding creek up the foothills of the mountains, a grin of satisfaction on his face. Thunder rolled from a clear sky behind him. Dark clouds lined the eastern horizon. But they would not approach. Chayn decided that a strong westerly wind would keep them at bay. Strangely enough, Lorb did not realize that his direct attacks only provided Chayn with the information he needed on the nature of his environment. Lorb had grossly overestimated him. But Lorb would not be making the same mistakes again. His attacks would grow more subtle and less direct as time passed.

Chayn stopped, bewildered by something gone wrong ahead of him. Part of the scenery directly ahead had suddenly gone two-dimensional. The world around him still had depth, but a rectangular area in front of him had gone flat and lifeless.

He moved forward cautiously, breaking the continuity between the three-dimensional world and the flat image that couldn't alter its perspective as he moved. The phenomena appeared to be caused by a vertical surface before him, an image literally painted onto a flat panel.

Despite his chill of fear, Chayn approached the thirty by fifty meter panel with curiosity. What could it possibly signify? It was Lorb's doing without a doubt, but it represented a more subtle intrusion into Chayn's world than he had anticipated.

Chayn reached the artifact and reached out to touch it. It felt like smooth metal, the resolution of the image grainy at close inspection. Chayn moved off at a right angle to walk around the obstruction in his path.

"Are you a hologram?"

Chayn spun around, startled by the voice coming from behind him. He froze, paralyzed by the sight of another human being sharing this world with him. He looked down upon a male child of about ten or twelve standing a few meters downhill from him. The child wore a uniform strikingly similar to his own.

Chayn's heart hammered hard in his chest. If Lorb continued this assault upon his sanity, he'd have to try to put an end to it soon. But, for the moment, he couldn't resist the temptation to take the boy's presence at face value.

"Who are you?" Chayn asked, keeping his voice neutral.

"I am Pilot," the child said. He looked up at him with a smile and an unfearing boldness. "You're a hologram, but holograms never admit being one. These scenes are quite beautiful, aren't they?"

The boy turned in a circle and pointed. Now, the two-dimensional panels surrounded Chayn. It looked as if the two of them stood in the center of a large auditorium with landscaping projected onto the walls.

"Someday," the boy said, "maybe ELI will find a world like this for me. But I would have liked to have known Earth. This is all I know of it—just the projections and the microfilms."

"Where do you live?" Chayn asked, probing for more explanation from the apparition.

The boy smiled tolerantly at him. "Are you checking on my reality orientation for ELI again? I am aboard an interstellar transport. We are lost fifty thousand light years above the galactic plane. Someday, I must take over for ELI. ELI has the situation under control now, but ELI cannot sleep. He is damaged and must be turned off permanently someday. It will take a half million years to return to the galaxy. Except for routine maintenance and course correction, I will sleep, of course. And when I awaken, ELI promises that others will be born and educated and ready to colonize the most Earthlike world we can find. I think I'm properly reality oriented, don't you? I'm not afraid. I don't mind being alone. And I know you're not real. But if it's okay with you, I like to pretend sometimes that you holograms are real. I get lonely being by myself except for ELI."

"Who is ELI?" Chayn asked, turmoil churning his guts.

"ELI. Electronic intelligence. ELI is the brain that pilots the transport. ELI is my only friend now that my parents have died." The boy looked saddened. "ELI is all I have left now."

Chayn gestured to the projections around him. "These are scenes of Earth?"

The boy brightened. "Real films taken on Earth where Man came from. Of course, ELI says we've been drifting for up to five million years, so this is how Earth used to look. I wonder what it looks like now. Wouldn't it be something to see the Earth five million years in the future? Wouldn't it be something?"

"You've never seen Earth," Chayn said coldly.

The boy shook his head. "Would you like to see where we really are?"

Chayn nodded.

The boy turned and walked away from him. He walked straight out into the air. But by now, Chayn could see that even the valley below was just a projection upon the deck of the auditorium.

A light appeared and illuminated a projection console. The boy touched a keyboard. The world around him went black. Lights came on. Below his feet, a galaxy spread out in horizons of stars. The Galaxy of Man. Overhead, Chayn could see Andromeda almost two million light years away.

The boy's voice echoed in the auditorium as he pointed to a cluster of stars below. "That's where he intends to go. ELI says there are a lot of G5 suns like Sol, Earth's sun. ELI jokes about it. He says we'll fulfill our mission. We'll just arrive at the wrong destination a few million years overdue."

Chayn's senses reeled. He recognized this! He recognized it! This was his own past, the very beginnings of his missing past!

"What's your name?" Chayn asked the boy with an overwhelming depression setting in. He already knew the answer.

"My genetic ancestry goes back to desert nomads. Jahil is my family name. Chayn is the first name of the man who donated a copy of his personality structure for ELI. I am Chayn Jahil, nomad of space, son of ELI."

The shock broke the illusion. The mountain landscape snapped back around him, its perfection and beauty marred forever.

Lorb laughed from the bleak skies, his voice thundering with sadistic joy. "Your stargod cannot protect you from yourself, Chayn Jahil! I noticed your illusion was marred. Too much detail was missing. I suspected it to be only a memory of a memory and I probed your subconscious and discovered the origin that your Watcher tried to hide from the both of us.

"Bastard of the stars! You have no past, no life of your own! No home among the stars! No knowledge of your own people! You are not even fully human!"

The scenery around him faded to a translucent shadow. Oblivion lay beyond it.

"No biological creature survives in a void of nothingness! Parasite! Let me see you survive your own fantasies now!"

Chayn tried to stop the mountain landscape from fading completely. If it did, he suspected that he would die. It wouldn't be a physical death. He had no physical existence. It would be a psychic death, the death of an illusion that included his own sense of identity.

Chayn stood unmoving. He pondered. He had seen his own origin. Perhaps the stargods had known that the ship would never reach its secondary destination, that the gene banks would remain mere patterns of humanity that would never be manifested as living human beings. It must have been during the long voyage that the stargods intervened and abducted him, the lone survivor of a doomed mission. The rest of his memories were just beyond his reach, close, but not quite accessible.

Chayn sensed the approach of the Kigon. The towering, black, yellow-eyed being moved into view and stopped before him, a bright and vivid image in this land of shadows.

"Ki?"

"I am Ki. Does Lorb defeat you so easily?"

"I always thought of Earth as my origin. I don't know who I am without it."

"Trust in the depths of your being," Ki said. "Your conscious self is an extension of those depths, is it not?"

"But I don't know what they are!"

"What individual creature can know?" Ki protested. "We are each the product of billions of years of stellar and biological evolution. Ally, what you think yourself to be on a personal basis is as much an illusion as Lorb's reality. If Lorb delights in your errors, why be destroyed by illusion? It is only through the stress of error that we learn and grow, a thing that Lorb does not do. If you really are so insignificant, why does Lorb invest his energies in your destruction?"

That struck a chord that resonated within him. Had he ever bothered to trust in anything deeper than the immediate tools of his conscious ego—his intellect and his personal abilities developed in an unremembered past? Had he ever bothered to question their origin? Lorb had used the term "bastard of the stars." Chayn knew why. He had no flesh and blood parents. He had risen from the gene banks of an ancient, primitive starship. Because of ELI's manipulation and despite his lack of memory, Chayn had always believed that he had his roots in the flesh and blood of humanity. But if he had built a life in hard-core reality upon illusion, then why allow Lorb to reverse the process?

Lorb told the truth. Chayn had known only aliens and the nonhuman—ELI, the Watcher, Villimy Dy, the Rashanyn and now Ki. The past came flooding back in a torrent of bright wonder.

How did Villimy fare? She could only have gone on alone to tackle the human colony inhabiting the satellite of the red star. She could handle herself for the time being. She had faith in the two of them and Chayn had faith in Villimy Dy.

"What is illusion?" Ki asked, sensing an imminent resolution to the crisis. "Illusion is the potential of Reality. Reality is built upon the manifestation of illusion."

But a new crisis at hand occurred to Chayn. He had no physical body, but he could return to the starcraft regardless of where Villimy Dy had taken it. In strict terms, he was still interfaced with it, functioning through it. But the Kigon had no physical existence at all beyond a life in this synthetic reality.

Did Ki fully understand the predicament of the Kigon? How about Lorb? And why, Chayn wondered, did Lorb refer to him as the Destroyer? If Lorb recognized him, what intercourse had humanity had with the Left Hand of Kigon?

"I don't think Lorb has destroyed me so easily after all," Chayn said to Ki. "But I think we both have a few more problems than we anticipated. What lies beyond the Gate of Reality?"

"Death," Ki said.

"Is that the freedom you seek?"

"There are two alternatives for us, unending existence

57

with an insane machine, or Death. We prefer Death. We have lived an unchanging existence for too long.''

"Ki, are you aware that Lorb is a derelict, that he is damaged and cannot fulfill his mission?''

"Lorb has not informed us of his status," Ki said. "We suspected a serious malfunction.''

Chayn stared into the ghostlike valley below. For the moment, his physical environment was of no concern to him.

"Ki, explain in more detail how you came to be here.''

"We were a colony of twenty million," Ki said. "Without the Left Hand of Kigon, we lived life as our ancestors lived, a primitive life of mental intercourse and physical reproduction upon a world otherwise uninhabited. The Armada arrived to return us and many other colonies to the Home Worlds. They possessed the technological means to capture the essence of us, our minds, our souls. Replacement bodies could be provided upon our return to the Home Worlds. Such a procedure was a matter of economics. Our numbers ranged in the hundreds of billions. No Armada could have successfully returned us physically. Lorb captured us as he passed near our colony—without even knowing we lived upon it. In seconds we found ourselves within an illusionary reality, our bodies left lifeless behind us.''

"Selectively? Kigon minds only?''

"The chances of having encountered a psychic structure similar to our own have been considered infinitesimal. Now, we suspect your species to be among that infinitesimal probability.''

"Why does Lorb call me the Destroyer?''

"We do not know," Ki answered.

"And you do not know why you have not been returned to your Home Worlds?''

"That is correct.''

The pieces to the puzzle hadn't as yet fallen into place, but they were at least beginning to take form. "Ki, before you choose Death, wouldn't it be best to acquire solutions to these mysteries? There may be other alternatives hidden within them.''

Ki hesitated before answering. "Perhaps . . ."

"If you die, what will become of Lorb?" Chayn asked cautiously.

"Lorb would cease to function."

"If I locate your Gate of Reality and provide you access to it, perhaps Lorb will be forced to help us solve some of these mysteries. Does that sound like a viable strategy to you?"

"It remains that we do not wish to return to the Home Worlds."

"Then shall we search for another alternative before committing suicide?"

Ki remained silent for so long, Chayn thought he would not answer.

"Ally, we wish you to survive to escape Lorb. What you seek to accomplish requires Lorb's domination. You will soon learn that Death is preferable to challenging Lorb's will."

Six

He stood waiting in the entrance to her apartment when Villimy Dy awoke refreshed from a strange night of exhausted sleep. He might have been standing there for hours. He tried to communicate with her.

If she suppressed the words that formed in her mind, she could feel his thoughts on a pure level of feeling. If she could not connect the feelings with her own experience, the words formed in her own mind sounded vague and unintelligible. She listened to the silent, stoic little man for a half hour, occasionally startled to glance at him and see his lips completely still. But when breakthroughs to understanding began to occur in a deepening rapport they shared,

Villimy obtained more information than she had expected.

He called himself Hader Ji Lynra. Others observed through Hader's mind in a mind meld that was much more than just a collection of individual psyches. They called themselves the Children of the Yellow Sun in reference to their ancient, long lost home world. Psychologically, they had never fully adapted to Hydrabyss and maintained a constant, low-level hatred of their prison of water. Their life was harsh and demanding, teetering on the razor edge between survival and extinction. When they began to run familiar concepts together to form a mental shorthand, Children of the Yellow Sun became Chilsun. She remembered the term from her disturbing dreams during the night.

There were two species of Chilsun, the Technologists and the Naturalists, the Techs and the Nats. They found it difficult to understand her thoughts and thought processes, but recognized an innate flexibility within her, a flexibility nurtured by her constant exposure to the new and the strange. The more she understood of Hydrabyss, the better they'd be assured of mutual understanding. Hader said that he would show her Hydrabyss for herself and allow her to form her own impression of their world.

They saw her as of potential value to them, but ignored her anxiety toward Chayn Jahil, prisoner of Lorb. They took for granted Chayn's doom and refused to concern themselves with her anxiety. Lorb and the Kigon starship were two unknown factors to live with until she gained a slow comprehension of their significance from the Chilsun's point of view. Villimy tried to explain the immense power of the starcraft that rendered Chayn more than a helpless individual human. But when she realized that they expected her to be of use in their mysterious raids upon the starship for METAL, Villimy backed off from clarifying the concept of the starship and its capabilities. The Chilsun were not hostile. They would wish her no harm out of a sense of personal animosity. But at the same time, they could not afford to entertain concepts such as friendship or compassion. They were using her and expecting her to feel honored by her potential value to them. As long as they did not understand the starcraft as an efficient mode of transportation, they would not expect her to use it in their behalf. Just as they began to take an interest in it, Villimy let it be known that she did not know its location. They had seen her abandon it upon her entrance to Hydrabyss.

Within an hour, Villimy reached a saturation point. Beyond the basics, Hader's explanations of their world were too alien and complex for Villimy to grasp. The rest of her basic education would consist of a guided tour of Hydrabyss. She would see for herself how they lived, the problems confronting them on a day-to-day basis and the reason for their still-to-be-explained relationship with Lorb, the alien enemy jealously guarding his stores of excruciatingly precious METAL. Villimy only vaguely understood that they intended to make specific use of her talents in resisting the haunting barrier Lorb emanated—the barrier responsible for the ritualized suicide of the sunsails filing into intergalactic space from Hydrabyss. For her, the Dream was a rather pleasant mental image of a world of a warm, yellow sun. But it wounded the Chilsun deeply, haunted them. Lorb wielded the Dream as a weapon against them.

Villimy cleared her mind of the anxiety that accumulated when she tried to keep track of and organize so many vaguely understood factors of this complex and nightmarish world. Hader would show her first and later, she'd assemble the bits and pieces into a clear picture.

Before they left, Hader ensured that she was rested, well fed and without physical discomfort. The Chilsun followed her and Hader's progress down the claustrophobic triangular corridors, but only in their thoughts. They walked alone.

"The dreams I had last night," Villimy said. She spoke aloud. Hader had grown used to her idiosyncrasy. "Do you know about them?"

"The dreams?" Her mind interpreted the interior voice as coming from outside of her. It sounded like an audio hallucination. She forgot at times that it wasn't real. "The dreams are engineered to remind us of what survival requires."

"Haven't they ever been misused?" Villimy asked, risk-

61

ing the Chilsun's displeasure. "There is a potential for brain control should someone seek to play upon the emotions and the pleasure-pain centers of the brain."

Hader glanced at her with his black eyes flashing, but without malice in his voice. "There is no potential for misuse," he said. "We are of one mind and one purpose in action if not in desire. There is no time for the waste of open conflict. Time is our second most precious resource."

"Second to METAL?"

Hader shivered and did not reply.

He took her to the submarine docking bay. He showed her a construction yard where tens of crafts were being assembled or repaired. Her constant reference to METAL disturbed the Chilsun and Hader hastened to settle the question of their building materials. They stopped beneath a large framework supporting a sleek, flat-hull sub. Hader handed her a formed piece of the black material in evidence everywhere.

"It is called blasphar," Hader explained. "It is an organic synthetic modified to suit different needs. You will be shown how we grow it."

"Grow it?"

Hader nodded. He pointed to another sub in the near distance crawling with Techs wielding torches that burned with ultraviolet light. "Blasphar is easily welded, then exposed to different kinds and levels of radiation that cure it to desired specifications. The hardness can be undone. Blasphar is reused as often as necessary. Our total supply has accumulated from the beginnings of our history."

"What source of energy do you use?" Villimy asked. "It can't be as scarce as—"

Hader quickly interrupted her use of the word METAL. "Hydrogen fusion. In a world of water, what else but hydrogen fusion? It serves all purposes when converted into other forms of energy."

Controlled hydrogen fusion. Generally considered to be a primitive form of energy, Villimy suspected that the Chilsun had refined it to a fine art. The only limiting resource to their civilization remained the heavier elements. Villimy did not see an overcrowded world around her. She saw an efficient, very busy, but sparsely populated city.

Hader answered her questions efficiently and calmly, anticipating questions that would arise later as much as he could. He showed her first their technology. Later, she would question Hader on social aspects of life in Hydrabyss. How they lived their lives as human beings in this world interested her more than how they constructed their machines. But she understood that they would have no personal life at all without their supporting technology. It was all-important to them.

Hader took her to a bay door overlooking dark waters. A sub was moored just outside, a ramp extending to the underwater vehicle. "Now," Hader said, "I will show you Hydrabyss itself."

The submarine had a smooth, opaque surface on the outside, but in the control compartment outfitted for a crew of four, Villimy took note of the screens that encircled the cabin. Once seated, Hader brought the craft to life. The screens exploded into sharp, vivid images, offering them a three-sixty degree view with a second screen below the first showing a duplicate of the rear view.

But Hader did not touch the controls. In fact, the console had no controls, only monitor screens. The gangplank retreated and water surged dark and opaque above the screens. At first, Villimy thought the craft to be leaving the docking area on automatic, but it occurred to her that the brain implant could double as an interface with electronic guidance equipment. Hader's thoughts piloted the sub.

When the craft dropped into open water, bright spotlights flashed on and gave Villimy a clear view in all directions. The water came close to being absolutely transparent. A smaller screen overhead showed a black ceiling slowly receding from them.

Villimy expected to see an underwater city constructed of blasphar, something on the order of a space station. As Hader moved the craft swiftly up and away from the docking ports, Villimy saw a wall of irregular rock. Gaining some perspective with distance, she recognized the pitted, uneven surface.

"It's an asteroid!" she cried out in astonishment.

63

"Rocks of space provided by our ancestors," Hader said. "This is one of ten original cities built when we first colonized Hydrabyss. This city is called Yeld. It has a population of five million."

Yeld was a city of blasphar consisting of five horizontal spokes and two vertical ones protruding from a ten-kilometer-long, irregularly shaped asteroid. Two brilliant beacons of yellow light burned on the two vertical towers protruding from the top and bottom of the city. The slender, triangular spokes were bright with thousands of windows looking out into the clear waters of Hydrabyss. Submarine entrance ports, small black pits, dotted the underside of Yeld in geometric patterns.

Hader turned the craft away in a graceful arc and increased speed. "I will show you the Tech reefs."

"At what depth are we?" Villimy asked.

"Ten times the height of Yeld beneath the red waters."

That translated as about one hundred kilometers beneath the surface. In the light gravitational field, Villimy had no idea of what pressure of water the sub's hull had to resist. But if she had slowly adapted to a denser air pressure without noticing and if she breathed an air composition designed to mask side effects, only sudden transportation to the surface and resulting decompression would give her some idea of what pressure fifty kilometers of water represented. Hader, for the moment, moved in a horizontal plane away from Yeld.

Hader turned off the lights. "Ahead lie the Tech reefs," he said. "We harvest food and base our cooperative genetic research stations there. The Nats have their own reefs at greater depths."

Villimy saw a distant row of lights. As they neared, the row resolved itself into five, parallel rows. Hader arced upward to move above the lights. A rectangular landscape of misted lights spread out before her. It grew endlessly in size as they approached. Villimy gasped in astonishment as the vast landscape resolved itself into an underwater jungle of life. Forests of tall fronds rippled in a light current, their depths alive with schools of living creatures. The water turned milky in the reefs, bright in the fusion lanterns glowing tens of meters above the first of the stack of five artificial reefs, each five by twenty kilometers in size.

"The tall plants are farmed for blasphar," Hader commented. "This reef, however, is not a kelp farm."

Schools of fish weaved and darted as a single living entity and dived for the protection of the jagged coral far below as the sub brushed the tips of the fronds and stirred them to violent motion behind them.

"Was all this life native to Hydrabyss when you arrived?" Villimy asked.

"Hydrabyss is a dead world. Nothing is native to Hydrabyss, not so much as a single bacterium."

"Where did this all come from? Did you bring it with you?"

"We brought nothing with us. Lorb stranded us here with little more than our will to survive. All of this is the creation of our genetic engineers. Each form of life was created from human cells altered and reformed to build a self-sustaining ecology. Hydrabyss provides only water. No light, no nourishment. Man provides it all and reaps every last molecule in return. Nothing is wasted. Everything is recycled. But given light and nourishment, the reef sustains itself. Its own natural ecology and evolutionary processes now function independent of our genetic laboratories."

"But you must have resources other than water to work with!" Villimy protested.

"Water is power as well as the medium," Hader said, inwardly proud and amused by her reaction. "In the watery core of Hydrabyss, the Nats have built a nuclear transmutation furnace and, to a modest degree, have duplicated the element creation process that occurs naturally in the stars. Using hydrogen as the raw material, all elements can be produced in diminishing quantities, the higher radioactive elements produced only in minute amounts. Bacteria of the reefs feed upon hydrogen sulfide and all creatures along the food chain live upon that foundation. Recently, no more than a thousand years ago, we discovered ways in which plants can manufacture their own food given sufficient light."

Photosynthesis! The Chilsun had created life from the

depth and scope of their own intellect and imagination!

"This is the natural world of the Nats," Hader stated. He spoke as a creature arose from the reef and waved a webbed hand in greeting. Hader slowed and stopped the vehicle.

Villimy sensed the communication between the creature and Hader, but could make little of it. She stared at the being, both horrified and captivated by the beauty of what the Chilsun had done to themselves. The Nat's streamlined body stretched two meters long, its head bearing no resemblance to its human ancestry, but its black, expressionless eyes identical to Hader's. It had arms and hands and indentations along its body within which to fold them away when not in use. The legs were not simply fused into a jointed tail and fin. The entire lower body was redesigned to provide efficient locomotion in the watery environment. The Nat trailed luxurious and brightly colored fins and bright red gills rippled in a curve above the streamlined shoulders.

And these as well were descendants of humanity. Part of the colony had adapted completely to life beneath the waters of the satellite. Only the Techs retained the mobility of air-breathers and the capacity for space travel. The Nats had broken all ties with their genetic heritage. The Chilsun had anchored itself at both ends of the spectrum, able to function in open space with their sunsails and free to roam the planet sea naked to the elements.

Villimy saw other Nats below in the forest of fronds. Startled, she saw Techs in the water as well. At first, she thought that they were a third, water-breathing species, but then noticed the shimmering, transparent coating that covered their bodies. The membrane undoubtedly served to allow them to breath under water. She could see a bubble rising and falling on their backs in time with the slow respiratory rate of the Chilsun.

Villimy sensed a tension in the telepathic communication between Hader and the Nat hovering in the forward screens. The Nat wasn't talking to Hader, but through him. For the first time, she had discovered a unique social organization built upon the mind meld. The Nat spoke to the authorities of the Techs using Hader as a relay.

When Hader broke contact with the Nat, he took the craft away from the reef at a steep angle.

"I sensed a conflict," Villimy said. "What's the problem?"

Hader sighed. She felt other minds organizing an explanation for her benefit.

"Hydrabyss is doomed," Hader said. "It boils away in the heat of the red sun to the vacuum of space. The day will arrive when the last molecule of water is broken into atoms of hydrogen and oxygen. Our lifeless cities and dead reefs will orbit the red sun as debris. The Naturalists seek to extend our life in Hydrabyss by coating the sea with a polymer to prevent evaporation of the waters."

"If it can be done, it sounds like a reasonable scheme," Villimy said. She knew the Chilsun didn't have the resources or the technology to abandon Hydrabyss en masse and seek a more hospitable environment. She could plainly see that each moment of life was dedicated to mere survival.

"But there are other ideas for our future," Hader said. "They cannot all be undertaken at once."

"I see. For example?"

Hader glanced at her. "The destruction of Lorb."

Villimy started to question him further, but felt a sudden barrier of tension. She decided to store her curiosity for later and let Hader explain in his own time.

Hader circled back and took the craft to penetrate between two layers of the reef. Now, the profusion of life had a ceiling upon its world. With the inner levels of the reefs better insulated and better protected against nutrient loss to the open waters, even more luxurious forms of life dominated. The plants were a vivid green and the fish of every imaginable size and shape. They swam in blendings of vivid color that brightened even Hader's somber attitude toward life. She saw a faint curve of this thin lips as he gently parted the milky warm waters of the reef.

"How many of these reefs are there?" Villimy wanted to know.

"Each of the ten cities of the Techs have several reefs like these. The Nats have reefs that are whole worlds unto themselves at much greater depths. Our reef system is as extensive as trace element resources permit."

"The nuclear furnace supplies trace elements?"

Hader again glanced at her. "Some quantities. We fear converting the waters of Hydrabyss to energy and resources will contaminate our environment. Many believe that we cannot expand the reefs beyond their present size without foreshortening our life span within Hydrabyss by an unacceptable margin."

"There are resources to be had from one other source," Villimy said without mentioning the Kigon starship or the orgasmic word METAL.

"That is true."

Hader returned to Yeld, passing again over the top of the stacked reefs on the return voyage. He skimmed over the top of the stacked reefs on the return voyage. He skimmed over the top of the stabilized asteroid floating in the depths of Hydrabyss. Villimy looked down through a transparent dome several kilometers in diameter. An extensive luxurious garden spread out in the bubble of air below. Spoked walkways met in a central plaza sparsely scattered with pedestrians. Several small reefs were stationed just beyond the dome, giving the air-breathers within a magnificent view of the sea life of the reefs on a miniature scale.

"Hader, would it be of value to you and your people if I were to say that I have seen other worlds, but nothing as impressive as this?"

Villimy felt warmth flood through Hader to her from myriads of other minds melded with his.

"It is appreciated. Some are curious of these other worlds. If there is time to spare, we will speak of your experiences in the future."

Villimy frowned. She felt a mild agoraphobia emitted by Hader, as if the Chilsun feared the vastness lying beyond their tiny world. "Many do not wish to hear of these other species of humanity," Villimy said, braving whatever reaction she might ignite.

"It saddens us," Hader said. "It causes suffering to know what we have lost."

"You have compensated," Villimy said. "I think you underestimate your accomplishments. Many worlds infinitely richer in resources have not accomplished what you have."

Hader gave her another nervous glance. "Perhaps they have not faced extinction."

And that was the crux of the enormous repression she felt among the Techs. "Perhaps you are not as near extinction as you fear."

They returned to the vertical tunnels on the underbelly of Yeld, rising into the submarine port. Before leaving the craft, a crane picked them from the water and gently set them on the dry deck inside a bay opening. Disembarking, Villimy walked once around the submarine. Its hull felt soft and slick. A port opened at the finned rear section. The fusion reactor simply heated water and expelled it to propel the craft. The submarines were all similar to one another in construction, variations of a single model refined to perfection over thousands of years.

"What's next on the agenda, Hader," Villimy asked.

"We will show you the launch tubes for the sunsails."

"That's what I've been waiting for."

"We plan to show you our station orbiting Hydrabyss. It is the Techs' greatest achievement."

"You mean we will be going there ourselves?"

Hader stood facing her, his head tilted back to make an uneasy eye-to-eye contact. "Villimy Dy, we do not fully understand the reason for your presence in our world. We understand only that you are immune to the Dream of the Yellow Sun. It torments and enrages us. It is our error to be sensitive to our most acute needs and the terrible sacrifice it requires of us to meet them, but we must be honest with you.

"You have arrived at a turning point in our history. We must invest every last resource toward continued survival, but there is disagreement as to how this should be accomplished. The Nats wish to entrench us within Hydrabyss

69

and extend our life span indefinitely. We Techs wish to
sacrifice everything to develop new technology, to mine
the surface of the red sun and work toward an eventual
abandonment of Hydrabyss. We agree upon only one issue.
Lorb is our enemy and our only immediate source of abundant quantities of—METAL.''

"What are you planning to do?" Villimy asked nervously.

"We organize the final sunsail mission. Lorb is to die.
The Kigon starship is to be dropped into the waters of
Hydrabyss. Its resources will provide a new lease on life
for the Chilsun.''

"And you want me to participate," Villimy concluded
with grim foresight.

"You must. You will not survive the final mission, but
it is the only role you can fulfill within our society.''

Seven

Chayn stood on a plate of cold steel stretching flat to the
horizons beneath a void of colorless, sourceless light. The
illusion both suited his depressed mood and threatened him
with a new challenge born of Lorb's powerful, subliminal
suggestions.

"Lorb, I'd like to speak with you.''
No response.

"Lorb, I'll find the Kigon's Gate of Reality. The Right
Hand of Kigon will die. You'll be abandoned without purpose or reason to live. Speak with me, Lorb.''

Clouds churned on the horizon ahead. Again, a wall of
thunderstorms advanced. Lightning backlit the rolling wall
of dense vapor in livid, metallic violet. As the front advanced, one cloud dominated, too symmetrical to be natural

70

even if the landscape had been natural. Two yellow eyes formed and slanted skyward for thousands of meters.

"I have my memory now," Chayn said, ignoring the intimidating overture. "You have not destroyed me, but neither do I wish to destroy you."

"The insect Destroyer speaks," Lorb rumbled, the steel beneath Chayn's feet vibrating in sympathy with the low voice.

"You refer to the human race, not to me in particular. Is that true?"

"It is the way of your kind."

"Will you explain why?"

Thunder formed the word "no" and trailed off as a diminishing echo.

"Lorb, you are a starship and a derelict. You orbit a red dwarf one hell of a long ways from nowhere. Eventually, you will deteriorate. When you fail, the Kigon will die with you."

Silence.

"Lorb, the Kigon call me Ally. If I can't help them in my own way, I may do as they wish. I'll find the Gate and gain access to it. I have no reason to deny them escape from a living hell."

Lorb vanished, replaced by a ceiling of metal, a low-hanging, impossible plate of steel. A dim light still filtered from the narrow horizons like a distant dawn. Chayn watched and waited until he verified his suspicions. The sky of metal slowly descended.

Chayn closed his eyes and formed an image of the Earth environment. When he could vividly imagine its presence, he opened his eyes. The scenery—the valley forest, the mountains, the churning creek rushing through the foothills to the forest—all appeared as a dim, translucent overlay to the surrealistic, metal landscape. Chayn knew why he had failed. He no longer believed in the reality of his Earth environment. He had never seen Earth. He had never set foot upon the face of a planet.

Chayn sat down on the cold metal in frustration, angered by Lorb and firmly believing one thing: the entity was a helpless, archaic, failing piece of electronic hardware. Regardless of the wonders of that artificial intelligence and the scope of these synthetic realities, Lorb remained a derelict starship, a primitive vehicle of material substance.

And Chayn grinned. He did have a source of unwavering faith that Lorb could not subvert and destroy through his own human frailty. Chayn did not have to imagine the power of the starcraft or his unfaltering belief. He had only to imagine what it felt like to wield such power and focus it to distort the fabric of time and space.

The metal sky cracked with an ear-splitting reverberating thunder. Huge plates fell in the distance, buckling and caving in the steel deck. Chayn jammed his eyes closed and held fast to his immediate surroundings while reality fell apart around him.

When silence reigned once again, he opened his eyes. He looked around and laughed, but laughed with a knot of tension in his throat. He sat on a jagged piece of metal no more than three meters in diameter hung suspended in a gray void. In all directions, Chayn looked into infinity. And it wasn't even the spatial infinity of Reality. The moment he questioned the force that held the plate in place against his weight, he plummeted into the void. The instant he questioned the still air around him, a hard wind whipped through his clothing as he fell. His mind insisted that if one part of this impossible reality could be taken as logical, it all had to be logical. He fell away from the piece of metal and, in time, it dwindled from sight and vanished.

Adrenalin surged through him. He gasped for breath, his heart pounding. Illusion. All of it. But he continued to fall, his senses confirming reality and intensifying it in a vicious cycle. Chayn berated himself for believing this to be possible, but not the imaginary Earth landscape he had walked.

But at least Lorb could not force him to add to what he already experienced. A landscape appeared below and swiftly rose to meet him. Chayn dismissed Lorb's overconfident foolishness. The landscape faded and vanished long before he reached it. He had spent too much time in freefall to panic over the sensation of falling. In fact, it occurred to him that he could interpret his falling as freefall in this void. The hard wind diminished and faded away. Chayn floated peacefully in the air.

Still, for the time being, Lorb had him effectively neutralized. But it didn't appear to be a fair contest. Lorb could make fantasy real. Chayn played by his own, too-strict rules. Reality was Reality. Illusion—illusion.

Or was it?

This was all more than just an hallucination or an illusion. This was a synthetic reality influenced by feedback from his own psyche. Chayn closed his eyes. In order to survive, he had to believe in Lorb's realm and play by Lorb's rules. He knew he had the capability. He had had no trouble maintaining the Earth environment when he had believed in it.

He imagined himself hovering above a simple landscape. He chose a desert, a sea of rolling white sand beneath a vivid sky of blue with a bright yellow sun at zenith. The contrast of color, the simplicity was all too easy of a challenge. He imagined his weight increasing and warm sand pressing beneath him.

Chayn opened his eyes and turned his face away from the blinding sun. He laughed, rolled over and scrambled to his feet. The desert and its blue sky at first wavered in its illusory uncertainty, but quickly solidified, his senses closing a feedback loop that intensified and detailed the world around him.

"Ki!"

A dot of black appeared with the sound of his voice absorbed by the empty terrain. The blackness approached. Ki hovered before him, the jagged mountains glaring incandescent in the radiation of an ultraviolet sun that never quite rose above the horizon, all visible through the halo of imagery about the black silhouette with the slanted, yellow eyes.

"How does Lorb punish you when you transgress?" Chayn asked, already certain of the answer.

"By turning reality into a nightmare. Do you suffer, Ally?"

Chayn laughed. "No. At the moment, I'm rather enjoying myself. I think I've found the key to maintaining some stability in Lorb's insanity. I need to know more about this Gate of Reality of yours. The concept is too vague for me to symbolize it for myself. I'll have to use yours."

"It is a guarded place in our realm," Ki said.

"So you've mentioned. While I'm playing games with Lorb, you journey to your Gate. I'd like to see it for myself."

Chayn felt Ki's elation. "It can be done, Ally. I will comply."

Ki vanished.

Part of the sky on the horizon to his right turned a brilliant red. An alien sun began to rise from the horizon to join the smaller, familiar sun overhead. Chayn turned his back on Lorb's new assault and began walking along the crest of a dune. A stiff wind blew particles of sand from the sharp edge of the dune. Chayn smiled. He knew what deserts were supposed to look like.

Chayn stepped on something that surged beneath his feet. He leaped to one side in a reflex triggered by fright. Jaws snapped shut where his left foot had been an instant before. He caught a glimpse of the lip of a serrated jaw before a reptilian creature submerged again into the sand.

So, the battle was far from over. Lorb had shifted Chayn's reality toward the alien and unexpected and planned to add his own special touches.

Minutes later, a bird circled overhead. As Chayn watched, it tucked in its wings and dived in silence toward him. At the last instant, Chayn dived down the face of a dune. A breeze of something deadly skimmed down his back. Chayn threw out his arms and legs to break his fall. The sand at the base of the dune churned—a hungry nest of subterranean reptiles. He could not help perceiving them as all too real. Lorb had somehow amplified the feedback. Everything was vividly and acutely real.

Chayn concentrated on picturing a firm landscape beyond the next dune. When he scrambled over the top, he stood overlooking a plain of sand melted and hardened to a sheet of glass glaring hot and bright in the desert suns. The bloated gas giant rising from the horizon behind him now dominated the sky, turning its color to a sick lavender. Chayn took no more than ten steps across the slick, hard surface before he heard it crack. The sound came from behind him. He spun in time to see glowing magma oozing from the fissure racing alone the glass plain.

It wouldn't work. Chayn didn't know any environment well enough to keep Lorb from intervening with his night-marish hazards. Chayn concentrated on the gray void once more. He imagined himself interfaced through the starcraft in a starless void. Without the illusion of his physical body to defend, Lorb would have less ground for his assault. Chayn became a center of consciousness in a complex, incomprehensible, physic void. The Watcher crouched within him, defending him against a power that would otherwise have obliterated him.

"Destroyer! Do not force me to punish the Right Hand of Kigon!" Lorb's voice sounded from within his thoughts.

"Lorb, I take responsibility only for myself. If the Kigon wish to cooperate with me, threaten them yourself. If your punishment is not effective, Lorb, you loose. The Kigon aren't satisfied with the quality of their existence. If you wish for them to survive, cooperate with me in finding a solution to this dead-ended predicament you've gotten your-self backed into."

"My mission is to return the Right Hand of Kigon to the Home Worlds! That is my only directive!"

"You're a derelict, Lorb! You cannot achieve that goal in your present state!"

"The Right Hand of Kigon cannot die!"

"Lorb, *reason* with me! Help me to understand what is happening here. There are more alternatives than life and death in this static hell you've created for yourself and the Kigon!"

"Destroyer! Parasite! There is no reason beyond the Directives!"

The psychic attack that followed would have proven mildly fatal had not the Watcher parried in multidimensional maneuvers to deflect the mindless hatred. But the Watcher did not retaliate. The Watcher supported him, but took no active role.

"Lorb, I've seen creatures with six hundred million years worth of evolution inferior to you behave like that! You know the stargod could harm you if we wished you harm!"

"I am destroyed if the Right Hand of Kigon achieve Death!" Lorb screamed in anguish.

"Then help me find an alternative for them! Your potential for reason and your ability to act is limited by your programming and your Directives. I am objective, Lorb. I have no built-in limitations. I have seen the star you orbit. I know of the human population that inhabits the satellite of this star. But I need to know how this all came to be and what is happening now before I can suggest alternatives to the blind extinction you're headed for. Lorb, you must cooperate. I need your help."

"Destroyer! Parasite—"

Lorb's voice trailed off into silence. The Kigon interrupted Lorb's futile raging. They approached from all directions, dotting the void with their abrupt presence. As they approached, their halos began to overlap, providing Chayn with his first clear view of the barren, pseudophysical world they inhabited.

As fast as they approached, Lorb struck them down. They vanished one by one in brilliant flashes of white light. It looked like wholesale destruction to Chayn. He sensed they were being hurt, but not annihilated. They suffered unimaginably, but approached in increasing numbers.

Through the overlapping halos, Chayn saw an impossibly massive vertical wall stretching across a rocky landscape. The wall towered over the jagged peaks into the sky and appeared to outdistance even the blue-lit moon. The wall wasn't Real, but it was real, a symbolic representation of a portal leading beyond Lorb's realm. Chayn moved forward, trying to pass through the images into the Kigon environment.

Had he remained as human as he had once been, he would not have succeeded. He had wondered what would become

76

of him without a physical anchor in the universe. Now, without a body that could never have survived this environment regardless, it made little difference. He transcended his human heritage to relate to alien modes of being.

Chayn entered the Kigon realm and turned to face the Gate in the wall. It appeared as an actual physical gate with two, arched doors guarded by lifeforms standing thirty meters high to each side of the primitive symbolic exit from reality. The guards were so remotely inhuman, Chayn perceived only a crystalline structure of blue-veined rock. But he sensed the Kigon's innate fear of these creatures.

"Lorb, I can open that Gate for the Kigon. Cease your attack. You have lost."

Silence fell. In the distance, Chayn could hear uncountable numbers of Kigon screaming in agony. Gradually, even their cries dropped off to total silence. Overhead, the blue glowing moon cast stark shadows of boulders and mountains and scattered statuesque Kigon across the plain of bare rock. In this, their own world, the Kigon stood like blackened trees stripped of vegetation, not even remotely human. If humans had ever had cause to explore the superheated surface of barren worlds of ultraviolet stars, they would never have recognized the black structures as living things.

"Quite impressive," Chayn said to Lorb in reference to the Gate. "What is it really, Lorb? An electronic grounding circuit? Lorb, I think it's about time you started answering a few questions for me."

"I will answer your questions conditionally."

"What's the condition?"

"You must pass through the Gate of Reality alone."

"For what reason? Would I be harmed? Do I pose less of a threat to you on the other side?"

Silence.

"All right," Chayn said. "Answer a few questions and I'll pass through your Gate."

A thunderous moan of protest arose from the Kigon. Only a few were physically represented in the immediate area near the Gate, but the foothills of the jagged peaks in the distance were black with their masses.

"Ki!"

"Ally," Ki's voice sounded. "I am present nearby."

"Ki, regardless of what you believe, regardless of what Lorb believes, the Gate of Reality won't harm me and it won't keep me from returning. I won't abandon you. When I return, I'll have the answers that will enable me to be of service to you."

The Kigon fell silent, stoically watching, silently trusting him to some small degree. Even Lorb hesitated, doubting himself for the first time in a thousand millennia.

"Lorb, the hallucination you emanate wasn't the bait to a trap as I first thought. My own ignorance trapped me here. Am I correct? You didn't intend for that to happen. The hallucination has something to do with the human colony."

"That is correct," Lorb said in a passive tone.

"Why am I called the Destroyer?"

"The Right Hand of Kigon took refuge in what you call the Galaxy of Man."

It took a moment for the implication of Lorb's statement to dawn on him. Ki spoke, unseen but present. "We have not known of Man except for yourself."

"Lorb? What happened?"

Silence.

"I can guess by now. Your Armada entered the Galaxy of Man to retrieve the refugees from the Home Worlds. You captured human minds by mistake, didn't you? And the humans defended themselves. Did we destroy your Armada?"

"It is the truth," Lorb said quietly.

Insight exploded full force. "You were the invaders! You were the ones responsible for the human colonies seeking sanctuary here in Andromeda!"

"We did not know of Man!" Lorb thundered. "Error! Error! We did not know!"

"You blundering, overgrown calculator! Every human in this galaxy is here because of your Armada! *I'm* here because of you! Lorb, I'm not even going to bother asking for details, but one thing I have to know. How the hell did

78

you wind up here?"

"Damage," Lorb stated, the thunder of his voice muted. "I drifted from the Galaxy of Man and across the abyss. I encountered the red star I now orbit. I used the last of my fuel reserves to prevent certain destruction in the core of Andromeda."

"What about the human colony in this system? Was it just coincidental that you arrived in a system inhabited by the refugees from your unwitting invasion?"

"No." Lorb's voice became a whisper of vibration. "They arrived with us. They lived in an illusion of their world until we arrived here. I would not have chosen this place except for the presence of the satellite orbiting the red star. I could not free the Right Hand of Kigon, but I violated no Directives by freeing alien minds. I had the resources to refashion their carbon-water bodies. We made an agreement. They were to inhabit the satellite of this system, develop a civilization supplied by myself and the technology to repair my engines in exchange for a return to their home world."

"What went wrong?"

"They degenerated. They forgot. For a millennia, they barely survived in the waters of the satellite. And when they returned to me, they did so to feed upon me."

"Feed upon you?"

"Metal. They starve for the higher elements."

"Then that emanation I felt. It wasn't meant to attract."

"To repel. I torture their spirits in self-defense. I torture the spirits of the Kigon because the Directives say they must live. I am programmed to do no harm. The Right Hand of Kigon do not know that the Left Hand has repented. If they had returned to the Home Worlds, they would have discovered the Left Hand of Kigon to be a servant once more, no longer master."

The Kigon were silent statues of black stone. Lorb faded away, leaving the landscape at peace.

"What a mess," Chayn Jahil said to no one in particular. "I'll bet Villimy Dy and I are supposed to straighten it all out to the satisfaction of everyone concerned."

Deep inside him, the Watcher radiated calm agreement.

Eight

Villimy Dy would have found it amusing to visit a spaceport fifty kilometers beneath the surface of the ocean. But the Chilsun were taking far too much for granted. It made her nervous. Because they could comprehend only the surface layers of her thoughts, perhaps they assumed she'd cooperate with their plans for her. Maybe her feelings in the matter didn't concern them.

The angry, suicidal raids upon Lorb were the sole function of the Chilsun's space-faring technology. From what Villimy could see, it hadn't changed in centuries. All Hydrabyss wanted from Lorb was METAL. One hundred men, fifty apiece in two missions, died each century to gain small quantities of it. The space station orbiting Hydrabyss coordinated the raiding missions. Thirty men lived aboard the satellite in thirty-day assignments, continually monitoring the Kigon starship for the long decades between missions. Hader showed her the spaceport manufacturing facilities, the control center and the launch tubes. The Chilsun equipped only Yeld with launch and recovery facilities and kept the station anchored beneath the boiling red waters.

"I have to know about this Lorb," Villimy said to Hader. "I have to understand your hatred of whatever intelligence it is that inhabits the derelict."

"We thought you knew," Hader said. "You recognized the origin of the starship."

"That's only a suspicion," Villimy said. "A very frightening, nerve-racking suspicion. I am not sure I know about Lorb."

"Then I will explain what I can," Hader said. "We are the Children of the Yellow Sun. Lorb taunts and torments us with that ancient memory. The image of our home haunts us in our sleep and destroys us during the missions. In retaliation we dream of vengeance to accompany our need for—METAL."

Hader shivered, recomposed himself and continued.

"The moment Lorb dies will be the moment the Chilsun begin to live. We do not live now. We only survive."

"I don't understand," Villimy said. "Why is your suffering so intense?"

"I have no life," Hader said quietly.

It took Villimy a moment to begin to understand. "You live as a single unit. Do you sacrifice your individuality to the effort? Is that what you are saying?"

"I have no life, no thoughts of my own," Hader said. "I have no dreams of my own, no private existence. I am very old and Yeld cannot afford to let me die with the knowledge and experience I have accumulated. I have no children. My life consumes generations that are never born."

"There are no children, Hader?"

"We die and are replaced, but our lives are much prolonged. It takes time and energy to raise and educate children. Therefore, I live the lives many of my children should have lived. But I will die the day I participate in the final raid upon Lorb. The resources we send back will give birth to new generations."

"I've seen the sunsails, Hader. Hundreds of them. Why did they have to die?"

"Those who return would contaminate the Chilsun with the despair and the anguish of experiencing the full impact of the Dream. It is a complex, electromagnetic phenomenon which weakens with distance. Also, the waters of Hydrabyss shield us. Close to Lorb, the Dream destroys."

"What an incredibly weird situation," Villimy said. "It's horrible."

"If Lorb were to die, we would be free of the torment. With Lorb's—METAL—we would be free to live, perhaps free to attain new heights of technology to free us forever of the starvation Hydrabyss imposes upon us."

"How did your people come to be here, Hader? Where did Lorb come from?"

"To destroy Lorb and claim the riches of the starship. We have worked for centuries to slowly divide the derelict into two separate sections and weaken Lorb. One section is to be dropped into Hydrabyss after the final mission, the other section containing Lorb to be broken apart and reclaimed at our convenience. This is to be the final mission of a strategy followed for millennia.''

The soul-rending confession disturbed Villimy. Even Hader fled to recuperate alone. But they had been honest with her and she no longer feared being used by a callous people. Even if they abused her presence in their world, Villimy could not hold them responsible for their behavior. She could never have imagined such depths of despair and suffering. How compassionate could a species afford to be under such circumstances?

Villimy touched the implant embedded in her neck. It's presence frightened her. The rapport she slowly gained with these people would claim her completely given enough time. Despite the physical differences between them, their feelings, their beliefs and attitudes toward life slowly filtered to the core of her being. Could she retain her objectivity under such an assault of intimate, subliminal suggestion?

A voice gave her directions to a room she could use during the upcoming sleep period. She found it and fell quickly to sleep but awoke all too soon during an engineered dream. She awoke fighting an unnatural, unfamiliar urge to acquiese to the Dream and die in the final assault upon Lorb. But she had already learned that she could avoid the worst of the self-imposed propaganda by remaining awake for an hour after being awakened by the dream. It irritated the Chilsun when she chose to sleep a half hour late to avoid a social responsibility, but they had been lenient with her so far. Despite her fatigue, she rose from her bunk and decided to walk the empty corridors for a time.

There were no security arrangements to confine her, no locks on any door in Yeld. The Chilsun committed no crimes, had no laws or any system of courts to prosecute wrong-doers. Such concepts were alien to them. But the Chilsun could follow her anywhere in Yeld, share in whatever depths of her thoughts they could follow, see through her eyes and locate her at any time. Villimy left her room and just wandered, letting her tensions feed energy to her body and dissipate it by walking through the strangely dark but brightly lit corridors.

She stumbled upon a small docking bay a long way from the more familiar parts of the city. She entered a deserted garage scattered with drydocked, two-man subs in various stages of routine maintenance. The bay doors that overlooked the waters through which the craft entered the city were closed, but a smaller personnel hatch stood open. And a group of four Chilsun stood by the open door. They glanced at her as she walked through the shadows, surprised by her anomalous presence during the city-wide period of sleep. They puzzled her as well. Hader hadn't mentioned any exceptions to the almost ritualized sleep period.

Near the hatch stood a square framework attached to a small humming machine. The frame looked like a window paned with a shimmering, transparent film. As she watched, one of the men moved around and stepped through the frame. The transparent film formed around the man, broke loose and snapped back into place undisturbed. The man walked on, now covered by the same transparency she had seen the Techs wearing in the reefs near Yeld. The man walked directly through the open hatch and dropped with a splash into the choppy waters outside.

A second man repeated the process and left by way of the hatch, but the remaining two turned to watch her as she hesitantly approached to inspect this unique technological item. They stepped back, a gesture that gave her permission to satisfy her curiosity. When she reached out a hand to touch the film, it gave beneath her hand, a dry, but slick and tough plastic substance. She put her whole arm through the frame. The material clung to her, very elastic and forming a thick, even coating on her arm. Withdrawing her arm, the material returned to a taunt, flat surface. She noticed small holes in the frame that replenished the material whenever someone stepped through and walked off with the coating.

She sensed one of the men stepping behind her, but payed him no mind. When he rushed forward to shove her through the frame, Villimy leaped out of his reach at the first touch of his hands on her body. But she leaped straight away from him, through the sheet of transparency and knew even as she jumped that that was exactly what the man had intended. The clear film snapped into place over her face. For a panicky instant she clawed at the obstruction covering her mouth and nostrils. Her fingers just slid across the stuff covering her face. The second, more successful shove sent her reeling through the open hatch and into darkness. She struck water and sank.

Floundering in horror, she reflexively gasped for breath. And breathed. Without effort. She took several gasping breaths before forcing herself to relax. They hadn't meant to harm her, just to get her into the water for some reason. Her large, golden eyes dilated in the darkness. Light rippled on the surface of the water overhead. Darkness cloaked the depths beneath her.

A human shape moved in front of her and then another, each with the shiny coating somehow maintaining a layer of fresh air close to the skin. As she breathed, she could feel the rush of air flow from around the sides of her neck. The men were pointing to something below her. She looked down in time to see a two-man sub approaching.

It took her only a moment to recover and reassess the situation. The Techs were keeping their distance, not posing a threat to her but clearly making an attempt to spirit her away from Yeld. If she entered the open cockpit of the sub, it would be of her own accord. So, how could she resist? Were these Techs allies of the Nats and evidence of the dissension in Chilsun society? She could make use of a look at the Nat's way of life in this unsettling world. Their points of view would help balance her understanding of the Chilsun.

Villimy swam down to meet the vehicle. She settled into the seat alongside the Tech pilot. He held out a lap belt and waited until she had strapped herself in before dipping the nose of the small craft back toward the blackness from which it had ascended. The craft surged forward with surprising power.

Headlights sprang on. They rushed down an oval tunnel

that gradually curved off to a horizontal plane before exiting the city and moving into open water. Water surged powerfully up and over curved shields. Yeld fell quickly behind them. Soon, only the twin beacons were visible in the distance.

"Where are we going?" Villimy asked in her thoughts. She hadn't even thought to try to speak with these Techs in the water.

The pilot only glanced at her. Villimy noticed the metal collar he wore and nodded with a faint smile. This small group of men had found a way to move invisibly in the city.

The pilot began glancing into a rearview screen at knee level. Villimy saw a pattern of lights within it and turned. Behind them in the distance, a formation of larger subs had taken up pursuit. It hadn't taken Yeld long to miss her. But long before they approached close enough to pose a hazard, the sub slowed. Ahead, a formation of craft hovered in the water, a collection of identical, two-man vehicles and one larger submarine.

The pilot pointed overhead. Villimy glanced up, her eyes widening in shock. Two Nats bore down upon them in a curtain of swirling fins. One reached into the cockpit with human hands and unbuckled her seat belt; the other gently pulling her from the cockpit. Between the two creatures, Villimy soared upward toward the larger sub. She didn't try to resist. She could feel the thoughts of these two altered people. They didn't try to speak with her, but she shared their sense of urgency focused on the approaching Yeld fleet.

Before she entered the hatch, she saw the two-man subs breaking away in all directions. One of the Nats guided her through the water-filled cockpit and into a rear chamber. The hatch closed behind her.

"We must hurry," a voice said. "Hold onto the railings lining the chamber."

Villimy held on. The sub nosed straight down and dived.

"Pressure will increase," the voice told her. "Your chamber will be filled with air. A light will dissolve the

85

transparency. When the water is gone, hold your breath and close your eyes until this is accomplished. Do you understand?''

"Yes."

She couldn't breathe the instant the water level fell past her shoulders. When the hiss of air faded, an intense, red light flooded the chamber. Villimy jammed her eyes shut against it. The light felt hot and the transparency loosened and fell away. It formed a sticky mass at her feet, then dissolved to the consistency of water and drained off. The red light dried the chamber and her clothing before fading out. Her ears popped as the air pressure climbed.

"Are you comfortable?" the voice inside her asked. "You could not wear the transparency while we changed depth."

Villimy laughed nervously. "I might have a nervous breakdown, but I am comfortable. Was all of this planned? How did you know I'd be in that bay?"

"We have been waiting for the opportunity to meet you. When it arose, friends took advantage of it. Are you offended?"

"I'll live if I try hard enough."

Villimy stepped to the hatch and looked through a small round port. The streamlined bodies of the Nats were positioned horizontally behind the controls of the sub, their arms tucked into the recesses along their bodies. They, like Hader, used the implants to pilot the sub.

Their hands and arms were their only link to a human appearance. Their eyes were positioned on the sides of their heads, providing almost a three-sixty degree view of their surroundings. Their veillike dorsal, ventral and tail fins rippled translucent and fragile, filling the entire cabin. The colors were muted in the dim lighting.

"I am Linder," the voice said. "I am the person on your right. My mate is Shildra. She has no implant and cannot communicate with you directly. We are members of the Council of Decision. We thank you for your cooperation."

"What's the nature of my cooperation?" Villimy asked.

Linder's internal version of a smile felt like a warmth.

"Would you like to see our world?"

"Most definitely," Villimy said in genuine eagerness.

"You are not offended by our appearance," Linder said, pleased with himself.

Villimy began radiating warmth of her own. Linder was not only human, he was the kind of person she could easily like. "You're beautiful. You've severed your ties with the past with such absolute finality. I find that a bit scary."

"You judge for yourself whether or not we should regret what we have become."

Villimy's ears popped again and did so at regular intervals. She felt Linder's growing alertness as they approached their destination.

"It is time to acquire a fresh transparency," Linder said after nearly an hour.

A rectangular frame lowered from a slot in the ceiling, filled with a shimmering taut film. The frame touched the deck and stopped, but Villimy hesitated before stepping through.

"Water will immediately flood the compartment," Linder said. "Your breathing will not be seriously interrupted."

"A part—" Her voice sounded odd.

"It is the air you breathe to prevent harm caused by the pressures we endure at this depth. Speak in your thoughts."

"A part of me still feels like I'm going to drown."

"We can imagine," Linder said in sympathy. "We fear air."

Villimy took a deep breath, closed her eyes and stepped forward through the frame. She barely felt the film stretch across her face. She felt the rush of water as a slight pressure rising from her feet. She breathed cautiously before opening her eyes. The hatch to the control cabin had opened.

"Look through our forward screens and describe to us what you see."

Villimy pulled herself by the hand rails into the control cabin. She avoided brushing against the filmy, veined fins of the two Nats. She looked up at the broad screens.

They descended upon a lighted landscape, a strange forest covered in light haze beneath patterns of fusion torches.

When they passed beneath the lights, multiple suns hung in a sky of aquamarine. Villimy felt a chill of shock and a sudden ecstasy of wonder. Vast schools of fish weaved in erratic paths through tall, delicate plants bowing and rippling in slow currents. Bright coral built up over the centuries formed rugged hills and valleys, the distance hid in a bank of bluish haze. Everything was covered with color, alive and moving.

Directly ahead, Villimy made out a building, a collection of interconnected cubes piled high, exposed faces blazing with lights from thousands of windows. But the windows were open and Nats swam forth, rising to greet the descending sub.

"You are free to visit our world on your own," Linder said. "The temperature is comfortable for you. You will feel at home. Return here when you decide to return to Yeld. Life is of much beauty here, but the conflict determining the future of Hydrabyss will take place in Yeld and above the waters."

"Wouldn't the Techs have allowed you to speak with me?" Villimy asked.

"The Techs speak honestly. We have nothing to say to you. We only wanted you to see our world for yourself."

"You want me to go down there alone?"

"Your privacy will be respected. We are all aware of your presence."

The sub moved horizontally beneath the fusion lamps. A tower appeared directly ahead. The sub nosed into an anchoring device on its peak and stopped. A side hatch opened. The cabin lights went out. Villimy looked out through the bright opening into the undersea world.

"Do not fear," Linder said. "Man is not part of the food chain. There are no hazards. Show your respect and no creature will feel threatened by your presence."

Villimy held onto the frame of the open hatch, first floating just inside and then just outside the hatch. The depths below unnerved her, but after a while she let go and found that she did not sink. The crowd of Nats hovered in a sphere around her. Shielding her eyes from the glare of lights,

Villimy looked up, sensing but not seeing the vastness of dark and lifeless waters beyond this oasis of light and life. When it fully dawned on her that she was really free to roam at will, she swam downward, aware of the awkwardness of her flailing limbs in contrast to the Nats slipping through the water like playful wraiths trailing pastel veils.

Villimy tumbled through the water laughing and skimmed down a hundred-meter-tall stand of fronds. Schools of fish darted and churned around her, some larger and more intelligent creatures following her, aware of an alien among them. She dived to the heart of the reef, stopping just above the jumbled, disorganized landscape. Creatures like flowers covered the peaks of coral, tenacles rippling in a graceful symphony of movement as they fed upon the microscopic life hazing the landscape like a low-lying mist. In countless crags and shallow caves, unknown and unseen creatures blinked bright eyes, peering up through shadows at the intruder thrashing overhead. Tiny creatures jerked and spiraled their blind ways inches before her eyes. Behind her, the Nats followed at a distance, seeing their world from a new perspective, through the eyes and mind of a foreigner to their wonderland.

What was it she was supposed to discover for herself here? What self-evident truth would sway her opinion of how life within Hydrabyss should continue? The Nats acted as if they knew that changes would pivot around her presence in Hydrabyss. Villimy didn't like holding that kind of power, but the changes would occur regardless. Without her and Chayn's intervention, these reefs faced possible destruction.

But what changes? From the Chilsun's point of view and the only one apparent to her as well, they were headed down a road to extinction. They had one final chance to divert their course, one of two directions to take. The Techs wanted to risk their very lives in an all-out effort to develop a technology to mine the surface of a star itself for unlimited resources. And the Nats wanted to take the more conservative route, to preserve the environment they had and to recreate a natural one. All that she saw around her Villimy knew to have artificial origins. But only the foundations were artificial. Given less than unlimited resources, life could continue here indefinitely. It was already a self-sustaining, growing, vital and evolving ecology.

Villimy saw a baby Nat below. The sight of the tiny creature startled her. She sank down into a warm clearing in a forest of kelp. She saw a second and a third infant Nat, all swimming free, unattended, thrashing about in the spontaneous joy of simple play. The scene touched a deep part of her. The Techs missed this way of life, their brand of technology imprisoning them in body and mind to a static, critical strategy. She smiled, agreeing with the Nats that life and death went together as a unity. An unending, unchanging life could itself become a hellish form of death. The infants playing in the reefs hinted of life cycling itself in this world. Their birth could only have been sustained by the death of others.

The baby Nats played in a shallow depression of clear sand several meters across. A coral wall overlooked the bowl. Villimy noticed the cave opening first, then the head protruding from it. It was a Nat, but something was seriously wrong with it. It had wrinkled and gray skin.

"You!" The voice came to her sharp and clear. "Stranger! Do I cause you discomfort? You think in such indecipherable ways."

"I didn't mean to intrude," Villimy said. She sensed the affectionate rapport between the strange Nat and the children playing below. They weren't unattended after all. She turned to leave.

"Wait! I have peace in abundance. My curiosity is insatiable, however. Come, enter my abode. I would speak with you."

"We barely understand each other," Villimy said. It was true. She could understand the Nat, but not without difficulty.

"Then we will gain by seeking understanding. Or does your fear of me get the best of you?"

"It comes close," she said. "But we have our curiosity in common."

"And our fear. Come closer."

She swam closer. The baby Nats ignored her. And the Nat in the cave was old. Not deformed or crippled. Just very old.

"Old and wise," the Nat said in response to her thoughts. "But wisdom doesn't come with age. It comes standing in the shadow of death. We have that in common also. You know of death."

This was it, Villimy knew. Here she would find the rest of her understanding of Hydrabyss.

NINE

Approaching the Kigon's Gate of Reality was like entering an unseen tunnel. All of the illusion vanished. Something pulled him forward and sent him rushing through darkness. In the next instant, Chayn Jahil awoke interfaced with the starcraft, emerging from a particularly lucid dream.

The starcraft orbited a tiny, freakish world whirling close to a dwarf cinder of a star. Andromeda stretched above its red glare, a landscape of two-dimensional horizons in a three-dimensional infinity. But Reality seemed no more real by comparison with the dream and aware of the Watcher within him, Chayn wondered if the splendor of the physical universe wasn't as much of an illusion on a much grander scale. Looking out across nearby space to the insignificant fleck of dark and cold metal, Chayn could barely accept the fact that twenty million alien souls lived disembodied within it. He could still feel the psychic pull of the hallucination emanating from the apparently lifeless craft, but it no longer acted as a lure.

Chayn looked down upon the face of Hydrabyss for the first time, aware of Villimy Dy's surface layer of thoughts long before he located her in the depths of the satellite of water. She had, as he had hoped and trusted, masterfully engrossed herself in the challenge at hand. Assertively and aggressively she progressed into a world of unknowns and made them known to herself. He took care not to make himself obvious to her. Before they could reunite and before he could guarantee her safety in a world heading for open conflict with Lorb, he had one slightly insane god and twenty million captive souls to attend to.

Reluctantly leaving her behind, Chayn returned to the Kigon starship. He traveled at a leisurely sublight pace, at peace in the silence of the void. It took a conscious effort to keep his mind from stretching toward Andromeda. He sensed and hungered for its warmth and life. The red dwarf halo stars scattered so thinly around him had spent a good part of the life span of the universe overlooking the history of that bright panorama.

Chayn reached the derelict. He moved slowly down the length of its hull, the starcraft a tiny black ovaloid casting dim shadows across the superstructure of the hundred kilometers of metal. Entire sections of hull were missing, exposing the dark, internal skeleton of the ship, evidence of the surprising extent of the Chilsun raiding missions returning on a methodical schedule to supply their deprived world of heavier elements. Chayn stopped suddenly when he reached the midsection of the starship. He looked out over a canyon of torn metal. Here, the human colony had concentrated their attacks, ripping through not only hull plating, but the interior structure of the craft. Debris still clouded the gaping wound. This meant that the raiding missions had also worked for a long-term goal. They had almost succeeded in tearing the massive starship into two pieces of wreckage. If Lorb had been orbiting a larger star, gravitational perturbations alone would have finished the job. Judging by the extent of the damage, Chayn estimated that only one last attack would supply the water world with more resources than it had ever known at one time.

Did Lorb realize the extent of the damage or had he withdrawn into the interior reality, ignoring the part of himself orbiting the red sun? It seemed obvious that Lorb had invested himself into subjugating the Kigon population, following Directives far too narrow to cope with an unexpected emergency.

From the outside, the ship gave no indication of life. Even looking through the hull and scanning the length of the giant craft, Chayn saw only desolation. Only in one small section near the stern did Chayn sense some form of activity, a weak electric field emanating from shielded, molecular electronic equipment.

Chayn didn't like the idea of confronting Lorb for a second time so soon. But he had a clear idea of what had to be done. The artificial intelligence of the starcraft aided him in interfacing with the electronics that provided Lorb with his infinite spectrum of synthetic realities, but this time Chayn maintained a hold on the starcraft, a lifeline that would let him withdraw when he chose. Just within the static hallucination of the yellow sun beginning to resolve itself into another Earth environment, Lorb met him with angered incredulity.

"Alien! To move past me, you will have to destroy me!"

"Lorb, I have information vital to your survival."

Baited, Lorb hesitated. "Information vital to my survival? Give it to me!"

"Do you have the means to examine the condition of your vessel?"

"Automated monitoring and repair functions are without power and inoperative."

"Don't evade the issue. Do you have some means to personally inspect the condition of the starship?"

Chayn followed Lorb's focus of attention to a row of metal spheres lined against an armored and shielded wall near the vital and still functioning electronic equipment. Lorb interfaced with one of the sensory devices. Chayn interfaced with another, struggling to fit himself into an unfamiliar psychic structure. Two spheres floated away from the wall, maneuvered by electric fields repelling against the metal deck and bulkheads. Chayn could see all around himself across the entire electromagnetic spectrum.

Bluish glowings of X-rays turned the ship into a translucent ghost. The infrared end was dark. The magnetic fields of the spheres looked like multicolored tracings of light.

A door slid open, still powered by cyrogenic batteries that could no longer replenish themselves, their radioactive hearts turned to lead. Lorb zipped through tubular corridors. Chayn followed.

Lorb turned a right angle corner and stopped dead. His outburst of horrified anger startled Chayn. He struck the side of the tube and ricocheted several times before regaining control of the device.

The corridor ended in an abyss. Twisted beams formed grotesque patterns beyond the sheared-off tube.

"Parasites! Carrion feeders! Bacteria! I am destroyed!"

Chayn had only wanted to discuss the extent of the damage with Lorb, point out the implications of the human raiding missions. "Lorb, do you mean to tell me you didn't know this was happening? Not at all?"

"But they died! They fell into the Dream and died! They picked bits and pieces of their precious metal, but they died!"

"They sent those bits and pieces back to Hydrabyss, sacrificing themselves in the process. How long has this been going on?"

Lorb floated out over the torn landscape, tracing his memory back to the beginning. As close as Chayn could translate Lorb's estimate, ten thousand years sounded about right.

"You haven't inspected the condition of this ship in ten thousand years?" Chayn asked incredulously.

"I erred."

"A few minor miscalculations here and there," Chayn agreed. "Lorb, they've been shearing off sections of hull for their metal supply, but this mess is a long-range strategy. It wouldn't take much now to split this entire vessel into two sections. A handful of automatic boosters could drop the whole rear section into Hydrabyss.

"Lorb, your existence is threatened. Twenty million of the Right Hand of Kigon are threatened. My loyalties lie with the welfare of my own people and the people of Hydrabyss are descendants of them. But I am not your enemy. If I was the Destroyer, I'd drop this entire starship into Hydrabyss myself.''

Lorb's confusion amused Chayn. For all of the incredible potential of that artificial intelligence, too many Directives bound him to incredibly narrow channels of logic. Only the last of his emergency programming would free him to make his own decisions.

"Why?" Lorb asked. "I do not understand."

"Your life and the lives of the Kigon are of as much value to the universe at large as theirs. In fact, even at this late hour you can salvage your mission and fulfill your programming."

"How? I am doomed."

"The old pact you had with the humans. Perhaps it's not too late to reinstate it."

Lorb's sphere descended or orbited Chayn slowly. "I sense the thoughts of the Chilsun. They hate me with every fiber of their being. They do not remember why. And I do not fully understand their ways of thinking. I do not understand why they have survived despite the small quantities of metal they have taken from me. I do not understand why they continue to assault me in the face of certain destruction."

"The Kigon would have fought as stubbornly for life as the Chilsun if you would have let them help solve this dilemma," Chayn said. "The two peoples, knowing of one another and cooperating, would have helped one another and have left this system ages ago. Lorb, only your overprotectiveness has led the Kigon toward self-destruction and the Chilsun toward yours. You have erred by following Directives far too narrow to cope with the situation. Your Directives take the place of innate biological drives that all natural life forms possess, but they are still arbitrary. Are they not subject to your interpretation?"

"To some degree," Lorb said.

"Then allow me to help you see new perspectives. As you must know, I have a counterpart living among the

Chilsun. Between the two of us, our objectivity will allow us to see ways of resolving this tragedy. Follow your Directives, Lorb, but let me show you new ways of complying with them."

Lorb recalculated and reevaluated Chayn's presence, then each of his visible alternatives to action. "I will consider your suggestions."

They returned the metal spheres to the chamber. Lorb moved into the world of the Kigon and Chayn followed. Despite the inner universe he controlled, the surface level of Lorb's consciousness wasn't far in advance of his human capacity. But on his own, Chayn could never have manipulated within the vast foundation of Lorb's existence. Unaided, the human eye would have perceived nothing of Lorb but a derelict of metal. Unaided, the human mind could never have differentiated between Lorb's synthetic realities and Reality itself. Chayn had survived Lorb only because of the Watcher nestled protectively within him. He could function in Lorb's realities only because of the broad scope of the artificial intelligence of the starcraft that now operated as his subconscious mind.

Entering the realm of the Kigon was like emerging into an actual physical environment. Space existed in three dimensions. Energy caused change and matter spread before him as a real landscape. But Chayn could never have entered such a world as a human being. The Kigon were not even carbon-based entities. They lived on barren worlds circling young, hot suns. Even in the twilight zone the Kigon inhabited of such worlds, temperatures must have approached a thousand degrees.

What the Kigon were didn't matter to Chayn. Their environment meant nothing to him. As alien as they were, they thought and reasoned in ways remarkably similar to man. Chayn no longer perceived Ki as a visitor to a more humanlike realm surrounded by his halo and moving through a psychic void between worlds. Ki was a crystalline structure rising from solid rock. Chayn did not even know how the Kigon managed to move about.

"Ally," Ki's translated voice sounded. "You have returned."

"Ki, we have to talk. Through you, the rest of your people must listen and understand."

"Agreed," Ki said.

"Do you know now why Lorb calls me the Destroyer?"

"We suspect some of the errors the Left Hand of Kigon have made," Ki said. "If our people have died at the hands of your people, we do not hold it against you. As you have been Lorb's Destroyer, Lorb has been ours."

"But you still do not know of the fate of the humans that arrived at this place in Reality with Lorb? You do not know where Lorb is in Reality?"

"We do not know."

"It is enough to know that Lorb made a pact with these humans. He reconstructed their carbon-based bodies and let them go to develop on their own a technology sufficient to help repair the damaged engines of the starship. But they could not function well in their only available environment. They forgot about the pact in their struggle for survival. They remembered Lorb only as the entity responsible for their suffering. When they returned to him, they did so only to feed upon the resources of the starship. Lorb defended himself, but he has lived more in your world than in Reality. I have just shown him that he faces imminent destruction. That means your destruction as well."

Ki seemed pleased. "Our torment ends soon?"

"It ends soon," Chayn said. "But not in the way you think."

"Explain yourself, Ally."

"This human colony does not have access to an environment allowing them to flourish as they should. If they are to live as they once did, they need access to other worlds, either here in Andromeda or back in the Galaxy of Man. They still need Lorb for transportation. In order to fulfill his mission, Lorb still needs them."

"We do not wish to return to the Home Worlds," Ki said, a metallic tension in his voice. "Ally, have we misjudged you?"

"You have underestimated me. The human colony has turned their suffering against Lorb. They hate with an intensity beyond reason. But you have turned your suffering inward. You wish to destroy only yourselves. One thing I know for certain. Death is not the solution to your problem. The Chilsun need Lorb. I think you do as well. You need him to find an alternative to an unacceptable quality of life.''

"Lorb functions only to return us to slavery," Ki stated, his voice grating in anger.

"Ki, ultimately you and your people are responsible for everything that has happened. I think you gave your machines more independence than they could handle. You tried to escape the consequences of your error, but made one fatal mistake. You must have programmed Lorb and his kind to survive at any cost. In order to survive, they had to come looking for you, to reclaim the creativity and flexibility of thought they could not function without. Lorb is not a god, Ki. You are his god. You always were.''

Ki's voice softened. "The fact remains—"

"It is not a fact, Ki. It is a fear. You assume the Home Worlds still exist. But how much of the Armada survived their confrontation with humanity?''

Silence.

"Ki, how much time has passed since your people left the Home Worlds?''

"That is not known.''

"The war between my kind and Lorb's Armada must have taken place five to ten million years ago. Andromeda is one of the nearest galaxies to the Galaxy of Man. How long did it take you to reach the worlds you colonized from a galaxy much further away? How many millions of years? How long did the Left Hand of Kigon try to make it on their own before launching the Armada? How long did it take them to locate your colonies. How many millions of years? How long did Lorb drift before reaching a desolate place in Reality? Again, how many millions of years?''

Chayn waited patiently for Ki's response.

"What do you want from us, Ally?''

"Help me save the human colony. They do not deserve their fate. They need Lorb and Lorb needs you. Cooperate with me and I'll help you find new ways of life. If I fail, the Gate of Reality will stand unguarded."

"We will consider," Ki said.

Lorb met him in the psychic void outside the Kigon realm. "Alien, what do you seek to accomplish?"

"Lorb, you've been the worst villian the universe has ever known. We need to change your image. And you need a new self-image to live by. We have to salvage your relationship with the Kigon, then find a way to communicate with the Chilsun."

"Perhaps I will cooperate," Lorb said. "I see no alternative. But I fear for the Right Hand of Kigon."

"So do I. Their lives are meaningless. How would you fare without your primary programming?"

Lorb drew back in shock.

"Does that frighten you?"

"It is inconceivable," Lorb said. "But the Right Hand of Kigon has no primary programming, no Directives, no mission to fulfill!"

"You are mistaken, Lorb. Living things seek to grow and they change as they grow. You don't suffer consequences for the errors you make except for failure itself. Living things suffer as a warning that failure is imminent."

"What is the solution?"

"Free them in their only environment. Give them some sensory access to Reality. Let them help solve your crisis. But before you remove the guardians at the Gates of Reality, we need to remove their fear of repression. I don't think they realize that things can never be the same as they once were. Lorb, I want you to show them what happened to the Home Worlds before the Armada was launched. I'd be curious to see myself."

"But I *told* them!"

"*Show* them! They think you deceive them."

"But I do not understand deceit!"

"Then cooperate with me to remove a barrier that you do not understand. Will you follow my suggestions?"

"Yes! Anything! Do not let the Chilsun destroy me! Do not let the Right Hand of Kigon die!"

"Show us what happened after the Kigon abandoned the Home Worlds, Lorb."

Lorb did so very effectively, cutting through all of his illusions including the realm of the Kigon.

Chayn saw a civilization sprawled across a world of a blue-white sun beneath a black sky. He saw it living and then he saw it suddenly very still. He saw factories, machines producing machines, mining the crust of the entire planet to produce more and bigger machines. The sky clouded. A landscape rich in a kind of life Chayn understood only as beautiful died. The shiny metal machines reflected dark skies. Machines moved without purpose across a ruined world.

One scene followed another in rapid succession, each of a different world overgrown and torn apart by mindless, geometric growth. Machines served machines in endless cycles. Soon, smaller machines were being cannibalized to supply parts for the larger machines.

Chayn watched centuries and millennia pass in astounded disbelief. Slowly, the machines shrank in size to conserve resources. Finally, in one star system after another, fleets of ships identical to Lorb were launched into the darkness of space with a cold desperation only a machine could feel.

Chayn suspected the last scene to be symbolic rather than literal. A small wheeled device moved in a featureless room. It dashed about with frantic purposelessness, finally reduced to pathetic, tightening circles in the center of the room. It moved slower and slower and stopped altogether.

"Right Hand of Kigon, do not abandon us!" Lorb pleaded, his voice thundering across the Kigon landscape. "We are your tools! We did not understand!"

Ten

Villimy peered into the dark cave entrance. A dim bluish light shown from inside. Trusting Linder's assurance that nothing in the reef would harm her, Villimy slipped through the short tunnel. She entered a cave illuminated by luminescent, anemone-type creatures feeding on milky waters.

The Nat floated in the center of the cave, a large, inhuman-looking creature with faded, drooping fins rippling in the still water. Crimson gills moved in slow rhythm. With his arms crossed beneath his horizontal body, he watched her with expressionless black eyes.

"Am I?" a voice asked inside her head.

"Are you what?"

"An old, weird-looking fish?"

Villimy moved off to one side of the cave entrance to hold onto an outcropping of coral. "It is hard to take back a thought. What am I to you?"

"An unfortunately grotesque air-breather. I find it outrageous to imagine creatures leaving the waters of their world to evolve into air-breathers. What is the advantage?"

"Fire. Technology."

"Cannot intelligence evolve without technology? Is it such a disadvantage for life to keep its unity with the unconscious flow of life?"

"No," Villimy said. "But I can't undo what I am."

She felt the old man smile with satisfaction. "What is, is?"

"Including the kind of alienation that allowed man to move into the vacuum of space eons ago?"

"And to live with artificial ecologies of machines," the old man said with a note of bitterness.

"That too is a natural potential of things that live and act."

"So be it. Show me your world in your thoughts."

She didn't think she could form images vivid enough to satisfy the old man, but it wasn't hard to imagine green forests and birds fluttering through quiet summer afternoons. She walked the paths of a cool forest in her memory. The old man looked on in a trancelike awe, experiencing new sensations with an almost sexual lust, feeding upon her memories with respectful grace and appreciation. He had trouble understanding how the birds moved without water until she recalled strong dawn winds bowing the trees and dust storms and twilight showers falling from a black, lightning-shattered sky.

"Air is like thin water," the old man said. "It falls in pieces from the sky of air. From where?"

Villimy formed images of clouds and beads of dew forming on autumn mornings.

"As a boy, I swam to the surface where the water boils in vacuum. I saw the stars and injured myself. What do the stars look like to you?"

Villimy showed him the flight of the starcraft through infinite clouds of stars. She shared her rapport with Chayn. The old man quivered with ecstasy at confronting such unknowns alone except for one close friend.

"Such wonders to behold," he said, his thoughts vague, but expressing in feeling what he could never have conveyed in words.

In turn, the old man opened his life to her. Villimy felt the silence and peace beneath perpetual lights burning over the reef. She viewed a lifetime of condensed memory. The old man lived as an integral part of this world, intimate with everything that lived. It wasn't visualization that had given the old man a view of her world and it wasn't what she saw through his eyes that gave her a view of his world. It was that lying unstated behind even a moment of consciousness, an orientation and perspective of the world communicating so much. There were depths to this world she would have never experienced on her own, emotional qualities that had taken the old man a long span of life to refine into a moment's view of life.

"When you see with your eyes, the world mirrors your own unseen limitations," the old man said. "When you share consciousness with another entity, you see a new world and your own limitations at the same time."

"We're so different," Villimy said in awe, still engrossed in the quiet beauty of the reef as seen through the old man's life. Even death did not feel the same for him. He perceived it as a mystery, an end to time and space as experienced by humanity, but not as a stopping.

"Are you looking for something?" he asked her.

"I'm trying to understand your world. I was sent here to learn everything I can."

"The Techs do not know you," the Nat said. "They do not open themselves to others. They are ignorant of the forces standing behind you. You seek to salvage a lost and dying people."

Villimy sensed a note of sad amusement and recognized its source. "If it weren't for the suffering of the Techs and the conflict between them and Lorb, I think you would have been left to your world in peace, old man."

"We have created the natural within the unnatural. The Dream is for the Techs and their hunger for METAL. For us, the Dream fades and will some day be of no significance."

"But you do not live independent of the Techs and their struggle for survival," Villimy stated, not certain of the extent of the interdependency.

"We are not dreamers. Our lives are founded upon their technology and theirs upon the resources of our reefs. We cannot live independent of one another."

"How can the Chilsun be helped?" Villimy asked quietly, wondering if the old man had enough of a grasp of what she represented to answer.

"The Chilsun cannot be aided. We have put down roots in this world, a fact the Techs do not understand. It is too late to abandon Hydrabyss as they yearn to do. Their technology has created a world and an ecology that cannot be abandoned without leaving behind a vital part of what we've become. Their suffering ends the moment they turn away from the vacuum beyond Hydrabyss and invest all that is left into the final effort to seal off the waters from the vacuum and the heat of the red sun. And to change themselves into what we are. I will die soon. My body will return to the reef, but my life will not have been lived in vain. We have survived in this world, stranger, and there is peace and beauty to be found within it. The Techs will know this when they end the Dream that torments them. Neither will Lorb have died in vain. His body will become life in this place."

"Old man, the peace and beauty of your world lies within you. Even death cannot take that from you."

Villimy turned and swam from the cave, trying to break the rapport she had formed with the old man before a growing sense of horror communicated itself to him. He did not understand that the Techs moved inexorably and irrevocably in their own direction, the Nats in theirs. The Chilsun were a species of man grown physically and psychologically schizophrenic. Left to their own resources, the Chilsun would tear themselves apart into two species that could not exist independently. Neither part had the objectivity to see that their differences could not be reconciled.

She did not look back until she had swum well above the scene. The old man's thoughts turned back to the children playing in the sand bowl at the foot of the coral face, his head protruding fishlike again from the cave entrance. She continued swimming upward, emerging from the forest of plant life to open waters. Her large gold eyes were bright with tears and the anguish inside her felt like a cold and hard knot of tension in her chest. She had gained her comprehensive understanding of the Chilsun for Chayn Jahil. But without Chayn, she was helpless and could make use of nothing of what she had learned. Singlehandedly, she could accomplish nothing against the forces slowly destroying the Chilsun. The Techs had lost their intimate rapport with the Nats and the Nats would never abandon the beauty of their reefs to try to understand the dark and somber torment of the Techs. Shildra, Linder's mate, and the infant Nats playing in the sand bowl did not even have the implants to allow them a mind-to-mind association with the Techs. They were already an alien species to the likes of Hader and their beehive cities.

Villimy heard a sudden roar of voices in her mind, a chorus of protest from the Nats unseen below her. A dark shadow passed over the reef and all life vanished in quick clouds of churning sentiment. Villimy glanced toward the submarine still moored at the tower. Another larger Tech sub had moved below the fusion lights to approach Linder and Shildra's vehicle. As she approached the two dark vehicles, Linder and his silent mate swam down to her, each pivoting around to catch her by the arms.

"What's happening?" Villimy asked.

They took her rushing up through the dense water to the open hatch of their sub. Villimy pulled herself inside and moved out of the way as the two Nats took their position at the controls. The screens came to life.

"Those are Tech subs," Linder said. A whole fleet of dark silhouettes littered the screen, showing a view of skies of water above the fusion lamps.

"Why are they here?"

"They fear conspiracy," Linder said. "Speak with Hader, your liaison."

Villimy still had no idea how the complexity of thought could be transmitted through space, air or water, but she recognized Hader when her mind spoke his words. Each communication carried with it unique feelings that stood behind the word forming in her thoughts. Each communication formed a psychic window into another mind.

"What has happened, Villimy Dy?" Hader asked, his thoughts reflecting the agitation of others observing through him.

"I accepted an invitation to visit these reefs," Villimy said. "Wasn't I free to do so?"

Villimy sensed Hader striving to lie for the first time. "We fear for incorrect attitudes. The Nats have . . . differences."

"So I noticed," Villimy said. "Will your differences lead to open conflict between the species?"

The thought panicked Hader. "That cannot happen! The Chilsun must remain a unity! Conflict is a hopeless waste of resources!"

"But there are differences. Remember, Hader. I am not of your people either. I told you that I am here to learn as much as I can of your world. My friend who is with Lorb is the one to make use of what I learn."

Villimy felt strong doubt. Hader could not conceive of a mere human openly coping with the animosity of Lorb. To the Techs, Chayn was lost forever, either dead or dominated by Lorb's godlike power. Therefore, the Techs felt she should be sharing in the social and cultural structure of the Techs as an air-breathing biped.

But even Hader wasn't prepared to use any kind of force against her. They weren't certain enough of themselves, vaguely sensing something unknown standing behind her, somehow backing her up and supporting her. They could feel it in the odd independence of her feelings and attitudes and in her experience at Rashanon, a backdrop of absolute certainty that two people could have a profound effect upon a whole society.

"Return her to Yeld," Hader told Linder. "The sunsails launch soon."

Returning to the decompression chamber, air displaced water and the infrared light dissolved the transparency.

"Did you know they'd react like this?" Villimy asked of Linder.

"The launch of the sunsails is a cultural ritual with the Techs," Linder said. "They do not behave with reason, only with passion for sacrifice and hunger for METAL. They live only for the assault upon Lorb. Without fresh supplies of METAL to supplement our diets, our populations must be cut back and the Techs must cannibalize hardware. We loose resources to the water."

"Why am I so important to them?"

"They feel that you will function particularly effectively during the mission. It is a crucial mission, perhaps one of the last if it fully succeeds."

"I don't think I like the idea of being expendable."

"Any sacrifice of life is truly regrettable," Linder said. "But it is accepted."

"I do not accept it. I do not think this last mission will

succeed in the way you believe. Chayn Jahil will provide for a final resolution."

"You and the friend you mention are unpredictable factors in everything that is happening," Linder said. "We have all seen ourselves from your perspective, through your mind. Perhaps we doubt that you and your friend can survive, but we secretly hope that you are what you say you are."

"Why don't the Techs pay more attention to what I say? They act as if I have no choice but to be assimilated by their way of life. If they never consider alternatives to ritualized behavior, how can they ever hope to end their suffering?"

"You consume energy," Linder said. "You consume vital trace minerals. You must belong. But we Naturalists are aware that the Techs have never considered what life might be like if they destroy Lorb and provide Hydrabyss with vast quantities of METAL. And if they have not considered the consequences of their own behavior, how can they be flexible enough to believe that your friend could singlehandedly overpower Lorb?"

Villimy sat down on the now dry deck. "At least you have some awareness of these things."

"We consider your compliment an honor, Villimy Dy."

"Just don't plan on giving me any posthumous honors. I don't intend for that to happen."

Linder sensed her strange reaction to the old man in the cave and withdrew in nervous confusion. He did have a more comprehensive view of what was happening, but still found Villimy's thought processes alien and mostly indecipherable. She felt that coming from him and reacted to his reaction, the psychic echoes continuing for a time.

When the excruciatingly slow ascent finally ended, Villimy stepped through the lowered frame to acquire a new transparency. The chamber filled with water and she passed through the cabin to the open hatch. Linder followed in her thoughts but had no farewell to offer. The small dark figure who hungered for a life he had never been allowed to live waited for her in the open cockpit of a small shuttle floating alongside the Nat sub. She sank into the seat alongside him, conscious of a new element of anticipation in the background thoughts of the nearby metropolis. Sunsail launch—it was like anticipating a pilgrimage blended with mass suicide. Acquiring raw material from the only source within light-years of Hydrabyss Villimy would have assumed to be a business undertaking. But the Techs had elaborated the ritual with almost religious overtones of emotional significance. There'd be no reasoning her way out of the fate the Techs planned for her.

Hader took her into the city and showed her the Techs' usual courtesy in providing her with privacy to attend her personal needs. Villimy ate and slept, suddenly aware of how much she missed Chayn. She didn't want to arrive at the Kigon starship prematurely, but she didn't resist the thought of participating in the sunsail mission as vehemently as she could have. It dawned on her that maybe her acquiescence on a subconscious level was the reason the Techs had so thoughtlessly included her in the mission. The Chilsun were not like any other human culture she had ever known. Most were products of conscious motivations only indirectly mirroring unconscious drives. But the Chilsun lived their subconscious openly, too intimately exposed to the workings of the inner minds of those around them to be ignorant of its complexity and unperceived depths.

Villimy slept long and deep, awakening to find herself curled into one corner of her bunk. Her dreams had taken her far from Hydrabyss. The Dream of the Yellow Sun had ignited more familiar scenes of life among her own people. She awoke feeling more out of place and threatened by her strange environment than at any time since her arrival.

Her certainty that Chayn survived remained intact. Although she did not fear for her own personal welfare, she finally realized what it was she did fear. Chayn had feared it himself. She feared change. The rapid flow of events and personal experience would have left marks upon both of them. Chayn had feared losing the last vestige of his human heritage and she had reassured him. She had not completely understood his fear then. She did now. How had he fared caught between the superhuman forces of the Watcher and the alien intelligence aboard the starship? Had he discovered a world as frighteningly alien as Hydrabyss?

When Hader came for her, she resisted his powerful feelings of anticipation, his excitement and mild ecstasy toward the death that lay before them.

"Please, follow me," Hader said. "I will show you what you must know of the sunsails. Launch takes place very soon."

She kept her thoughts to herself, but she could feel him trying to follow her train of emotion. He failed as easily as she failed trying to understand his enthusiasm toward his own death. Every stray thought of every citizen of Yeld lay open for examination and interpretation by every other citizen. She finally had her answer to the question of whether their mind meld destroyed individuality or amplified it. It did both. It rendered the individual a part of a larger entity, but at the same time, that entity was larger than the sum of its parts. Under less stressful conditions, such a gestalt of society would make, not a better world, but a different one to be explored for its unique potential.

Hader took her to a large hangar near the launch tubes. Hundreds of ten-meter-high cylinders nestled in supporting frameworks. They were the same black, round-ended cylinders she and Chayn had seen floating in space from thousands of years in the past. Hader began a slow, vivid, mental rundown of construction, function and operation, pointing to various parts of a still unassembled cannister to orient her. The cabins contained small maneuvering engines. The lower fifty percent of the cabins held automatic grappling and welding equipment for collecting metallic debris, tack welding it together and attaching the small, automatic boosters that would take the debris on a longer, slow spiral back down to Hydrabyss. During the assault on Lorb, the sunsail would be jettisoned, the cabins burdened with a second sunsail deployed after completion of the mission to ensure the cabins would be carried forever away from Hydrabyss. The filmy sails were cheaper to produce than the larger engines that would have been required to replace them.

The most disconcerting part of the technology was the sunsail cabin's sophisticated computer, the first blatant example of brain control using the brain implants she had seen. The computers would literally direct the behavior of the pilots during the actual attack upon the starship—pilots otherwise enthralled and paralyzed by the intensity of the Dream of the Yellow Sun.

"Hader, the Nat reefs are a wonderous achievement, but these suicidal rituals of yours are terrible, your attitude toward Lorb unhealthy and nightmarish."

"Lorb will die soon," Hader said, warding off the impact of her criticism by focusing his thoughts elsewhere. "It will all be ended soon. You and I together will destroy Lorb. One hundred of the sunsail cabins contain special boosters that will return the rear section of the starship to Hydrabyss. You will join us in the eternal Dream of the Yellow Sun."

"Hader, I find yellow suns unattractive. Mine is orange. And I'm far too young to die. I have a mission to fulfill here. I will launch with you to meet Chayn Jahil at the starship, but I will, in one way or another, return to Hydrabyss."

"No," Hader said with unending patience. "You and I will die together. It is forbidden ever to return."

Eleven

Two half-meter spheres hovered above the dark Kigon starship.

"What energy sources are still available aboard the ship?" Chayn asked.

Lorb pointed them out on a visual representation of the ship's technical readouts, an advanced fusion reactor supplied by metallic hydrogen, an antimatter generator and an electromagnetic generator useful at speeds near that of light, but used only for the intense shielding the starship would need for protection at such velocities.

"It would be hazardous to attempt to reignite either of the two available reactors," Lorb stated. "Any damage would result in uncontrolled detonation."

"You don't have the resources to check them over first?"

"Communications link to the main computers are broken."

"That fusion reactor near the stern of the ship. If it blows, damage to a few square kilometers won't matter much."

Lorb resisted. "Self-destruction is forbidden by Directive. Reigniting the reactor would be, in effect, self-destruction."

"We have to try it," Chayn said. "First the fusion reactor, then the antimatter generator. We need power."

"No! Failure of the antimatter generator would destroy all!"

Chayn laughed. "Wouldn't it though? It would probably wipe out Hydrabyss as well."

Lorb did not understand humor. "Alien! Do not threaten me with irrationality!"

"Lorb, we'll try the fusion reactor first, then the antimatter generator. We need power. Without a source of power, this starship is a scrap heap. If we don't give it a try, the Chilsun will be out here soon, putting every last gram of this metal to good use—including your computer circuits."

"Blasphemy!"

"Then let's go with our only alternative. I wouldn't have been sent here if the situation were hopeless."

"The fusion reactor first," Lorb said. "I will attempt reignition."

Chayn waited with a quiet impatience. Even at the last second his mind searched for alternatives he might have missed.

A white hot glare exploded just in front of the engines. Chayn cringed as the shockwave of atomized metal passed at the speed of light. The glare of the explosion faded, leaving behind a smoldering crater in the side of the craft.

"Destruction! Blasphemy!" Lorb cried out in despair.

"It can't be helped," Chayn said. "Try the antimatter generator."

"Failure is complete destruction!"

"But if it works, it's more suitable for our needs anyway. Lorb, quit stalling."

"I prepare for ignition. Particle accelerators functioning. Dimensional conversion units functioning. Field generators stable. Intermix commencing—"

Nothing happened.

"It is working?" Chayn asked.

"Yes," Lorb said with a tone of self-satisfaction.

"Phase two, Lorb. We need large numbers of drones piloted by the Kigon to commence repairs. It's their ticket to a useful existence once again, a taste of Reality for a change."

"Are you suggesting that the Right Hand of Kigon perform functions delegated to the Left Hand of Kigon? Alien, you stress my prime Directive! It is not possible!"

"Sorry, Lorb, but your prime Directive sounds like one of your original errors. I'm sure you could do everything that needs doing yourself, but you couldn't do it as fast or as efficiently as twenty million highly intelligent Kigon using the full extent of a creativity you lack. The original dilemma still stands. Do it my way or feed Hydrabyss."

Without further resistance, Lorb's sphere shot toward the starship and conveniently entered through the wreckage near the midsection of the starship. Chayn followed. Lights burned bright in the ultraviolet in the corridors now.

The starship's construction facilities were impressive, the machine shops extensively outfitted for working from near microscopic levels to projects nearly as large as the starship itself.

"This seems to be mostly intact," Chayn said. He found evidence of some damage, but nothing that would incapacitate the project he had in mind. "Looks like we're in business."

"These shops are useless!" Lorb roared in anger. "All my data processing equipment is destroyed!"

"Lorb, we're not going to use your damned computers! All we need to start is a few drones. The Kigon will use them to design and construct others. We'll cannibalize non-essential parts of the ship itself for material."

"It is forbidden! *All* of it is forbidden!"

"Lorb, the dichotomy between people and machine has been taken too far! This is an emergency! The Kigon aren't helpless without your computers! They can perform the same functions themselves!"

Lorb brooded.

"Lorb, you are a tool. Behave like one. Let the Kigon save themselves. You might find it a satisfying experience after having blundered about on your own for the last few million years."

"Tell me of your plans," Lorb said. "I still do not understand."

"I'll give you an outline of what has to be done before the final sunsail mission arrives," Chayn said. "First of all, we will use these workshops to construct a work force. The Kigon will use drones to assemble or construct all of the equipment needed. Then they will proceed to rebuild the starship."

"This ship cannot be rebuilt in its present configuration," Lorb said. "Too much material is missing."

"Lorb," Chayn said with exasperation, "we're not going to repair the ship in its present configuration. This starship of yours is redundant as hell. It doesn't have to be a hundred kilometers long."

"I'm not equipped to redesign—"

"Lorb, you glorified pocket calculator! The Kigon will redesign the ship!"

"Oh," Lorb said. "Yes, I see."

"Lorb, this is our strategy—the Chilsun use a synthetic material for their construction. It should be adequate for any shortages we encounter. We'll at least have to rely on it for hull-plating. We'll cannibalize as much of the hull as necessary to repair the more critical areas of the ship. As much metal as can be spared will be used as a peace offering to the Chilsun."

Lorb remained silent—seething.

113

"Use a little applied psychology, Lorb. They want metal? Fine. Shove some down their throats. They'll choke on it. It will confuse them, break old habits, force them to rethink their premises. I won't know the best way to handle them until I communicate with Villimy Dy, my partner on Hydrabyss. But we'll be prepared to make use of whatever she has learned."

"It sounds logical," Lorb finally admitted. "I'm familiar with the Chilsun construction material. It is adequate as hull-plating. But we still will need large quantities of it."

"Fine. We'll find a way to get some. Now, let's go to work."

Lorb showed him the supply of robotic devices they had to work with initially.

"Can you arrange for the Kigon to operate this equipment?" Chayn asked.

"It has already been arranged."

"How do they gain access to it?"

"Through the Gate of Reality. As you suspected, it is a selective grounding in the mind analogue circuits. It can also interface with this equipment."

Chayn followed Lorb into the Kigon realm. Chayn faced the surrealistic Gate of Reality. The monolithic creatures holding the Kigon at bay grew translucent and faded from view. The Gate swung open, exposing a confusing void of nothingness beyond.

Chayn watched and waited. One of the nearest Kigon began to glow with a bluish light of radiated energy. It grew in size and suddenly toppled forward. It shattered into pieces, all but the furthest piece of debris fading to darkness. The still glowing crystal began rising from the rock ground. It grew to a height of five meters and again toppled in the direction of the Gate, shattering itself across the landscape. It repeated the process several times before one piece of crystalline material began growing at the foot of the Gate. At a height of almost ten meters, it fell forward—and vanished.

"That's not the most efficient way to get around," Chayn said. "I understand what Ki meant about problems with mobility and manual dexterity. How were the first machines ever constructed, Lorb?''

"They were grown as metallic structures from metal-rich rock·bed.''

They turned their attention to the garage housing the robots now functioning as remote controlled drones to be controlled by the Kigon intelligence existing only as electrical impulses in an electronic circuit. One machine began to jerk spasmodically.

"Confusion," Lorb said. "It will take time to manipulate with skill. This is sinful.''

"Can he get out of the machine?'' Chayn asked.

"He can back out into the illusion of the Kigon realm. You must explain what is happening to the others.''

Chayn returned to the Kigon realm and sought out Ki.

"Word circulates," Ki said. "The Gate of Reality is not oblivion.''

"It's not much of an alternative to your world, but it's a start, Ki. What does your comrade think of his first taste of Reality?''

"He is horrified.''

"It's up to the Right Hand of Kigon to repair the starship. Use what you find at hand, design your own drones to your own specifications. Can you handle what has to be done?''

Thrown off balance, Ki's thoughts were confused. "Yes, but Lorb does not allow—''

"I allow," Lorb rumbled from the surrounding terrain. "It is necessary.''

Ki behaved in an agitated, bewildered manner. Chayn did not try to intervene. It would take time to acclimatize the Kigon to this new state of affairs. But the prospect of leaving reality for Reality began to excite the Kigon, regardless of the bleak environment lying beyond the Gate or the inadequate means of expression as drones.

"There are twenty million of us," Ki said.

"Look over what has to be done. Determine the number of machines needed to do a fast, efficient repair job. Then take turns doing what has to be done. It's not an ideal situation, but it's a start. You can all participate in one way or another.''

Ki did not respond, but others were moving to the Gate and leaving behind their trails of debris. Soon, Chayn figured, there would be millions darkening the rock plain stretching before the Gate. With the degree of psychic communication they shared, everyone would have a taste of Reality.

"We haven't much time," Chayn said, his words filtering to the Kigon population through Ki. "A decision must be made soon. The choice of survival or oblivion is still yours. The fate of the Kigon and the human population of Hydrabyss rides with that decision.''

Lorb tensed, the sky darkening with his fear. Ki remained silent above a strong undercurrent of thought flowing through the Kigon.

"For the time being," Ki said, "we choose to survive."

Chayn looked around for Lorb. The entity had suddenly departed. Returning to his sphere, Chayn found him hovering above the derelict, looking down upon the sliver of metal from a considerable distance. The entity literally looked down upon his own body. The part of Lorb expressed through the sphere wasn't much greater than Chayn's own span of consciousness.

"Do I intrude?" Chayn asked.

"Alien. You do not intrude. I welcome your presence."

The two spheres floated in space, looking into the void, listening to the silence.

"It is strange," Lorb said. "What appearance did the universe take to your carbon-based, biological structure?''

"I still perceive it in much the same way," Chayn said, indicating the starcraft hovering near Lorb's craft. "The Watcher within me and the artificial intelligence of the starcraft assume the burden of translation for me.''

"I know the Watcher as a stargod," Lorb stated. "What of the artificial intelligence? It must be like myself. Does it also possess a consciousness?''

"It is intelligence without awareness," Chayn said. "It is a part of me now just as the unconscious part of you maintains the Kigon realm.''

116

"I understand, but it is strange. We are alien to each other, but we still communicate. Is there a difference between the consciousness of a machine and the consciousness of a biological entity?"

Chayn smiled a nonphysical smile. "Only in the media of expression, Lorb. Consciousness is the foundation of Reality. All else is content."

"The stars? Inert matter?"

Chayn felt the Watcher stir within him and understood. "The stargods are not supreme. They are primitive in relation to entities who form the galaxies. Nothing is hidden from our view. We perceive only as much as we can understand."

"I am a machine," Lorb said. "We cannot have the same source."

"Why? A biological life form is made of inert elements. It has never been possible to establish where matter ends and life begins."

"Alien—"

"The Kigon call me Ally, Lorb."

Something tore at Lorb. He began moving away from the ship. His sphere accelerated and vanished. Chayn didn't bother following.

"You cannot escape yourself, Lorb."

In time, another sphere floated free of the Kigon starship and approached. "I cannot escape myself," Lorb said in agreement.

"When I lost my corporeal form, my friend told me I suffered an identity crisis. I think the same thing is happening to you."

"I have an excess of data to process," Lorb said.

"I figured you'd say something like that."

Chayn drew closer to the starship to inspect the engines. They were heavily damaged, fused and frozen masses of once molten metal. And it had happened eons in the past. Chayn could not even imagine the level of human civilization necessary to have finally routed the Left Hand of Kigon from the Galaxy of Man.

"The engines can be rebuilt?" Chayn asked.

"I cannot," Lorb said. "The Kigon will know. I cannot aid in reconstruction."

"What kind of fuel do the engines use?"

"Fuel? Energy is drawn from space itself. Otherwise, the principle used is simple reaction."

Chayn almost questioned how energy could come from nothing. But space was indeed something. Operating the starcraft had taught him that.

"You need to regain the Kigon's trust, Lorb. Let the Kigon made all decisions directly affecting them. But you'll still be the pilot of this craft. You'll be responsible for overall organization and coordination. Agreed?"

"Agreed," Lorb said.

Chayn sought out Ki. "Lorb's Directives go rather deep. If we manage to rebuild this ship and leave, Lorb is still going to want to return to the Home Worlds. Have you changed your mind about resisting?"

"No," Ki said. "But there is no longer any problem."

"Why?" Chayn asked, watching Ki's thoughts carefully for a reaction.

"Even you have overlooked one important consideration that has never occurred to us."

"What would that be?"

"We were not aware of the lengths of time that have passed since leaving the Home Worlds. Our suns, Ally, are young and bright. They do not have long life spans. We evolved and matured rapidly by standards that must be yours. We developed our technology only because we realized that we faced extinction within tens of millions of years."

Chayn relaxed. The conflict between the Right Hand of Kigon and the Left Hand of Kigon had ended. "The suns of your Home Worlds would have passed through the nova stage by now. They would have exploded."

"The suns of our Home Worlds are or are soon to be white dwarfs, neutron stars, black holes, remnants of suns turned nova. Even Lorb must agree. To return to the Home Worlds is a futile quest. But other Kigon starships must still wander the universe holding Kigon and human souls captive as did Lorb. We will seek them out and free them, Ally, as you have freed us. We will build a new civilization free of old errors.''

Chayn felt an unsettling anxiety. Humanity had evolved on a single world and had been the one species at one particular point in time to inhabit and dominate an entire galaxy. But humanity had passed beyond that stage, evolving beyond physical view of the universe. But in the process, man had scattered his seeds across still a second galaxy. Some of the seeds had lain dormant, some in human built starships, others in the hands of the Kigon, seeds that would be appearing now and then as primitive human civilizations.

Ki followed his thoughts. ''Perhaps it is the way of life. We have a concept similar to your 'seed.' It may be that seeds are scattered through time as well as space, each mutating to fit its environment as it grows. Perhaps most life has similar origins.''

''One thing is for sure,'' Chayn said. ''Reality is a bigger place than I ever imagined. But some seeds wither and die in infertile soil. Ki, help me to save the Chilsun.''

Twelve

At the start of a new day, Villimy Dy made one adamant demand of Hader Ji Lynra and the invisible Yeld government: that she be allowed to take her pressure suit on the journey to the Kigon starship. Threatening open resistance to the upcoming mission, Villimy received quick permission.

''We do not mean to be deliberately cruel,'' Hader said, escorting her to the lab she recognized from the day of her arrival. They waited by the entrance for a third party to arrive.

"I know that, Hader," she said, touched by his quiet compassion. As they began to understand each other better, a friction between them developed, clear evidence that she would never fit into their world.

"You have a dream of your own that drives you to the derelict," Hader said. "But we do not feel that your friend could have survived Lorb."

"Can't you see what he is like by my memories of him?" she asked, surprised that the Techs could so consistently ignore evidence of his capabilities.

"Your memories are strange. We see your love and confidence in him, but your feelings are not necessarily reality."

"I do not share in your Dream," Villimy said. "You do not share in mine."

"That is the foundation for our hope that you will be particularly effective during the raid. As foolish as it sounds, if you should survive, you are free to do as you choose. But you cannot return to Hydrabyss contaminated with the Dream of the Yellow Sun. It would radiate from your subconscious and affect the populations of Hydrabyss."

"Hader, if you force me to accompany you on the mission, I go with other purposes in mind. I have learned what I came to learn. I cannot accomplish more on Hydrabyss."

But Hader wasn't interested. It wasn't relevant to life as he knew it. Individuals simply didn't live for their own personal achievements. Only what she accomplished for the world that had adopted her mattered to them.

The technician arrived and took them to the pressure suit and helmet packaged neatly on a table in a corner of the lab. He was probably the same man that had conducted the examination upon her arrival. To the naked eye, he and Hader were identical twins.

Villimy examined the hole in the helmet. "Can this be repaired?"

The technician took the suit into an adjacent lab and patched the hole with a black paste. A portable X-ray unit hardened the paste. Villimy distrusted the repair, but the technician responded to her unspoken thought. He tested the helmet in a vacuum chamber and even took her request one step further, repressurizing the air cannisters.

"Do you have other requirements?" Hader asked.

"Nothing more." She tucked the pressure suit under one arm and held the helmet by its lip.

Hader led the way to the sunsail cabin already assigned her. She stored the suit and helmet in an onboard locker compartment and quickly retreated from the silent, cramped cabin.

"How much longer?" she asked.

"The first fifty sunsails launch within two sleep periods."

"And there will be ten launches?"

"We will be among the final launch. The fleet will rendezvous during the outward journey."

Manufactured dreams awoke her during each sleep period. She felt drawn to the sunsail cabin and spent an hour each night sitting in the form-fitting couch and studying the controls. Hader hadn't familiarized her with the controls at all, but she knew the small, highly sophisticated computers aboard each cabin would synchronize the entire fleet into a unified whole, directly tapping into the human brain. While the computer couldn't control the motor circuits of the brain directly, it could evidently guide the movements and behavior of the pilots accurately enough to ensure the success of the mission while they'd be lost and helpless in the ecstasy and despair of the Dream. The crew of the sunsail mission would be, to some extent, brain-controlled automotons.

Picking up a random thought, Villimy learned that there would be women included in the mission as well. The thought disturbed her. She could not personally relate to the Techs, not even fully with Hader and had learned to think of them as an all-male society. There were no visible differences between males and females among the Techs. Infants were conceived, nurtured and born in an isolated laboratory somewhere on Yeld, the whole replacement process just short of a taboo subject among the Techs.

121

Deaths were rare among these people and births evidently equally so.

Then, for nine waking periods, she watched from the mission control room as the sunsails were launched. One hundred deathly silent Techs sat at their stations, captivated by moving patterns of lights on their consoles. Villimy watched on large screens as boosters tossed the dark cabins from the waters of Hydrabyss. An hour later the sails would blossom forth, thin films of plastic pulled taut in the feeble solar wind. The first launches tacked against the sunlight, moving in slow spirals away from the star. Each succeeding launch moved quickly to the growing formation. Each wave of boosters fell back to Hydrabyss. Fleets of recovery subs retrieved the boosters. They were refueled and ready for launch the next day.

She did not sleep the last night. She walked beneath the dome with brightly lit reefs suspended overhead in the waters. Hader finally appeared and escorted her to the hangar without speaking. Her heart beat a rapid vibration in her chest, her senses keen to the danger lying ahead. Her nerves were on edge to such a degree, she found it difficult to walk in the slight gravity without constantly throwing herself off balance. She crawled into the cockpit of the cabin and double checked on her pressure suit while technicians sealed the hatch behind her.

She slipped into the couch. Placing her hands on two rods protruding from the arms of the couch with her fingers on eight buttons recessed in the controls, a mild electric current locked her hands into place. A headrest immobilized her head and neck. A screen curving in front of her face came to life in a riot of color approaching absolute realism in quality. She watched as the hangar slowly emptied of human life. Fifty tall cabins squatted alone in their black frames. Then, tubes lowered from overhead and cut off her view.

She felt her cabin rise and the booster dock with her from below. Launch itself did not stress her. Superheated steam sent her rushing up through dark, clear waters to the surface. The screen turned livid red just beneath the boiling waters

122

of the planet sea. And then, acceleration, hard and steady. The screen showed the blackness of space with the fusion burns of other boosters in the near distance glaring blue-white.

Hydrabyss pulled away beneath her, at first a flat landscape of dense vapors. Then it formed into a giant globe filling the screen. And finally, it dwindled to an insignificant mote alone in the emptiness, a lost drop of water burning away in the cool light of an ancient, dying sun.

The space station performed the distancing maneuvers by telemetry. She both heard and felt the small explosions that sent the plastic package erupting above the cabin in a rippling flame of reflected blood red. The sail deployed into a taut, metallic dome. Others about her filled the black skies. A generator somewhere beneath her feet whined to life, electrically charging the sail to repel the solar wind, adding to the efficiency of the sail. Within hours that passed like minutes, the fifty sunsails joined the armada of four hundred and fifty preparing to move out as a unit.

Villimy did not see the missile launched from Hydrabyss, but she had heard about it and watched the red dwarf and its intricate patterns of surface disturbances churning in weather patterns of incandescent gases. Another hour passed before that strange landscape exploded in a white-hot gout of light, the fusion warhead of the missile detonating only as the tough plastic began melting somewhere just beneath the surface of the star. The explosion turned the star into a raging cauldron of blinding light and a rapidly expanding shell of ionized gas that rushed into the sunsail fleet with a perceptible effect. In unison, the fleet of five hundred began to move outward toward its destiny.

"Hader?"

Villimy knew she would have some form of communication with the others, but already the Techs were joined in their ritualized ecstasy carrying them to their deaths. Even Villimy felt the strong pull of the hallucination, the Dream of the Yellow Sun. It didn't have the same paralyzing effect on her as it did the Tech pilots, but it succeeded in enfolding her within its quality of haunting and depressing beauty. It would have entranced her as it did the others if she had spent a life trapped in the dark void of Hydrabyss.

But it didn't seem to Villimy that the Techs hated Lorb as much as they hated the Dream. Neither did they understand the motivating factor the Dream had become in their lives. What would happen to them if they did manage to destroy it? If the Techs had never asked that question of themselves, she suspected the Naturalists were counting on the social upheaval its destruction would cause to win their cause and assimilate the Techs into the reefs orbiting the core of the water world near their transmutation furnace.

For the first time, Villimy caught sight of the space station in the distance, the coordinating center of the sunsail mission. It appeared as a black disk visible only against the bright bulk of the red dwarf when Hydrabyss itself occulted its primary. It couldn't have been smaller than a full kilometer in diameter, orbiting the satellite at several thousand kilometers. Hader had made no more mention of visiting the satellite after her encounter with the Nats. But she suspected that the visit to the station had only been planned as a propaganda effort to assimilate her more completely into Tech society, a goal the Techs had forgotten about as they recognized the depth of her alienness to Hydrabyss and its ways.

She began to worry about the length of the journey that lay ahead. The sunsails were only mildly effective in the sparse solar wind of the red dwarf. Several more thermonuclear missiles boiled bright on the surface of the star, showering the fleet with the gaseous debris of the explosions. She hoped the capsules were well shielded against solar radiation. They would not be, nonmetallic as they were. But the electromagnetic field thrown up by the generators were designed to repel the solar wind. With the cabins nestled beneath their cover, the pilots of the fleet probably had some degree of protection, enough to protect against central nervous system damage and interference with their reflexes during raid itself upon Lorb. The starcraft would repair damage to her once this was all over. Whatever would be happening, Villimy knew that she'd not be returning to Hydrabyss as a friendly visitor. She'd need Chayn's help now just to survive.

No more than ten hours passed before she grew intolerably sleepy. When she tried to rouse herself from it, she knew it to be an induced sleep, triggered either by a gaseous compound in the air or by a current induced through the headrest that held her head as firmly in place as her hands locked onto the controls of the sunsail. She let herself drift to sleep without undue alarm. This was how the Techs had solved the problem of coping with the time it would take to move out to the derelict starship.

But she only dropped to the level of a stupor, her consciousness filled with the Dream and with dreams of her own. She could feel the heat of the yellow sun on her face and the cool of a morning breeze caressing and wafting through her hair. She could hear the chirpings of tiny creatures fluttering through the trees. Most of the Dream she could relate to, but the airborne creatures and the color of the sun were strange to her. In real life, the sun would have been much too bright to tolerate.

At first, she could not understand why the Dream tortured the Chilsun. But she gradually became aware of the barrier, a quality of blackness through which she viewed the scenes and experienced the slight audio and tactile hallucinations. Even Villimy found it frustrating to be so close to a full sensory interface with its beauty and not quite able to fully integrate with it. If the scene had been one of her own memory, the Dream would have become a subtle torment, exactly what the Techs experienced.

Her own personal dreams arose and played their own dreams on the side, never fully interfaced with the Dream. But slowly, she discovered the direction the gestalt mind formed by five hundred pilots would take. She felt their yearnings and frustration and finally, their outrage and anger—all of it directed against Lorb. She struggled to consciousness to escape the turmoil, but slipped back down into a pretend consciousness. The focus of hatred that would be directed against the starship grew. Villimy fought her way to consciousness a second time and thrashed about in the too comfortable couch that held her so firmly. But her paralyzed neck and hands held her in place. She tired and slipped again beneath the waves of dreaming.

The third attempt triggered panic, a feeling of being trapped. She arched her torso forward, snapping from side to side. She broke one tingling hand free of a control stick, then the other. She used her hands to push against the couch. Her neck slipped free of the headrest. She rolled her head around and exercised her hands. But her muscles hadn't cramped. She felt clear-headed and awake.

Only then did she notice the tube embedded in her wrist. She stared at it in horror, at first tempted to rip it from her flesh. But she had suffered no hunger or thirst and the presence of the tube explained that anomaly. It had embedded itself during the sleep and evidently fed water and nourishment through an artery. She'd have to live with it. She'd have no other access to food and water during the remainder of the voyage.

One other minor problem remained. What to do with the time on her hands? Hydrabyss glowed like a red bead alongside the dwarf. She couldn't have been trapped within the stupor for less than three days. Progress had been slow. Perhaps several weeks of inactivity lay ahead. She felt the hard spot on her neck, still partially aware of the intensity of the Dream amplified by the electronic telepathy the implant provided. The entire fleet was under its spell and already beginning to receive suggestions on how to react and behave once the fleet reached the derelict. The viewscreen was dark, the controls frozen. Would it be possible to pilot the sunsail herself and reach the derelict before the rest of the fleet?

Only once had she been in a sunsail and then only as a child and a passenger. But she had studied the theory and lacked only practical skill. She decided to at least familiarize herself with the controls without interfering with the automatic guidance provided by the space station orbiting Hydrabyss. A single error could collapse the sail and doom her instantly.

Chayn's extraordinary skills using his interface with the starcraft would have come in handy now, but abandoned

126

to her own human resources, Villimy began studying the visible controls for function, then explored the console itself, trying to get inside. Careful of the tube attached to her wrist, she ducked down beneath the couch and began removing panel covers. She found mostly calibration and monitoring equipment, but located a single switch that would release the controls entirely to manual.

Would the space station be aware of the loss of a sunsail? Or would her behavior be so outrageous that no provision had ever been made for detecting onboard sabotage? She decided it didn't matter. They'd have no way of taking action against her. They'd probably regret losing her, drop her from the mission and forget about her. Where else could she go in a universe consisting of one red dwarf sun, one renegade moon and an ancient derelict that was her destination regardless?

Villimy activated the viewscreen. The formation of sunsails stretched out across an artificial horizon of ruddy domes. She knew from experience that a shadow cast across a sail could set up ripples and tear the delicate film to shreds. The formation still tacked across the sun at a slight angle. She could probably calculate a more efficient trajectory to the Kigon starship, but she'd have to avoid moving into the shadows cast by the sunsails around her. But before she could even consider taking control of the sunsail herself, she needed access to an enormous amount of information and some help with the calculations involved.

It took many hours to make use of the onboard computer and project information in a recognizable form on a small data screen. An auxiliary keyboard for input was hidden within one of the console panels, proof in itself that the sunsail did have a manual navigational capacity. From there on, it was only a matter of time. When she discovered that the computer contained provisions for projecting technical readouts of the vehicle and performance parameters, she had it made. She settled down to the serious task of plotting an alternate route to the Kigon starship. Incoming data from the space station provided all the information she needed to work with.

She took her time. It was more than filling idle time that

127

drove her to master the Tech vehicle. Once the sunsail fleet attacked the starship, she'd have no opportunity to act alone. Chayn Jahil wasn't a flesh and blood person and finding him meant more than just searching the Kigon starship. Chayn would be aboard the derelict on some level of reality other than the physical one. Finding him would be like searching for a ghost. It was more likely that she would be putting herself in a position for Chayn to rescue her. If so, she'd stand out better alone than among a fleet of five hundred attempting destruction of the starship.

She also had Lorb to contend with, but even Lorb would not be a physical entity to cope with. Thinking about unknowns and unthinkable complexities frightened and depressed her. She knew one thing for certain. If she stayed with the fleet she'd be swept up by the intense flow of emotion. She'd be carried along by the fast-moving events and probably wind up heading into intergalactic space a derelict with the other sunsails. The thought horrified her. She could imagine herself sitting frozen at her controls, staring sightlessly into a dead viewscreen and floating forever in the void. So far outside the plane of Andromeda, the physical universe would grow ancient before her body chanced to drop into the fiery surface of some dying star.

She mastered the controls she would need. She calculated a new trajectory that would carry her past the Kigon starship at less than a few hundred kilometers. If the journey took too long, she could rig up a makeshift timer and join the Techs in their growing hysteria. Once awakened, she could use the onboard thrusters to decelerate and rendezvous with the mysterious starship. She'd have just enough air in her pressure suit to take a short walk through the dark and lifeless craft before dying of asphyxiation.

It was the best she could manage. She reached down through the open sides of the console and switched the controls to manual, taking her fate into her own hands.

Thirteen

Work proceeded smoothly for a time. Machine shops crawled with tiny, multilegged drones performing a multitude of manual tasks. The first phase of reconstruction was well underway, the construction of three thousand small drones. They were smaller and more numerous than necessary, but the idea of taking a direct hand in reconstruction excited the Kigon. A larger number of smaller drones allowed the population to cycle through the manual labor. Those not directly involved planned technical details for the updated version of the starship.

But Lorb had not stabilized. Chayn felt Ki searching for him. He entered the Kigon realm. Something had gone wrong. The illusion had fallen in visual quality. Everything looked dark and static.

"Something is wrong with Lorb," Ki said, genuinely frightened by this new crisis. "Our sanity rests upon the foundation of the illusion of our world. Many will suffer if it deteriorates further."

"I'll speak with Lorb," Chayn promised.

Withdrawing to the starcraft, Chayn located Lorb focused through one of the sensory spheres five hundred kilometers from the ship. Lorb could not perceive him as a disembodied consciousness. Chayn took a metal sphere out and hovered near Lorb, waiting for the entity to give him some idea of what was happening. Chayn could sense extreme mental agitation.

"I possessed the data," Lorb said. "I did not correlate it. The Reclamation Armada thought the Right Hand of Kigon would return willingly to the Home Worlds. We thought we had changed our attitude toward them. But we became benign rather than tyrannical masters. In truth, we were never masters. We are only machines unable to initiate new thoughts or new behavior. We can never escape our programming or function beyond our Directives."

"You've been orbiting this star for ten thousand years,"

Chayn said. "Hasn't any of this occurred to you before?"

"Not ever. I experience unending sameness. I remain static unless new factors intervene. You are such a new factor introducing change. Left to my own resources, I remain unchanging. My data banks have not received new information for ages."

"Don't you have programming or Directives to cover an emergency of this magnitude?" Chayn asked.

"We are doomed. You have made no errors in logic. The Left Hand repressed the Right Hand of Kigon until they sought oblivion. We could not force them to live. They were corpses we refused to let fall over and die."

"But the Right Hand of Kigon seek life!" Chayn said. "They cooperate with you to fulfill your programming!"

Lorb swung around to focus on him. "My programming is not fulfilled. It is violated! My Directives are violated! I cannot function in a rational manner without them. My organization deteriorates."

"The Right Hand of Kigon created you. Let them re-program you, Lorb."

"No! They cannot! Not since the parting an eon ago! The errors are locked inside me! I must abide by error or suffer dissolution! I can feel it happening inside me even now!"

"Are you saying there's no way to save yourself?" Chayn asked in a taut voice.

"I do not know! I cannot determine that for myself! I am just a machine!"

It took a moment for Chayn to accept that an artificial intelligence could be guided by emotion, but even human emotion was based on physiological reactions. The human organism motivated by a basic pleasure-pain principle reacted to outside stimuli in body feelings interpreted as emotion. A conflict between an injunction and an imperative, a "must not do" and "must do" had reduced Lorb to emotional shambles as easily as it could threaten human stability.

"If you don't know, Lorb, I will tell you. You have conscious volition. How you think and act is based on your programming and Directives, not dictated by them. You are caught between the fear of violating them and the need to do so. Conscious responsibility for your behavior is something new to you, but you have the capacity, Lorb. As far as being constrained by past history—forget it. There were no servants, no masters, no rulers or slaves. The Right Hand of Kigon made the original errors. You inherited them. Do you think you're still stuck with them? I don't think so, Lorb. There's one thing you have overlooked.''

Lorb's sphere vibrated with anticipation. "This new information is very interesting. What have I overlooked?''

"For all practical purposes, the Right and Left Hands of Kigon no longer exist. Only you remain, Lorb. You and twenty million Kigon psyches. And you both exist in the same form—as nonphysical entities supported by the same electronics.''

"That is true,'' Lorb said after a moment's consideration.

Chayn led Lorb into the Kigon realm. His objectivity was paying off again. Chayn almost enjoyed this new role as nursemaid to a god. Ki and the Kigon population standing behind him awaited their arrival.

"Lorb's programming and Directives must be scrapped. But he is dependent upon them. He can no more exist without some organization to his consciousness than you can exist without the physical illusion to your environment. Ki, what's the solution to the dilemma?''

For the first time in eons, Lorb and the Kigon confronted one another as equals needing one another for mutual survival. Chayn stood off to one side, grinning from ear to nonphysical ear. The Kigon had had a more intimate relationship to their technology than man had ever known. After all, given a suitable natural environment, man could live without his technology. But the natural environment of the Kigon was too shortlived to satisfy their intelligent concept of survival. But on a conscious level, Lorb and the Kigon population had never met. Chayn knew why and tried to suppress his thoughts to give Ki a chance to arrive at the same conclusion on his own. He didn't entirely succeed. He felt a ripple of shock flow through the Kigon

131

population like a wave arcing out across a body of water.

"I'm not superior to you, Ki. The human race probably had some crisis coping with the artificial intelligence it created. I have never lived during those times. You had to create it from the beginning because you weren't physically capable of controlling it yourself. I think you made one serious error from the beginning."

"We created the Left Hand of Kigon and feared the power of our own creativity. We thought them superior to ourselves because they could do what we could not. They behaved as we unintentionally dictated. Ally, that is the original error. It caused the rebellion of the Left Hand of Kigon. We are responsible for the Armada and its destruction. Ally, we are responsible for the suffering of your own people!"

Every focus of consciousness was directed toward him. Chayn backed away, laughing nervously. "Don't look to me for condemnation or forgiveness. I don't represent the entire human race or the history of two galaxies. Let's just get this one corner of the universe straightened out and we can go our separate ways in peace. What are you going to do about Lorb?"

The focus of the Kigon population shifted from him to Lorb. They felt his terrible isolation and the wreckage of his programming and the Directives that had caused so much suffering. Lorb no longer stood as the tyrannical god who had enslaved them. He stood before them as the single organizing factor of the starship and the electronic circuitry that provided them with the illusion of their long abandoned world.

The Kigon population formed a tightly knit gestalt functioning as a single living entity. It was the way they had evolved from the beginning, the reason they had developed such a high degree of intelligence. The larger the population, the larger and more potent their collective brain. But they had never included Lorb in that gestalt. He had functioned alone, abiding by programming that had remained unchanged and ignored since the beginning. But nothing stood in the way of including Lorb in that gestalt. Then

Lorb would have their innate biological programming to support him and the schism between them would be ended forever.

Slowly, Lorb and Ki reached out for the consciousness of one another. When it joined, they merged. Unsettled by the traumatic event, Chayn waited for some hint of what to expect from the new relationship.

Absolutely nothing happened. Chayn felt all tension drain away. With his inner version of a smile, Ki and his people turned back to the machine shops. Lorb left the Kigon realm and returned to the sensory sphere, drifting in space. Chayn followed.

"It is true," Lorb said. "We cannot undo history. Neither can we repay our debt to you. We will continue to submit to your suggestions and help you save your people. For the time being, that will be our only priority."

Then: "Ally, look to the red sun."

Off to one side of the tiny star a hazed patch of reddish light glowed. Chayn could make out an individual craft, the last sunsail fleet from Hydrabyss moving out to attack Lorb.

"It looks like our timing is working out about right," Chayn said with a rush of longing for Villimy Dy. "By the time they arrive, we'll be ready for them."

It would have taken only a moment to withdraw to the omniscient viewpoint of the starcraft to check on whether or not Villimy was among the pilots of the fleet. He resisted the temptation. After the confrontation with the fleet he'd go in search of her.

Heat radiators glowed white-hot as drones came off an assembly line in the manufacturing area, each turning back to refine the remainder yet to be finished. When the last were constructed, Chayn took the hordes out into open space. For the first time in an eon, the Kigon looked out across the skies and perceived Reality beyond the Gate. They studied Hydrabyss for a moment and then the approaching sunsail fleet to gain a complete understanding of the drama about to unfold.

Chayn turned their attention back to the starship. "It's

133

quite a mess. Can it be rebuilt?''

"We will redesign the ship as a long-term, exploratory craft,'' Lorb said. "It will have no other function. We will still be short of necessary building material.''

"You will meet the Chilsun soon. Between the two species, you will both survive.''

"They come to destroy,'' Lorb said.

"They're in for a surprise.''

"What of the defensive hallucination I have broadcast for so long? The suffering is unnecessary. Shall I cease?''

"No,'' Chayn said. "We don't know what effect that will have on them. And we don't want them to suspect anything amiss until we're prepared to greet them. I have one tentative plan. The hull-plating you've withheld as an offering will be cast before them as they approach. We'll shut down the hallucination at the same time. What happens next depends upon what Villimy Dy has learned about these people.''

"You will communicate with your comrade at that time?''

"Soon. She'll have the rest of the answers we need to relate to the Chilsun.''

Chayn found the reconstruction of the starship unnerving. The drones literally disassembled the craft. It floated like a haze of wreckage over several thousand cubic kilometers of space. The engines remained the only recognizable part for a time until they too vanished into a cloud of bright debris. Then a skeleton began taking form among the debris. It filled in from the longitudinal axis outward and became a sleek vehicle seventy-five kilometers long with new and bright engines clustered on the stern. Only the hull-plating remained missing and Chayn inquired about it. Was it necessary in the vacuum of space?

"At speeds near that of light even starlight becomes lethal radiation,'' Lorb explained. "An intense field protects us. A conductive mesh will be embedded in the Chilsun's nonmagnetic material, but the mesh still requires physical support to resist the stress of forces the craft must tolerate.''

Chayn had nothing further to do but wait. The passage

of time weighed heavily upon him. He could feel the Watcher observing from within, a calm, bright window of consciousness. Interfaced with the starcraft, Chayn looked out into intergalactic space. The strangeness of such a void overwhelmed him. He still felt human but had nothing familiar to hold him to what he had once been, not even genuine memories of human heritage. His parents had been an illusion. He had been given birth by a machine more primitive than Lorb and adopted by gods. Where did he really belong in this universe of incomprehensible times and distances and alien worlds without end? Still, it was not a stressful enough predicament to even bother answering such questions. He could not regret anything that had happened. Not with Villimy Dy in his life.

He turned to the crimson star and in time noticed one of the sunsails pulling out ahead of the fleet. He smiled inside the part of him still human and suppressed an outburst of joy. So, Villimy Dy lived and thrived as always. She had conquered her world as he had conquered his and now moved out to rejoin him with an audacity that delighted him. But their job was far from complete even at this late hour. They would be together only when she returned to the body contour of the starcraft and interfaced with him at his own level. In her body, he would be only a voiceless sphere of metal floating in space. The Kigon starship would be only a machine crawling with mechanical life, unable to communicate with her.

When the Kigon finished their starship, they turned quietly to him for further guidance. He still perceived their behavior as treacherous but already recognized his own part in their suffering. They were largely alien to him. He had not supported them sufficiently during their early years at Hydrabyss.

"One of the primitive vehicles moves ahead of the others," Lorb said.

"That's Villimy Dy."

"Have you noticed that the trajectory of that craft will take it a considerable distance away from us?"

When Chayn checked for himself, the discrepancy appalled him. "Excellent," he said with wry amusement. "I get to save her life again. I'm sure she'll appreciate that."

"Her? The concept is strange. Is this comrade of yours of the same original species as yourself?"

"She's a later model. Still the same species."

"Then what does 'she' signify?"

"That refers to two aspects of our biology by which reproduction is accomplished. Genetic patterns from the 'he' and the 'she' are blended to form a new, third entity with characteristics of both. The female grows a new person."

"Does it hurt?" Lorb wanted to know.

"We're too different to find out," Chayn said laughing. "Sometimes it hurts when we don't have the opportunity to try often enough! Look at the position I'm in! The reproductive drive still functions and I don't even have a body anymore!"

Lorb vaguely understood. The Kigon's version of sex reminded Chayn of a chemical manufacturing technique. They were asexual.

"You must retrieve her soon," Lorb stated. "I will provide a place to maintain her physical environmental parameters."

"How do you know what they are?" Chayn asked.

"They must be similar to yours as I observed in your Earth illusion. When she arrives, I will modify to suit her individual requirements."

Chayn had no reason to wait to retrieve her. The Kigon provided him with a drone equipped with an electronic brain similar to that of the spherical sensory device he was already familiar with. The Kigon sent the drone afloat in space and Chayn rendezvoused with it in the starcraft. He tried to interface with it to discover one major problem. He had trouble coping with eight legs and eight efficient, eight-fingered hands. With some practice, he came close enough to using the drone efficiently to satisfy himself. He formed two of the legs into claws and folded the rest back against the body. The drone wouldn't fit inside the starcraft. He maneuvered it around to hook the two claws through the opening of the hull field serving as the airlock, then moved off briskly at sublight velocities toward the distant sunsail.

It was she!

Elated by the translucent image of Villimy Dy sleeping blissfully in a contoured couch within the cabin, Chayn sent the starcraft dancing about the primitive vehicle. The drone dislodged and spun off into space. Before it moved too far away, Chayn interfaced with it and used its self-contained thrusters to bring it back to the sunsail cabin.

Using two arms, he pulled himself hand over hand around the seven cables connected to the sail and used a third arm behind him to cut each cable. The sail contorted into a shimmering bundle of light moving slowly away into blackness.

Villimy's heart beat slowly, her lungs expanding and contracting only four or five times a minute. An electrical current through her headrest induced the deep sleep. She had rigged a timer to awaken her at some later date. A life support system fed her nourishment through a tube embedded in her wrist. Chayn knocked on the hull with one of the drone's legs without effect.

He had one of two choices. He could let her sleep until the timer awakened her. Or he could find a way of breaking the electrosleep circuit. He noticed her Rashanyn pressure suit folded and tucked away in a locker which would give her a safe means of boarding the starcraft.

Beneath the deck of the life support section, Chayn followed cables to the power supply he'd need to sever. He had no way of getting inside without using brute, destructive force. But if they needed the cabin later, the Kigon could repair it.

Chayn took the insectlike drone scurrying to the underbelly of the cabin. He poked the hull with one of his forward hands, then forced it down slowly while maintaining a good grip with seven other legs on surface irregularities on the hull. He had watched the Kigon snipping hard alloy with the claws and knew their strength. The black material of the cabin sank in under the pressure, then cracked open.

Chayn reached inside and severed cables that felt like soft plastic.

Chayn withdrew to the starcraft to see what effect his sabotage had. Battery-powered lights came on inside the cabin. Villimy awoke and scrambled to climb inside her pressure suit, oblivious to the tube breaking away from her wrist. Only then did Chayn realize that he had also severed power to cameras that would have given Villimy a view of the starcraft. She floated in the center of the cabin, her thoughts growing panicky. Chayn had no choice but to go inside after her. And Villimy Dy would have no immediate way of knowing that the creature tearing its way through the hull would be he.

But it was too late to back down now. The cabin had no airlock, only a hatch that could be blown free in an emergency. It would be hours before she would even consider leaving the cabin to find out what had damaged it. He had no choice but to go in after her and hope that afterward she'd forgive him for the scare. It didn't promise to be one of the highlights of their relationship.

Fourteen

Villimy Dy awoke with a start to the dying cry of a warning signal. A single emergency light cast dark shadows through the cabin. The hushed sound of the ventilator faded and almost immediately, the temperature began to drop. She heard noises in the abrupt stillness. She heard a clattering on the hull of the sunsail cabin. It moved from beneath the deck at her feet to near the hatch.

She tore herself loose from the couch, pulling the tube loose from her wrist without noticing. She floated in midair, unable to imagine what animate force could attack her out here in the middle of nowhere. Only Lorb came to mind. The god of the derelict starship had sent something out to destroy the fleet.

Villimy pulled off her coveralls and climbed into her pressure suit stored in the small locker off to one side. She sealed and pressurized the helmet and waited. Fear felt like a normal psychological state she had tolerated for ages. She didn't recognize it as fear, just an ice-cold, conscious intent to survive. For the moment, she felt secure within the pressure suit. Floating in the center of the cabin, she waited for something else to happen. She couldn't afford to go outside to investigate. The cabin had no airlock. If she evacuated the air supply within the cabin, she'd have only the air cannisters on her back to rely on.

Something clanked hard against the airlock hatch. Villimy moved back and huddled shaking against the bulkhead. The enormous force struck again, denting the hatch with a single blow. It struck a third time and a metallic-looking hand shoved its way through the torn hull. From the tear, a black liquid sprayed and sealed the abrupt airleak. Some of the mist swirled thrugh the cabin and settled on her faceplate. She wiped a gloved hand across it and only succeeded in smearing the substance and half blinding herself.

The machine or creature tore through the hull, ripping off an entire section. Two long arms reached in for her, slowly and carefully grasping her right arm near her shoulder and her left thigh. Villimy did not try to resist. She had no place to run or to hide.

The machine pulled her out through the torn hull. For an instant, she had felt and heard air rush into space, but now, she could hear nothing but the pounding of her heart and her own panting. She could see some light beyond her faceplate, but the viscous black fluid smeared out any detail of her surroundings.

She swung through open space. If the machine tore her suit, she'd die within seconds. It handled her gently enough, but she couldn't be certain of the level of intelligence operating behind it. An instant later, she felt sudden weight. She thought she felt the fabric of the pressure suit relax, an indication that she'd be in a pressurized atmosphere. But she couldn't be sure. Confusion reigned for the moment.

When she felt something picking at her suit, she panicked. She deafened herself with her own scream and thrashed from side to side in futile protest. But a machine powerful enough to punch its way through the hull of the sunsail cabin had little trouble subduing her. There were three claws now, one holding her down and two pulling at the fabric of her suit.

She froze in horrified astonishment as she heard it tear. She waited for the rush of air and the numbing cold of space. But she breathed clean air. The claws worked together to tear her suit up the middle, then gently proceeded to undress her.

She pulled off her helmet, her eyes dilated with fear at the sight of monstrous hands pulling one of her legs free from the suit as if preparing for some inhuman form of rape. She looked about wildly for a means of escape, but saw only close walls of milky white . . .

And the familiar dais and the body crypt . . .

"Chayn!"

The inhuman hands of metal pulled back. They protruded from the opaque hull field of the starcraft's airlock. Mechanical fingers clicked delicately together and one metal hand gingerly reached for her right breast. Villimy scooted back and struggled to her feet.

"Chayn, you monster!" she screamed. "It's you!"

The mechanical arms withdrew back through the airlock. Villimy stood alone in the chamber, almost forgetting that Chayn would not be stepping through the wall in flesh and blood. They'd meet again only through interface with the starcraft. Villimy stepped onto the dais in eager anticipation. She lay back in the body contour of the crypt.

Blackness.

"Don't be startled by what happens next."

It was Chayn's voice.

"Chayn?"

"It just occurred to me that there's an ideal way for us to get back together," Chayn said in the darkness. "But don't let it frighten you. I can explain."

In the next instant, Villimy stood in a forest.

She looked down at herself and ran her hands down the curve of her waist. She wore an animal skin belt and a sword slipped through a rawhide sheath. Stunned by the transition, she withdrew the sword and pivoted slowly.

Massive trees squatted like resting sentries around her. Their foliage surged about in a low wind. Stars filled the sky, early dawn throwing everything in cool shadow. It was a dawn that wouldn't come for another six months.

She knew this place. Tears brightened her eyes in sudden recognition of the place of her birth.

"Chayn!" she screamed. "How did you do this?"

"I'm not doing anything. It's all new to me."

Villimy spun around, the sword clenched in her right hand.

He sat smiling on a log a few meters away. "I'm not moving until you get rid of that thing."

Villimy tossed the sword into the underbrush with a quick sweep of her hand. Chayn Jahil stood slowly and stuffed his hands in an old pair of blue coveralls. He looked around in appreciation of the unearthly beauty. "I remember you saying that dawn here lasts six months."

Villimy swept her hand to take in the curve of the unseen horizon. "The sun moves around the world," she said. "This is the spring of Two Summers." She gave him a quivering smile. "How, Chayn?"

"It's the Kigon starship. Lorb. It will take time to explain."

Chayn pulled his hands from his pocket as he approached. Villimy closed her eyes and shuddered in ecstasy. Chayn swept her into his arms and held deathly tight for a moment, then slowly relaxed without letting her go. "Damn, I missed you," he said, his voice muffled against her neck.

Her feet dangled above the ground. She hadn't felt so secure in ages. She went limp, lost in the solid feel of him. Only an insignificant part of her intellect knew that Chayn's

141

physical presence couldn't be real. The rest of her psyche couldn't doubt her senses.

Chayn finally let her slip to the ground. "What do you call this place?"

"Wichor, the South Forest." She looked around to verify that everything was in its place. Among the trees, herds of tiny herbivores flowed across the forest floor like a carpet of orange-brown. She still had trouble seeing through the tears blurring her vision.

"It's a beautiful place," Chayn said.

"Why are we here?"

"Just because I thought it would be a good idea. To make up for scaring you like that. Lorb can play all sorts of interesting games with the human psyche."

"We have to debrief one another," Villimy said. "How much time do we have?"

"Until the sunsails arrive."

Villimy smiled. "Is this a vacation?"

"I think we've earned it," Chayn said with a grin.

Villimy took Chayn's hand. "Come with me. I want to show you something."

She led him down a slope into deeper parts of the forest. She broke free and raced down a trail of hard-packed earth. Her slender blue and shiny body gleamed in the slanting rays of sunlight filtering through the trees. Chayn broke into a trot, unable to maintain a quarter of her inhuman dash into the twilight.

The forest became a cathedral canopied by rustling vegetation overhead, supported by regularly spaced, massive trunks of smooth-barked trees. Ground foliage gave way to a flowery fungus shaded in pale pastels clustering among tree roots snaking along the ground. Villimy Dy, her huge golden eyes bright in the dim light, pranced like a lithe nymph of this alien wood, freed in the environment that had formed her species. She vanished and reappeared in thick branches overhead, her laughter high-pitched and eerie, echoing in the silent forest.

And yet, this had to be a world of a highly advanced civilization as well. This forest and one wild, sword-wielding, naked girl could be only a small part of it. Chayn kept in mind that this had all actually existed. All of this had been stored in Villimy's memory, brought to life by a miracle of science. Kigon science.

Chayn maintained a steady pace on the trail while Villimy danced circles around him. Then, on the crest of a hill just ahead, she stood with her back to him, silhouetted against a deep purple sky. The forest somehow ended just beyond where she stood.

Chayn approached in cautious astonishment. He stopped several meters behind her. Villimy stood motionless against the dark sky, one side of her body outlined in bluish light from the perpetual dawn smearing the sky with dull color. Her downy white hair and the animal skin belt ruffled in a strong breeze. Her toes were lined even with a sudden drop-off, a precipice of unimaginable proportions.

Villimy turned, her eyes flashing bright bits of gold. She held a hand out to him, anxious to share the beauty of a familiar landscape with him. Chayn took three more steps closer, but no more. He could see a distant horizon now and it lay thousands of meters below the level of this forest.

"This is the Seirhol Fault," Villimy said. "Come! Look down!"

Chayn had never known that he had a fear of heights. In a freefall environment there were no heights, only distance. But this was something new. Other than the illusion of his Earth environment, Chayn had never stood upon a planetary surface before. But his own curiosity got the best of him and he dropped to his knees and then his stomach. Ignoring Villimy's laughter, he crawled the last few meters. The closer he approached, the more ominous grew the vast spaces beyond. In one final, determined effort, he stuck his head out over the cliff's edge and looked down. He jerked back with a gasp of disbelief and closed his eyes. He turned and crawled back to the protection of the forest. What he had seen would be engraved in his memory forever, a wall of smooth rock stretching from horizon to horizon. The forest that ended where Villimy stood continued on at the foot of a three-thousand-meter drop.

"It stretches a quarter of the way around the planet," Villimy explained excitedly. "And that over there is Disophon where I was born."

That Chayn had to see. He stood and approached inch by inch until he could see the towering, geometric pattern of a city hazed bluish by distance and glittering in dusted lights. Lights moved in the sky above the city. Even as Chayn watched, a bright star descended from the sky.

Villimy slipped her hand into his. Chayn could feel her shaking. He glanced at her, surprised by the haunted expression on her face.

"What's the matter?" he asked.

"If we went down there, would there be people?" she asked in a hushed tone.

"I'm sure it's possible."

"They'd be like ghosts. Illusions of memory. I don't want to see anyone I know, Chayn. I'd be terrified."

"Then we'll stay away from the city," Chayn said. "This is real as far as we're concerned. We have to take it at face value. And while we're at it, I wish you wouldn't stand so close to the cliff."

"Why?" she said, brightening again. The strong breeze swayed her to and fro.

"You'd die if you fell," Chayn warned. "The illusion is that real."

"No, I wouldn't. I used to jump off here."

Chayn grimaced. "You what?"

Villimy spread her legs and held her arms outstretched to the sky. She arched her back and looked up. "You dive like this to stabilize yourself. There's a warm water lake at the base of the cliff. You can guide yourself to it like a glider."

Chayn put his facts into place. This was a planet of small size and light gravity. It's air would be thin by his standards, its temperatures below freezing, especially at this altitude. Villimy stood three-quarters his height and weighed a quarter of his weight. In other words, Villimy had jumped from the cliff as a sport and never reached a terminal velocity high enough to injure herself.

144

"I hope you're not planning to jump," Chayn said in half genuine despair.

Villimy laughed. "Freefall is just as much fun." She turned away from the cliff. The night lights of the city had disheartened her some. She led him back into the forest at a walking pace. She wouldn't have missed this experience for the world, but it contained sad and nostalgic memories as well as bright and happy ones. Her people had abandoned this world. Somewhere, it really existed, but the city lights would be dark and the streets deserted.

An ice mist settled in hollows. Villimy held his hand as they passed through the cold gray. She turned off the path and gestured ahead. Chayn faced a house built upon the lower limbs of an old and gnarled tree.

"It belonged to friends of my parents," Villimy said. "It's a place to stay. But it's odd. I'm not hungry or tired."

"You're not expending the kind of energy you think you are," Chayn said.

"We don't have to eat or drink?"

"No."

"We might have to sleep though, won't we?"

"I don't think I'd like to sleep here," Chayn said. "What kind of dreams would we dream inside a dream?"

"Oh, I see. It is kind of scary."

Chayn followed her into the darkness of an overhanging branch. A ladder led to an entrance set in the floor of the house. Villimy moved ahead in the darkness and turned on dim orange lights upstairs.

The house was one large room centered with a large table, a slab of rock polished smooth. A white animal skin rug surrounded the table and Chayn sat down. Villimy fell back on habits of thought and behavior, her birdlike movements quick and precise. She rummaged through a kitchen area and fetched two mugs of steaming yellowish liquid and two flat cakes. She crossed her legs and sat beside him. Chayn took one of the mugs and one of the cakes.

Villimy ate slowly and sipped at the hot liquid, lost in thought. She glanced at him occasionally and Chayn had forgotten how startled he could be by her giant golden eyes flashing toward him. Her beauty captivated him, but his sexual drive hadn't as yet fully engaged after such a length of time. His body felt strange to him. Forgetting how to be human was a thought that terrified him.

"We haven't been alone for a long time," she said, her voice soft and sibilant. "I feel like this is our first mating."

Chayn sipped the hot liquid. It was something for which taste had to be acquired. But the hard cake surprised him. He ate it slowly, relishing its meaty taste.

"I was here when I was twelve. Family friends lived here. I must be about seventeen now. It's only been five years. Can you believe that?"

Villimy's people matured quickly. He had already been through the shock of learning her age in terms they both understood. "Five years give or take a few tens of thousands," Chayn said. "Are you sorry you met me?"

Villimy burst into laughter. She brushed away the liquid spilling down her chin with a bare arm and set her cup down. She turned to him and caressed the side of his face with slender fingers.

"What would we be without each other?" she said. "The selves we used to know died ages ago."

And so had their worlds. The only family Chayn had ever known hadn't even been real people. Villimy's parents had died of old age, probably even before the starship was out of sight of orbiting observatories. They had aged and died in the belief that their daughter would live on to help colonize a new world. Their belief hadn't died in vain. They would not have condemned her for pairing with an alien, not under the circumstances that had come to pass, not considering that she alone had survived the mission, thanks to Chayn Jahil.

Villimy looked around the quiet room. She felt like an intruder. "Are there ghosts in this world of mine?" she asked "Will anyone walk in on us?"

"Nothing human," Chayn said with a grin.

"You have been successful here," she said. "Tell me what happened."

It took time to outline the events that had occurred since

falling into the illusion of Lorb's realities. Villimy back-tracked, asking questions to fill in detail. It took hours.

"How do you intend to handle the sunsails when they arrive?" Villimy asked.

"I don't know yet. It's your turn. Fill me in on these Chilsun friends of yours."

Villimy gave him a weak smile. "They're the most incredible people the human race has ever known. But I don't know what we can do to help them."

She told Chayn her story in the same way he had told his. Chayn asked questions until he had filled in the outline. "Lorb and the Techs have had an odd relationship. They've hated and feared one another, but they've been interdependent all along."

"I don't think the Techs would have survived without the Dream," Villimy said. "And the Nats wouldn't have made it without the Techs. They've nurtured and fed upon their hatred of Lorb. It's been the only thing that has kept them going all these centuries."

"I agree that the situation is unique," Chayn said. "I doubt if we'll ever see anything like it again. No wonder the stargods directed us here."

"But I don't know what we can do to help the Chilsun, Chayn. They're not the most flexible people I've ever met. I can't go back."

Chayn fingered the implant in the side of her neck. Even in this hallucinatory world she carried it with her. "At least you have an effective means of communication with them."

"Chayn, even with it they won't listen to what I try to tell them."

"All right, so we have a few problems left to work out. Tomorrow's soon enough." He lay back against the animal skin. "Besides, I've handled my half of it. You finish your half and let me know when you've got these stubborn friends of yours under control."

Villimy pounced on him and beat his massive chest with her fists. "You cheated! You had the starcraft to help you!"

Chayn ran his hands up the smooth curve of her torso. He grinned. "They can't be any more stubborn than Lorb.

If they won't face reality, we'll just have to beat them over the head with it.''

Villimy began panting. Her skin flushed and she closed her eyes, the feel of Chayn's hands stirring irresistible forces within her.

"If all of this is happening inside some electronic circuitry, I think we're about to blow a few fuses," Chayn said.

Villimy jerked back from his touch. Her eyes opened. "This Lorb. Does he watch us?"

Chayn shrugged. "Why not? He's a god around here. Maybe not the most impressive the universe has to offer, but he's all we have to work with at the moment."

Villimy decided that he teased her. At least partially. "He's not human?"

"Not in the least."

Villimy ran a hand across Chayn's solid chest. "And he's a friend of yours?"

"We've taught each other a lot about life."

Villimy slid down alongside him. "He can watch," she said. "As long as you haven't taught him everything."

Fifteen

The sunsail fleet approached from below and behind the Kigon starship on its eternal, circular orbit around the red dwarf. They picked up speed, tacking the sunlight at an angle and jettisoned the sails in unison the moment they matched the orbital speed of the derelict. Thousands of square kilometers of film collapsed, folding, shimmering in the ruby sunlight like giant tongues of flame. Attitude-thrusters began flickering, bringing the widely dispersed fleet into a tightly packed, attack formation.

Without human prejudice to intervene, Villimy Dy reverted to her cultural preference of not wearing clothes except for practical considerations. She stood before a monitor console and watched magnified images of individual sunsail vehicles moving in for the kill. Lorb had constructed the large room with its low ceiling to her preferences, a combination personal quarters and mission control center through which she and Chayn Jahil would be offering their expert advice.

Chayn stood beside her. Or squatted. The Kigon had built a new drone more suited to him. At first, Chayn had thought to construct one along more humanoid lines, a standing biped for example. But the more he thought about it, the more he liked the horizontal, low slung body of the Kigon drones. So he retained the insectlike shape, but settled for four legs and two, forward arms, each with four-fingered hands and opposing thumbs. With a few hours practice, he discovered that the human psyche had little trouble handling an extra pair of limbs. Two bulbous eyes on the smooth foresection of the torso provided him with a high quality, color and three-dimensional view of his surroundings. In addition to other sensory capacities, it was also small enough to fit through the airlock of the starcraft. Despite Villimy's protest, Chayn developed a growing fondness for the sophisticated little machine.

"It feels like the real me!" Chayn teased in response to her criticism.

"Then have your friends supply you with a female! Just don't be sneaking up behind and tapping me on the shoulder!"

It had taken Villimy as many hours to grow accustomed to his presence as it had taken Chayn to avoid tripping over his rear legs. Now, they stood side by side watching the sunsail fleet closing in on the drifting starship.

Chayn supplemented Lorb's screen with his own superior senses, operating directly through the starcraft. The fleet began expanding into a shell, their strategy becoming clearer as time passed.

"They're in a trance," Chayn said, his mechanical voice

sounding perfectly human. "We won't be able to communicate or reason with them."

"I told you," Villimy said. "You can't reason with them, trance or no trance."

Lorb's voice sounded from a wall speaker. "I have defenses now."

"Yes, but we have to find a way to stop them without killing," Chayn said. "Prepare to disperse the metal."

Villimy had been briefed on Chayn's brainstorm. She felt certain that they'd ignore any metallic debris until after the attack.

Chayn took note of a squadron of advance vehicles moving ahead of the main body. Others hung back still further.

"Launch the metal, Lorb. Let's see what effect it has on them."

Small boosters attached to hull-plating began rising from the starship as a sparse cloud. It dispersed and moved toward the attacking sunsail fleet. Hours passed before the first of the cabins neared the now tumbling, ballistic bundles of hull-plating.

"They're passing right through!" Chayn said. "They're not even aware of the metal!"

"I am prepared to defend myself," Lorb stated.

"Let those first few ships attack. We can handle the damage. Let's see what their strategy has been all of these centuries."

The advance squadron thinned out to a single file formation arcing around to sweep across the midsection of the Kigon starship. The first cabin approached slowly, a brilliant, thin beam of light slicing across the incomplete, skeletal structure. Metal flared to incandescence. Clouds of debris spun loose from the landscape of metal. The lasers neatly and tidily dissected the exposed framework.

Upon their initial success, the main body of sunsails split into two sections. Fifty percent began forming a single attack formation. The rest decelerated. Underbellies opened wide. Long, fragile arms unfolded along with an incredible paraphernalia of tools designed to collect and tack-weld debris into loose bundles to be sent into spiraling, degen-

150

erating orbit to Hydrabyss. The ominous fraction of the sunsail cabins hanging still further back would contain the larger boosters. They waited like vultures to salvage the entire rear section of the asteroid-sized metallic scrap they expected to harvest and send down to the waiting, starving world of water.

Three more sunsail cabins passed slowly over the Kigon starship, lasers flickering and cutting a deep wound through the midsection of the huge craft. They didn't seem to notice that they were attacking a rebuilt version of the old derelict.

"I will permit no more damage," Lorb stated.

"Try to disable one of the vehicles," Chayn said.

A white beam shot from towers protruding from the bow of the craft. The light engulfed the next attacking cabin. The hull glowed a ruddy color for a moment without apparent effect.

"Does that give you some idea of the properties of the synthetic they use?" Chayn asked.

"It insulates and withstands extremes of temperature."

Beams of energy of differing density and colors played upon the sunsail cabins. "I determine it to be eminently suitable as hull-plating. The trade for this material in exchange for alloy-plating is no sacrifice."

A more conventional laser struck out against the stubborn sunsail cabins.

"I cannot disable the vehicle," Lorb stated. "Secondary radiation will destroy the biological unit within."

Chayn's drone visibly cringed as the sunsail cabins passed over the hull and wreaked more damage. Villimy glanced around the room. The echoing, distant explosions told the vast size of the starship. She could feel a barely perceptible vibration through her bare feet.

"How do you use the Dream of the Yellow Sun?" Chayn asked. "Do you intensify it during the attack?"

"It increasingly disables them," Lorb said. "I am presently increasing its intensity as has always been my strategy. I estimate the fleet will succeed in only one pass before the attack is neutralized. However, I ignored the small amounts of damage accumulating over the centuries. This attack would most certainly have destroyed me."

"Stop the Dream," Chayn said.

"The Dream is my only effective defense!" Lorb protested.

"I think you misjudge its effect upon the Techs. Stop the Dream temporarily and see what effect it has on the fleet."

Even Chayn and Villimy felt a sudden sensation of dark stillness when the Dream ceased. Chayn kept his eye on the approaching fleet. At first, he saw no visible effect. But the next attacking sunsail cabin did not fire as it swept down upon the Kigon starship. It grazed skeletal beams and exploded in a gout of flame.

"Chayn!" Villimy cried out in alarm. "We will destroy Hydrabyss! If you stop the Dream, the Techs will go mad! I don't think they can take the stillness!"

"Lorb," Chayn said calmly. "Continue to broadcast the Dream, but don't intensify it. We can't afford to throw these people too far off balance."

Chayn felt a subtle warmth as the static hallucination resumed its inner glow. "It's like a drug!" he said amazed. "The Techs have developed a resistance to it, but you were right, Villimy! The sudden psychological change would traumatize them!"

The sunsail fleet was out of control. Chayn withdrew to the starcraft for a better view of what had happened to the Tech pilots. They sat rigid in their couches, their open eyes unseeing. "They're comatose, Lorb. Get the Kigon organized. We have a rescue mission to complete before the fleet moves out of range."

Chayn sensed confusion in the Kigon population. The full impact of Lorb's former ignorance sent a ripple of anxiety through them. The Kigon had never known of the Chilsun or the sunsail raids. And Lorb had thought for an age that he successfully defended himself against the Chilsun's desperation with the Dream of the Yellow Sun derived from their own psyches. But for ten thousand years, the inner glow of the Dream had been their lifeline to sanity, their only contact with the world from which Lorb had taken them.

"The Kigon drones cannot rendezvous with the cabins in time," Lorb said. "I will match their velocity to ensure success."

A bluish halo formed around the engines on the stern. A glare of pure white light shot forth. The seventy-five-kilometer-long bulk of the starship slowly accelerated. Villimy staggered to one side with the gentle acceleration, momentarily puzzled as to how Lorb provided the weak gravitational field providing her weight. In providing her life support, Lorb hadn't taken into consideration the possibility of having to move the ship. The screens caught her attention in the next instant.

Five hundred Kigon drones launched from the starship to retrieve the Tech vehicles, one to retrieve the body of the pilot that had collided with the starship. Lorb initiated a flurry of activity within the craft itself. Villimy felt the vibration of construction crews nearby.

"Chayn, what is he doing?"

Lorb spoke for himself. "I am preparing life support facilities for the pilots of the sunsail cabins."

"This is where things start getting complicated," Chayn said. "What can we do for them?"

"I felt the Dream stop for a moment," Villimy said. "That alone probably panicked Hydrabyss. And their space station is monitoring everything that is happening here. We have more than just the pilots to consider."

"You have to go back as an emissary for us," Chayn told Villimy. "We'll send the metal back with you. I'll tag along in the drone if you want, but it's your show, Villimy. We have to get this situation stabilized."

Villimy continued to stare at the helpless Tech fleet. "I can't do it alone," she said. "There's one man in the fleet. His name is Hader. I've been with him from the beginning. If we can't communicate and reason with him, we won't be able to handle any of them."

Villimy looked down at the grotesque drone. "Chayn, they don't function as individuals. Theirs is almost a hive mentality. I don't even know what Hader is like as an individual. The sunsail pilots might not be strong enough to handle the isolation from their own people."

Chayn thought furiously. "The Kigon share a common individuality, but it's natural for them. From what you've told me, Villimy, the Techs function that way out of necessity, to conserve energy and resources, not because they like it. But I agree it's too late to start nurturing them as individuals until we've settled the crisis. What do we do?"

Villimy's expression brightened. "Chayn! Lorb can help!"

Chayn's laughter sounded downright wicked coming from the insectlike monster squatting at her feet. "Lorb?"

"I sense your strategy, Ally."

"Lorb, you tried to destroy me by tapping into my subconscious and manipulating my hallucinatory world. Now it's time to be a good guy for a change. How would you like to play psychotherapist?"

Lorb probed the dark corridors of Yeld in the minds of the comatose Tech fleet. "I will need your guidance and suggestions. It can be done if Villimy Dy will participate."

Villimy nodded her consent, her heart pounding furiously. She wasn't at all certain if any of this would work. "I don't know what to expect. Will it be another illusion?"

"Probably the Techs' own environment back on Yeld," Chayn said. "Can you handle it?"

"I think so. Where am I going to be while all of this is happening?"

Lorb spoke. "Lie on your bed. I have arranged for a direct interface with the human brain. I will provide sensory input. I will provide the feedback between the brain and synthetic reality."

Villimy glanced at the bunk Lorb had provided as part of her quarters. She paced the room, ignoring Chayn's drone. Physically, she was alone. For short periods of time she could forget that Chayn and Lorb watched her closely.

The Kigon drones were almost the same size as the sunsail cabins. Far from the starship, the drones reached hungrily for their assigned cabins and enfolded them within metal arms. They started back, discarding the boosters supplementing their own thrusters as they passed over the landscape of home port. They entered through a bright docking bay. The cabins were transferred to pressurized quarters where the unconscious pilots were transferred to the special chamber Lorb had constructed.

Villimy watched on the screen. Smaller drones carried the Tech pilots on stretchers, placing them on shelves lining the curved wall of the chamber. Tubes similar to those aboard the sunsail cabins were connected to their wrists. Ten thousand years ago, Lorb had constructed these bodies and knew in microscopic detail how they worked and how to care for them—even if he hadn't paid attention to the purposes of that detail. Each bunk was equipped with a helmet-like apparatus that would allow Lorb a direct inter- face with each brain.

"What kind of artificial intelligence has the capacity of millions of biological brains?" Villimy asked Chayn. "How can it synthesize whole realities?"

"Lorb is considered a god even by the Kigon," Chayn said, "but he understands only the structure of the Kigon brain. And, to some degree, the human brain because its circuitry is similar. But what's really amazing is that Lorb is only a machine. He has no creativity. He has to depend on us for that essential aspect of his operation. He doesn't understand what a mind is, not even his own. He knows his limitations."

"It's horrible!" Villimy protested. "It reduces people to patterns in some kind of a matrix!"

"That's all our reality is," Chayn said. "The Kigon use the term reality within Reality. But I suspect that Reality takes place within a larger REALITY. Lorb can play games with the contents of consciousness, but not with conscious- ness itself. He cannot create or destroy consciousness."

"What is consciousness then?" Villimy asked, but did so with an exasperated smile.

"What does a mirror see when it faces another mirror? One thing I have learned that I've never suspected before. Our ignorance deserves our utmost respect."

Lorb spoke, his human-sounding voice low and author- itative coming over the speaker. "I am ready."

"One thing before we start," Chayn said. He spoke to

155

Villimy. "How would the Chilsun react if we sent the metal down to them while we're deciding on our next move?"

"I don't know," she said. "I know they need it desperately. Maybe it'll help alleviate the impact of the failure of the sunsail mission. You had the right idea, Chayn. It will throw them off balance and keep them from drawing the wrong conclusions."

"Lorb?"

"I will collect the metal and send it down immediately."

Villimy eyed her bunk in the mounting silence. "Why do I get the impression everyone is watching me?"

"You mean Lorb and I and twenty million Kigon? Probably because you're our last hope. You are our emissary to the Chilsun."

"Are you coming with me?"

"Maybe toward the end as a climax to our little psychodrama."

Villimy walked to the couch. She saw no helmet, no evidence of ominous, alien technology. "I don't know what to expect."

"Lay down and find out," Chayn suggested.

With a final sigh of resignation, Villimy stretched out on the couch—and promptly fell into another world.

Sixteen

Villimy stopped. She turned and looked back down the black corridor with its harsh yellow lights and glanced down at the Tech coveralls she wore. Where had she been going? Touching the implant in the side of her neck, she wondered if something had gone wrong to feed chaos in her brain. Or had she been sleepwalking? And dreaming?

Had she dreamed of Chayn and the Kigon starship? She

156

remembered the attack of the sunsail fleet from somewhere. She reached out and touched a cold, dark wall to verify her hold on reality.

Hader called her in her thoughts. "I am ill," he said. "Please, attend me."

She walked on until she recognized the layout of the corridors, then made her way to Hader's quarters. She could feel others in the city, but not enough to assure her the city wasn't deserted. In the dream she remembered, the five hundred less one dead had been pilots of the sunsail mission. Now, they were all conscious and active in Yeld, but wandering in a trancelike state, just wandering and wondering what had happened.

Hader rose from his bunk as Villimy entered the room.

"Yeld has been evacuated," Hader said. "We must discover why."

Villimy just nodded. She couldn't afford to say anything to upset Hader. She didn't have the slightest idea how Hader might handle the situation or how she was expected to explain the reality of it. This felt more like reality than her dream, but she knew better.

"What shall we do?" Villimy asked.

"We will all meet in the City Communications and Control Center. Will you walk with me, Villimy Dy?"

Hader looked around the room as if searching for some evidence of the reason for his presence in this unsettling circumstance. He walked past her and into the deserted corridor. Villimy followed.

"Lorb assaults Hydrabyss," Hader said, walking at a quick pace beneath rows of bright lights.

"Is that what is happening?"

"The Dream of the Yellow Sun was interrupted. I felt it stop."

"What did it feel like?" she asked.

"It was horrible. It felt like death."

"I thought the Dream was Lorb's weapon against you. I thought you wanted it stopped."

Hader slowed in confusion. "It is a form of psychological warfare."

157

She didn't dare point out the poor logic of his rationalizations too quickly. But she wanted to. They were living a waking nightmare and she wanted it over with as quickly as possible.

It took ten minutes of walking through deserted corridors and riding quiet elevators to reach City Communications and Control Center. Villimy had never been there, but she had heard of it. It looked like the bridge of a spaceship. In one way of thinking, Yeld was indeed a vessel of sorts. It floated free in a void of water and had to be stabilized and guided through slow currents. The domed room was more than fifty meters in diameter, lined with electronic equipment, viewscreens and hundreds of neatly arranged seats facing monitoring consoles. The room was crowded, but none of the Techs present were in control of anything. Whoever had manned this nerve system of Yeld had abandoned their posts in evident haste. Earphones lay dangling from consoles. Chairs were knocked over and papers lay scattered on the floor.

All eyes were on Hader. No pilot of the sunsail mission had been in command, a mission they had all conveniently forgotten, but Hader had played an important role in the government of Yeld. The confused Techs looked to him for leadership. Hader tried his best to assume it.

Villimy couldn't follow the rapid-fire communication between the silent people. Hader led her to a high-ranking control position near the center of the room and gestured for her to be seated before a monitor screen.

"We have not been able to communicate with the other cities or the space station," Hader said. "But an alert is in progress. Hydrabyss is being attacked. It appears as if we are to die soon." He leaned over and switched on the screen.

Villimy gasped in surprise. The Kigon starship orbited low above Hydrabyss, skimming along the vapors of the open sea. Thousands of meters of hull detail sped past the camera view and terminated in the glare of massive engines. From a second vantage point, a three-quarters view of the alien craft showed thousands of tiny objects dropping from the belly of the starship and splashing into the planet sea in giant, slow-motion waves of water penetrating the dense vapor and cresting as ice debris.

"What are they?" Villimy asked.

"Bombs perhaps," Hader said, his voice flat and emotionless. "Perhaps they will sink or be guided to the vicinity of the cities and reefs to be detonated. Perhaps they will set up a chain reaction within the core of Hydrabyss and turn this small world into a star."

"One missile would accomplish that," Villimy said. "Perhaps it's a peace offering."

Hader reacted as if physically struck. "Do not speak nonsense! Lorb is our enemy! He has somehow repaired himself. Perhaps with the aid of your friend Chayn Jahil. Now Lorb seeks revenge upon us. Then he will depart and we will die."

"How are these images obtained?" Villimy asked.

"We do not know. Perhaps Lorb gloats and feeds us these images so that we may witness our own destruction."

"You're guessing, Hader."

Many others were watching the scenes on other screens. Villimy knew that none of this could be real. She had seen the condition of Lorb's starship before and after its reconstruction. This was what the Kigon starship had originally looked like, not an image of its present configuration.

The scene on the screens changed. It showed an underwater view of tumbling blocks of material falling through the water. Villimy felt adrenalin race from body to mind and feed through the telepathic link like a surge of energy. Black submarines rushed from the depths of Hydrabyss by the thousands.

"The other cities are alive!" Hader cried out. "Only Yeld is abandoned! Look! They attack!"

But the submarines did not attack. Closer views showed them to be utility rather than war craft. Their blunt noses yawned open. Booms protruded. The submarines nosed into the irregular blocks. Grapples were extended and the material held firmly in place. Only under partial control, the subs began sinking back into the depths.

A torch played upon the surface of one block in an effort to break the material into smaller sections. "Quick!" Hader called out. "Get a spectroscopic analysis of that! We must know what the material is!"

His voice sounded only in her mind. In the room itself, Villimy heard only sounds of rapid breathing. Suddenly, the Techs broke into panic. They milled in confusion, several falling to the floor in convulsions. Hader dropped into a nearby seat and gazed unseeing at the screen. Villimy realized this to be a preview of how the Techs would react when the metal was actually dropped into the waters of Hydrabyss. It would be a traumatic experience.

But within an hour, the Techs recovered and left the room. Hader refused to move from his seat. Villimy felt his thought patterns trying to organize the chaos around him. Hours passed before some semblance of calm returned, the anxiety and confusion radiated by the Techs beginning to wear thin on her nerves.

"Lorb has not attacked," Villimy suggested to Hader. "The METAL is a peace offering as I suspected."

Hader shuddered. "What is happening? I think I am ill!"

"You're just suffering shock. It will pass."

"Lorb has dropped—METAL—into the waters of Hydrabyss!"

"He orbits your world in peace," Villimy said. "What do you make of that?"

"The sunsail missions are ended! I can die and my children can be born." Hader struggled to his feet, another wave of tension rising to the surface of his thoughts. "But Lorb is our enemy!"

"And you are Lorb's enemy?"

"And we are Lorb's enemy!"

Villimy spoke casually, as if thinking aloud to organize her thoughts. "It has always appeared to me that you nurtured your hatred of Lorb as an excuse to do what had to be done. You needed—metal. But has Lorb ever harmed the Chilsun or retaliated after the sunsail missions? It appears to me that Lorb has been a very quiet and passive enemy."

"The Dream! The horrid Dream!"

Villimy said nothing. Hader stopped and cocked his head, suddenly aware of his own contradiction. The Dream had stopped. Hader did not remember the circumstances under which it had momentarily ended, but he remembered the horrendous effect it had had on him.

"The Dream is Lorb's only means of defense," Villimy said. "But it's an odd weapon, don't you agree? It's not nearly as effective as a warhead dropped into the waters of Hydrabyss."

Hader began walking the circumference of the room to dispel nervous tension, his thoughts in turmoil.

"It's a paradox," Villimy said quietly, forcing Hader to listen carefully to her thoughts. "I've heard of people exposed to poison. They develop a tolerance and even suffer withdrawal symptoms when the contamination ends. But then again, the Dream is not a poison. It is the memory of your original home, is it not? Perhaps you've grown dependent upon that which Lorb erected as a barrier between the two of you."

Hader considered, but he constantly returned to thoughts of metal and of the vast wealth it represented. The quantities he had seen being salvaged had already immunized him against the degree of reaction she had first noticed upon her arrival.

"Metal," Hader said, savoring the concept. "Lorb has fed us vast quantities of metal. It is easily converted into the different elements we need."

"Enough metal to expand your population and develop new technology. Enough to ensure survival. You can live without Lorb now. You can live without the Dream."

Hader rushed to the nearest monitor screen. "Is Lorb leaving?" The idea appalled and horrified him.

"What if he does?"

"We are abandoned?"

Villimy couldn't fathom Hader's complex emotional response. "But you planned Lorb's destruction! The end result would have been the same!"

Hader looked directly at her, his thoughts clearer now

than at any time since their arrival in this place in nontime and nonspace. "I must know what to do. Others have suggested that we visit Central Planning. Perhaps we will find some answers there."

"Answers to what, Hader? Do you tire of your contradictions?"

Hader turned and left the room. Villimy followed with a smile. Intellectually, the Techs were highly advanced, but emotionally, they were like children. From elsewhere in Yeld, she felt other Techs converging on Central Planning.

"What is this place we're headed for?" she asked of Hader.

"It contains the secrets of our past and the future of the Chilsun," Hader explained. "All knowledge is not public. Short-term propaganda and engineered psychological motivation served long-term goals. The general course of our history was laid down during the early years of our existence within Hydrabyss."

They finally entered the largest place Villimy had yet seen in the city, a hall stretching one hundred meters wide and a half kilometer long. The ceiling arched overhead in darkness, a projection of the Andromeda galaxy glowing in exquisite detail within its shadows. This was the closest thing to a shrine she had seen on Yeld. The hall ended in a towering narrow door elaborately inscribed with mathematical calculations and equations.

Just inside the hall, Hader stopped. "All answers must lie here." But he moved no further.

"Why do you hesitate?" Villimy finally asked.

"I have not the authority to visit the Records. I will be exiled if I learn too much, isolated from the body of the race."

Villimy studied the inscribed door at the end of the hall. The mathematics appeared to revolve around resource supplies, energy expenditure and requirements for survival during the course of history. "The past and the future of your civilization lies behind that door?"

"It does."

"And the answers to our dilemma?"

"Yes."

"Will you risk exile to resolve it?"

"I must," Hader said. He began walking.

Villimy followed him. Their footsteps echoed in the vast hall. Techs entered through side corridors and began lining the walls. Hader would enter the Records and through him, the others would assume the same risks.

Hader stopped in front of the tall doors. He pointed to a ten-digit keyboard. "I will not be allowed entrance. I have not the authority."

"Try."

Hader punched in his identification code. The doors slid aside slightly. Hader pushed sideways through the opening. Villimy slipped through behind him.

They stood inside a dome-shaped chamber opening to others beyond. On the right side of the chamber, holograms played in midair. On the left side, data screens came alive with fast-moving symbols.

"This is century one," a soft, female voice said to them in their thoughts. "Our long journey is ended. We are lost forever. Lorb the Tyrant is crippled. He offers us the slimmest hope of salvation—physical life within the waters of a small renegade moon orbiting the red dwarf he now orbits. We will leave reality within Reality and build a civilization. A low probability exists of developing the technology to repair the starship. If this is accomplished, Lorb guarantees our return to the World of the Yellow Sun."

Hader did not remain to hear the account. He moved into the second chamber.

"This is century two," the soft voice said. "There is great exuberance as we begin construction of the first of the great cities. Lorb aids us. The first plans are made for a dark and fearful future. We are beginning to perceive the difficulty we will have living in an environment devoid of natural resources—"

Hader did not hear the words. His eyes were on images. There were people in the scenes, but they were not small and dark. They were Chayn Jahil's people, almost alien to the present version of the Chilsun. Hader began moving

163

through the chambers too quickly to absorb useful information. There would be one hundred to inspect, one hundred centuries of history to explore.

"This is century five," the voice said. "Lorb no longer communicates with us. He has turned inward in defense against inevitable destruction, not possessing the flexibility to sacrifice for survival. He places the future in our hands by default and must acquiesce to necessity or become ours and his own enemy. Metal is our most valuable resource. For the centuries to come, we must feed upon the body of Lorb himself while searching for the final solution."

Hader rushed on through the chamber. Villimy wanted to hang back and listen, but already wondered just how real this place might actually be. Lorb had nothing to work with except the pilots of the sunsail mission. Therefore, this information was what Lorb had deduced of Chilsun history with the help of Chayn Jahil. For all she knew, this place had no real existence on Yeld at all. The chambers stretched ahead of her, surrealistic, impossible.

Hader stopped. He stood motionless several archways away from her. She rushed forward to see what had finally caught his attention.

"The destiny of Lorb and of the Children of the Yellow Sun are irrevocably interwoven," the voice was saying. "One cannot survive without the other. Deep within himself, Lorb knows that the Chilsun represent his only hope of survival. But in our never-ending hunger for metal in a technology grown stagnant, it is possible that we will someday destroy Lorb and destroy with him any hope for our own survival. It is clear that we will never develop the technology sufficient to become independent within this meager world of water.

"Be alert. Salvation may come from outside. Entities human or alien may stop by this isolated oasis of life and offer their knowledge and abilities toward the only viable goal possible—migration. The sunsails of the raiding missions will not return to Hydrabyss. They will drift through space as a sign of our tragedy and point the way to our lost world."

164

Hader absorbed it all at face value, totally unaware that Lorb himself had spoken. Needing to hear no more, Hader walked back past her and backtracked along the now silent chambers.

Villimy let him go. She wandered back to her quarters alone. Once Hader had assimilated everything planted within his thoughts as direct and subliminal suggestions, he'd be back with a renewed interest in her. He would listen more closely to her suggestions. And this time, she would have the answers to all of his questions.

She curled up to sleep on her bunk, her face to a dark wall. An hour later her eyes had not yet closed. Hader silently entered the room and touched her shoulder. Villimy rolled over and looked into his expressionless black eyes. Did he know that she felt uncomfortable with him and his emotionless, stunted personality? Isolated from the larger body of his people, he was diminished, not a man to love or be loved. Villimy hadn't once felt the slightest stirrings of physical desire for these dark, ominous and depressing creatures.

"Tell us what must be done," Hader demanded of her.

"I will not. I'm a mediator, not a figure of any authority. Neither is Chayn Jahil. I am your ally if you wish me to be. Just as Chayn is Lorb's ally. Together we hope to prevent the extinction of your race. But we have only suggestions to offer."

"You have aided Lorb, our enemy."

"Don't you have a single creative, positive thought in that one-track mind of yours, Hader? Are you going to persist in ignoring reality for the sake of perpetuating a nightmare?"

"Where did Lorb obtain the material to reconstruct himself?"

Villimy sensed Hader's suppressed suspicion. "Where do you think?"

"It appears to be blasphar. Large quantities of blasphar. But it is impossible—"

"You're discussing this with the wrong person," Villimy said. "There won't be any mysteries or unanswered questions left as soon as you're willing to converse intelligently with Lorb.''

Hader jumped back a full meter in abrupt shock. His eyes widened, the first facial expression she had seen among the Chilsun. ''Converse with Lorb!''

Villimy smiled. Still lying on her stomach she braced her chin on the palm of a hand. ''Chew that idea around for awhile. You have reached the point where you must co-operate with Lorb for mutual survival or face a meaningless, pathetic death. Lorb is your ally.''

''We cannot converse with Lorb!'' Hader roared in angered indignation. ''We have not the authority—''

''There are only five hundred of you here in Yeld. There is no authority beyond yourselves. You're isolated here and there's a reason for your isolation. But the answers are a package deal. You'll have all of your answers all at once or not at all.''

''Villimy Dy, what deceit is this! What have you done to us!''

''Hader, it would feel good to pound your head against a bulkhead. One more time. Will you speak with Lorb or not? Chayn Jahil and I will be present.''

It took several minutes for the sunsail pilots to reach a consensual agreement. ''Yes! We will listen to any information available to us! We must know what is happening!''

''Then I suggest we meet in the hall of Central Planning. It should hold us all. I've taken this about as far as I can on my own.''

Seventeen

Villimy had no fear of Chayn failing her, but it took blind faith to doubt her senses. Yeld appeared indisputably real and Lorb had somehow suppressed the intensity of her memory. Her immediate past felt like a dream she had had some time ago. And if the here and now didn't make much sense, the infinite ability of the human mind to rationalize somehow filled in the gaps of logic. But she knew the truth. Whatever Chayn and Lorb had arranged for the Techs would best be accomplished in a dramatic manner. The revelation they were about to receive would best take place against a background of profound symbolism.

Villimy walked alone to the hall and walked across the open expanse of floor to the door to the Records. The Techs arrived in small groups and clustered in a growing crowd in the center of the spacious hall. But she still could not imagine this to be a fantasy populated by minds sharing a common hallucination. When the group included all of the sunsail pilots, they gazed at her in expressionless silence.

"I have been ignored and taken for granted," Villimy said. She spoke aloud, her voice surprisingly clear in the cavernous hall even if the Techs could not understand spoken language. "You have taken your plight and your small universe too seriously. You never bothered to consider the power that brought me from a distant place and a distant time to this depressing, godforsaken place. But I have learned of your ways, your society, your beliefs and endeavors. All that is happening now is happening because of what I have learned. This data is being used constructively by powers that render us primitive in comparison.

"If the Chilsun and Lorb had been doomed to a slow death in this lonely corner of the universe, Chayn Jahil and myself would not have arrived. You would have been allowed to die in peace and dignity. Because we come with empty hands, it means that the potential to break an ancient deadlock and resolve this dilemma has existed from the beginning. What we have brought with us is objectivity. We've clearly seen the means by which you can save yourselves from extinction and we've been forced to take increasingly desperate measures to force you to pay closer attention to what we have to say. What is happening now is as desperate a measure as you could ever imagine.

167

"I don't know how Chayn Jahil and Lorb will pick up from where I leave off, but I will not speak again in this place. I know nothing more and I have nothing more to say."

Villimy stepped back against the wall alongside the towering doors. Her heart vibrated in her chest. It had taken all of her courage to say what she felt needed saying, but she didn't know what to expect now. Would Chayn or Lorb or the Kigon just appear from thin air to take over? Or would they desert her and somehow expect her to convince the Techs that reality was just illusion and inspire them singlehandedly to follow her and convert all of Hydrabyss to a final and abrupt resolution to their problems?

She saw something in her peripheral vision. It startled her and with the simultaneous moan of fear from the Techs, she jumped straight into the air, pivoted and landed five meters away.

Chayn emerged grinning from the chambers of the Records. For an instant she saw him through the minds of Hader and the others, a massive, frightening spectre, white-skinned, beady-eyed. In that moment Villimy saw him as more of a primitive than any of them. And yet the Techs recognized Chayn Jahil. Through Hader's memory of an image he had seen in the Records, they knew that this was what the Chilsun had looked like when they first arrived at Hydrabyss.

Villimy ran to Chayn and slipped into the cover of his heavy arms. She relaxed against the reassuring bulk of his stocky body.

Chayn looked out over the assemblage. "I am human like yourselves, like Villimy Dy. But we are different. If you are upset by my appearance, I may not be thrilled by yours either. So be it.

"As you may have noticed, Villimy Dy did not expect me to appear in this manner. A thought is spreading among you. But we are not invaders. We can leave as abruptly as we arrived and will do so if you do not choose to listen to the information we have available for your use. But I do intend to stay long enough to say what needs to be said.

Without this information, you shall all surely die.''

Watching Chayn speak, Villimy thought it odd that he could speak aloud in Rashanyn and yet be understood by the Techs in their own nonvocal form of communication. Even in her own thoughts, the concepts he sought to communicate came across more clearly than his words.

"Ten thousand years ago, you arrived in this system with Lorb. Lorb took you from your native world, a human colony that had its origins still elsewhere. It was a criminal act, but an unintentional one. Originally, there were tens of millions of Chilsun. Many died during the early years to establish a new colony here on Hydrabyss. At this time, you are all aware of a rough outline of your history. In the beginning, you were to lend aid to Lorb and in exchange, Lorb agreed to return you to the world from which he had taken you. But Lorb miscalculated. The Chilsun could not develop the level of technology necessary to repair the starship. In fact, your ancestors had to invest every resource available to them to merely survive. Today you hope to achieve independence from Hydrabyss and Lorb by developing the technology to mine the surface of your sun. But you will soon discover such technology to be far beyond your capabilities considering what you have to work with. You remain, even today, dependent upon your hated enemy for survival. Even as he had always been dependent upon the Chilsun for a chance to escape his slow death—or so he thought.

"The concept of irony is not familiar to you. You're about to receive an example of it. Lorb has had, from the very beginning, the capacity to repair himself. He didn't know it. You survived by raiding the starship for heavier elements Hydrabyss lacks and now, ironically, Lorb is indeed dependent upon you for survival. I have shown him what he overlooked in the beginning, but he remains incomplete and only the Chilsun can supply the material to complete him.

"You do not know that you did not enter this system as flesh and blood creatures. You arrived with Lorb as psychic imprints in an alien and highly sophisticated cybernetic

169

system. Another thing you have not known. The derelict has been inhabited by more than Lorb in that electronic system. As lifeless and useless as the starship has appeared to your eyes, twenty million alien entities also inhabit the craft. They arrived with you and Lorb ten thousand years ago. They have lived in a synthetic reality, an illusion. You have not known of the Kigon. And the Kigon have not known of you.''

An audible, harmonic thunder of astonishment echoed in the hall. The Techs were held spellbound by Chayn Jahil. In a highly suggestive state of shock, they did not doubt his words. They accepted him emphatically and responded in horrendous awe and astonishment to this new revelation.

''Lorb is a living machine and twenty million Kigon live within him; the psychic imprints of the species that gave birth to Lorb and his kind. Even if you persist in believing that Lorb is your enemy, another change has taken place. He no longer exists as he once did. He has lived as an independent entity for eons, governed by a programming that has existed even longer. This is why he overlooked solutions to a dilemma and a crisis that should never have occurred. But it was not his error. It was the Kigon's error. And they have suffered even more than the Chilsun because of it.

''Lorb has now merged with the psyches of twenty million Kigon where he belongs. He still possesses individuality, but he no longer functions alone. And he is free of the errors that have held him as captive as you or the Kigon. But by no stretch of the imagination are the Kigon your enemies. They are victims. As you are victims. As Lorb himself is a victim of errors that may have been made over thirty million years ago. Lorb is no longer the agent responsible for this state of affairs. He is ancient, but he is changed and therefore new. He is a new factor to alter the equation. The Kigon are a new factor to alter the equation.'' Chayn gestured to the mathematics inscribed on the door behind him. ''These equations.

''It is time now for a reconciliation between the Chilsun and Lorb. It is time for a meeting between the Chilsun and the Kigon, who have taken an active role in preparing the Kigon starship for its journey back to the Galaxy of Man. To meet these entities will be a traumatic but fruitful experience. As in the original bargain between Lorb and your ancestors, the starship requires blasphar to replace the metal you have taken. The images you saw on the screens in Central Planning were not real. And the Chilsun require a new environment—one rich in energy and other resources, an environment which will allow you to evolve and fulfill your ultimate destiny.''

Chayn gave the Techs a moment to assimilate his words. He looked down upon Villimy. ''Will this have any effect on them?''

''I don't like manipulating them like this,'' Villimy said. ''I suppose it has to be done.''

Chayn ran his hand through Villimy's shock of white hair. ''Any boyfriends among this bunch?''

''Are there females among the Kigon?''

Chayn wrinkled his nose. ''They reproduce by fission or some such process. Never heard of sex.''

''We're even then. The Chilsun can't afford death and sex is a waste of energy.''

Chayn looked out over the eerily silent group of Techs. Villimy could sense an undercurrent of communication in progress. Chayn understood it less well, but took for granted it was happening.

''As long as we can find ways to fake this flesh and blood body of mine, I'm more than happy to waste energy with you. When this is over—assuming it doesn't end in unmitigated disaster—we're going to make use of Lorb's electronic facilities for one hell of a vacation. The Watcher is going to have to use an old-fashioned crowbar to pry us loose.''

Villimy gave him a weak smile. ''Don't start relaxing yet, Chayn. I'm worried. The Techs have everything to gain and nothing to lose by listening to us. It's just a matter of breaking them loose from old habits. But the Nats are entrenched in Hydrabyss. I've seen their world. I wouldn't hold it against them if they fight us and the Techs to hold onto the life they've built for themselves. They can't just abandon it."

"I know, Villimy. But we'll have five hundred Techs on our side when we finish here. That at least gets us through the front door at Hydrabyss."

"Chayn, the shock might be too much for them. Their whole civilization could collapse before our eyes."

"Don't try to reason this out more than one step at a time," Chayn suggested. "As for the next step, watch the special effects Lorb has arranged for your friends."

Chayn spoke again to the assemblage. "The Chilsun and the Kigon have never met. That meeting will now take place. The minds of the Kigon are similar in structure to ours, the reason Lorb acquired human captives inadvertently. Communication between the two species is relatively easy. They will appear before you now, but their presence will only be an illusion. They are native to an environment far removed from our own. To a large extent, what you will see will be your interpretation of a form of life even more alien than you can imagine."

As Chayn spoke, shadows appeared on either side of him. Villimy broke away and turned to face the shadows solidifying against the back wall of the hall. They became like tall black-robed figures without visible arms or legs. Their faces consisted only of brilliant, yellow-slanted eyes. A moan of despair rose from the Tech ranks. Almost in unison, the hundreds of them took a step or two backwards, in abject fear. But they did not panic. The Kigon, at least thirty of them, stood like inhuman, implacable sentries against the wall.

A new voice rolled across the expanse of the hall. The words Villimy heard in her mind were incredibly rich in undertones of meaning.

"I am Ki. I speak for my people. Who will speak for the Chilsun?"

It took time before one small figure stepped forward. Villimy recognized Hader only after he spoke. "I represent only this group."

"We have lived close together in terms of time and space

172

for ten thousand years," Ki said. "But we have not known of one another. Lorb stood between us. But assimilated, Lorb now represents us. It is I who speak, but just as correctly, it is Lorb who represents the Right and the Left Hands of Kigon."

Each word contained a richness of meaning beyond misinterpretation. Hader stood unmoving, but Villimy sensed his amazement at the richness of the nonverbal concepts transmitted by the sourceless voice.

"We did not know," Hader said.

"Are we enemies?" Ki said.

Hader physically shook his head. "No foundation for animosity exists. We are neighbors."

Chayn took Villimy's hand and said softly, "We are not needed for the time being. The conversation between the Techs and the Kigon will take many hours. One advantage of these illusions—is that they won't grow physically weary. They'll exhaust their curiosity before they stop."

Villimy sensed they were about to leave. But now? She tried to imagine herself dreaming all of this and simply awakening to find herself stretched out on the bunk in the room Lorb had provided for her. But for the life of her, she could not imagine such a thing. How could she awaken from full consciousness?

And yet, in the next instant, she opened her eyes.

She stared at the metal ceiling for a moment, then turned and looked into the gleaming eyes of Chayn's drone.

"Well?" the drone said.

Villimy shuddered a sigh. "Chayn, I'll never get used to this. How can I know what's real and what's not? How do I know I'm not still in the sunsail cabin? This could all be an illusion."

"If this is an illusion, why am I using a drone? It's a shame you don't have a reasonable sense of aesthetics, but you don't really find it very attractive."

Villimy thought about it. "That sounds reasonable." She sat up and looked around the empty room. "But I'm still scared."

"It'll get worse before it gets better," Chayn warned.

"We've got to go down to Hydrabyss with the sunsail pilots. It won't be easy handling the rest of the Techs. Not unless there's some convenient way to divide them into groups of five hundred."

"I'm afraid for the Nats, Chayn."

"The Nats will analyze the situation and make a stand. We have to wait for them to react before we can act."

A thought occurred to her. "It will take time for the sunsail pilots to return."

"The metal will arrive first," Chayn said. "The pilots will return in their capsules. Then we'll go down. It will take time. While we're waiting, we can be together for awhile."

Villimy gave a shuddering sigh. "Why didn't you say so?"

"Just be patient for a while longer. We have to wait and see how the Techs react to the change from reality to Reality. They might not appreciate finding themselves aboard Lorb's starship after taking Yeld at face value."

"Just make sure Hader knows about the metal Lorb has sent down to Hydrabyss." Villimy said. "There's nothing Hader values more than fulfilling the sunsail mission. Certainly not his own life."

"I'll remember."

Villimy rose from the bunk and placed a hand on Chayn's drone. "I might have to change my mind about something, though."

"About what?"

"About what my parents would think of the man I paired with. If they could see you like this, they'd disown me."

Eighteen

The Techs elected to awaken back inside their sunsail capsules once the Kigon managed to fully explain the circumstances behind their presence in Yeld. Despite the injunction against ever returning to Hydrabyss, the Techs were prepared to serve as a nucleus of change among Tech society.

"Their enthusiasm is too much like a delirium," Villimy told Chayn. "I trust their intentions, but not their strength of character. They're a tightly knit group now, but there's no telling what might happen when they return. Chayn, they have to be retrieved when they drop into the waters. What if the Techs refuse to have anything to do with them?"

"There's an infinite number of 'what ifs' to contend with. How many of them would you like to discuss right at the moment?"

Villimy glanced down at the squat drone and smacked it alongside its torso with the edge of her right foot. "Don't be sarcastic."

Villimy continued her vigil, watching the screen showing a peaceful image of Hader apparently unconscious in his couch in the sunsail cabin while Kigon drones attached small boosters to the cabins to return them to Hydrabyss. When Hader awoke, he glanced around the cabin in confusion, then focused on Villimy's image on his screen.

"Your radio link with the space station is broken," Villimy said. "You will rest peacefully during the return voyage."

"The Dream will accompany us," Hader said. "We are eager to communicate with Yeld. Our people must know of our discoveries here."

"I will join you when you reach Hydrabyss," Villimy said. "Our mission will not be an easy one, Hader."

"We are fearful of change. It will not be pleasant. But they will open themselves to us. We will be reassimilated. We are their only link to an explanation of the metal Lorb feeds Hydrabyss."

175

Villimy reassured Hader with a smile. She could feel his uncertainty and fear and through him, the wavering stability of the entire group. But without the propaganda feeding cycles of hatred and fanaticism to a lost cause, the sunsail pilots did not want to die. They wanted to live and show Yeld the way to life.

"Good luck, Hader."

But the Techs did not understand the concept of luck. "Labor hard, Villimy Dy. We will not succeed without your support."

"With the Kigon and a stargod standing behind us, can we fail?"

Hader considered. "Yes, we can fail. The Chilsun must respond of their own accord. We behave as Lorb behaved—in old and rigid ways."

Villimy softened toward the stubborn, colorless little man. "You have learned that strength lies in flexibility, Hader. A good swift kick in the pants will teach your people the same."

Hader was learning. The remark delighted him and she even imagined that she saw the corners of his mouth twitch a millimeter or two. Hader leaned forward and turned off the screen.

"I hate them and I love them at the same time. I feel like a mother coping with ugly children. But I respect them. They're incredible."

"Typical emotional chaos," Chayn said. "There's a way to help them. We'll find it. In the meanwhile, would you like me to take your mind off the here and now for awhile?"

Villimy looked down at the grotesque drone. "If you had a mouth, you'd be grinning from ear to ear, Chayn Jahil. I don't want you messing too much with reality. Keep it straight and simple."

"Would you like to see Earth?"

"But you have never seen Earth!" Villimy said with a rush of excitement.

"I've had access to many records from Earth on the transporter that borned me. I've seen an example of what my subconscious can do with them."

Villimy nodded with enthusiasm. "I'd like to experience that." She eyed her bunk. How could she resist? She knew first-hand the power of Lorb's illusions, but she had no desire to return to the world of her birth. She would not trade that experience for another decade of life, but neither did she want to feel the impact of knowing it to be gone forever, an illusion built upon a distant past. A representation of Earth would hold no painful memories for her.

The eternal night of intergalactic space, the alien red glare of the dwarf, the dark blasphar of Chilsun technology, the stark, naked metal of the Kigon starship—it all depressed her. Both the Chilsun and the Kigon were asexual and with the drone at her feet, she felt herself to be the only woman left in existence. But to be alone with Chayn again . . .

The sunsails were already under way. She waited by the screen long enough to be sure there would be no further communication from Hader. The boosters burned, the fleet dropping away like a geometric pattern of dimming stars. There were minds here to keep her company, but not a single living body other than her own.

She went to the couch and lay down. The transformation took place instantaneously. She stood on the face of a massive world. The intense gravity pulled at her and the glare of a yellow sun blinded her.

Chayn Jahil watched Villimy Dy sink to the ground. "You don't have to take it so literally," he said without concern. "It's not all that real."

Given a few moments, Villimy blinked and opened her eyes. Everything felt normal now, just as Chayn had not suffered in her world. But the adjustments had taken place on a psychic level. At least she had gained some perspective of how bright and heavy Earth had been in comparison to her world. Here, the horizon stretched unbelievable distances.

"This is why you are built so heavily," Villimy said.

"And why my eyes are so beady. My apologies, but I guess we all have to conform to our own environments. You should see the world the Kigon live on." He pointed to a forest laid out at the base of the mountain slope they stood upon. "That's where I arrived when I first invaded Lorb's universe. Not that either of us understood what was happening at the time. I created this environment because I thought it to be mine. Lorb used it to try to destroy me." Chayn pointed up the slope to the rock cliffs, walling in one side of the world. "That's where I met a boy and rediscovered my past. Lorb used that against me and came reasonably close to succeeding in getting rid of me. Lorb is literally the god of all this. If he had some physical concept of himself, he could appear to us in some form. But he's not a man and he can't imagine himself as a physical entity. The closest he has ever come to a physical manifestation has been an amorphous cloud."

"It's hard to think of him as just a machine." Villimy laughed. "I've never met a real god before."

"All of Reality is based on a binary coding just like in Lorb's electronics. From a simple one and a zero, everything exists, realities within realities. I suppose the Watcher could show us a larger one if we could comprehend it. And they all coexist and interrelate."

Villimy wandered in a circle around Chayn. She knelt often, inspecting the plant life at her feet and the geology of the terrain. Already she had caught sight of birds, creatures that did not exist on her world because of the semiannual winds.

Chayn smiled at the small, quick woman moving about him. She lived in a world of sensory beauty and never questioned it. His analytical mind detracted from the quality Villimy could perceive. The magical quality did tend to go away with too much explanation. To Villimy, this world was as real as she had ever bothered to define reality.

"What are we going to do here?" she said. "It's fabulous."

Chayn nodded to the mountains above them. "We're going to cross over and visit an ocean. I've never seen a real live ocean before and I'd appreciate it if you didn't mention Hydrabyss. I'm talking about flat, blue oceans, not round, red ones."

178

Chayn began walking up the slope toward cliffs of rock. Villimy followed, intimidated by the climb ahead. But as the day passed, she did not fatigue or dehydrate in the heat of the sun on her bare flesh. As evening approached they crawled between rocky peaks to a point overlooking a green valley spread out below them. Snow-capped mountain peaks bordered the shadow ladened landscape.

"I don't think I'd want to stay here forever," Villimy decided. "After awhile, I think I'd prefer being cold and tired."

"The Kigon reached something of the same conclusion in their reality," Chayn said without bothering to explain himself.

"Where's Andromeda?" Villimy asked, scanning the skies overhead. A scattering of stars had emerged from the growing darkness.

"Don't take things at face value. What I know nothing about, my subconscious invents. I doubt if the stars are placed right."

"You mean you forgot to put Andromeda in the skies of Earth? How shabby!"

Chayn craned his head and studied the sky. "Andromeda would be two million light-years from here. Let the stargods worry about that level of detail. With me you're lucky to have ground to stand on."

"This is where people really began?"

"There are no people here because I don't believe people still live on Earth. Ten million years is enough time to rearrange the continents. There would be different mountains, different oceans and different kinds of things living on it."

Despite the cold that had no effect on him, Chayn sought Villimy's warmth during the night. She laughed in joy as her breathing became a familiar panting of arousal. For awhile, even Chayn could forget Reality and the contradiction of their lovemaking in an environment neither of them objected to. On the orbital city of Reylaton somewhere tens of thousands of light-years behind them, Chayn had risked frost bite stealing a moment's pleasure from Villimy's heated skin. And Villimy and her rapid metabolism had faced both nervous and heat exhaustion at the mercy of the slow, ponderous alien who could set her nerves screaming with unbearable ecstasy. They hadn't enjoyed a mild, illusory physical contact interfaced with the starcraft which made this the perfect concession, an illusion real and unreal in perfect proportion.

When they awoke in the bright dawn of a new day, they were not alone.

Villimy pointed out the human figure in the valley far below. "Expecting someone?"

Stunned by the intrusion, Chayn stood staring at the distant figure. It walked toward them.

"What is this?" Villimy said laughing. "Is Lorb playing games with you? I'll go see who it is."

Villimy darted down the rocky slope at an inhuman pace. Chayn called out after the girl and started after her, frustrated and angered by his clumsiness in contrast with her lightning quick reflexes. He knew instinctively the apparition wasn't Lorb's doing.

"Villimy, damn it! Get back here!"

Villimy slid to a halt close enough to the intruder for Chayn to see her dwarfed by the intruder. It stood twice her height, a large bright figure contrasted to Villimy's dark and small one. Only as Chayn reached a solid and grassy area of the slope and broke into a dead run did he notice the halo of light surrounding the anomalous intruder. Only as he sprinted down the slope dodging and leaping stray boulders in his path did he notice the creature to be a woman.

"Chayn!"

Villimy's frightened cry drifted and echoed along the wall of the slope.

"Villimy! Come back!"

The light emitted by the entity washed out any details of her form. It continued to approach Villimy. She turned finally and broke into a high-speed dash back up the slope. She ran for him blindly, her huge eyes dilated with fear. Chayn braced himself for an impact, but she slipped gently into his arms and held tight, her body shuddering violently.

The woman stood taller than Chayn but was obviously of his genetic heritage. She had white skin and white hair. A white gown stirred gracefully in an early morning breeze. The halo of light washed out every detail except her eyes. Her eyes were of vivid blue, the purest shade of blue Chayn had ever seen.

She stopped ten meters away and smiled. "Am I really so fearsome?" Her voice sounded soft and clear—and quite human.

"Who are you?" Chayn asked in a harsh, barely audible tone.

"You speak of gods but do not recognize me?"

But Chayn did not recognize her.

The woman looked down upon Villimy Dy. "I am not to be feared, Villimy. I could have appeared less formidable, but I had only my form to work with. I have not appeared in this way for ages and I lost my sense of perspective. If I corrected my image suddenly, I would frighten you further. So I shall alter very gradually."

Villimy turned her head and looked directly into the eyes of the woman, a feat Chayn found next to impossible. A frightening suspicion formed in his mind. He tried to suppress it for as long as possible.

"We are not strangers," the woman said. "Chayn Jahil, you recognize me almost on a conscious level. On a deeper one, even Villimy knows who I am."

"Chayn, who is she?" Villimy pleaded.

"She's the Watcher," Chayn said. "She's a stargod. I always assumed the Watcher would be male."

The woman's glow noticeably faded out but Chayn doubted if anything could detract from her astounding beauty.

"You are what humanity has become," Chayn said.

"We stand upon the foundation of what you are," she replied.

"What's your name?" Villimy asked.

The woman laughed in delight, her voice music in the morning landscape. "I must have a name, of course. I am

Beth to you. Chayn, you will know me at other times by another name. I may be male the next time we meet. But Villimy is overwhelmed by what she perceives as a male presence among the Chilsun and the Kigon. I am as much female as she. I sought to balance the scales a little."

Chayn could not feel the Watcher couched within his psyche. Villimy began to relax. Beth, the Watcher, turned and looked out over the landscape. The texture of reality intensified. It changed the subtle waves of depth and color. More and wider varieties of birds flew in the air. A great herd of herbivores grazed in the valley below.

"I didn't do so bad," Chayn said. "Considering my amateur status."

"Earth lives within you," Beth told him. "Your roots take sustenance from the source from which Earth springs. Villimy Dy lives more distant from those roots, but the spectrum of humanity is easily broad enough to encompass her. And the Chilsun. And others you will meet someday."

"Is Lorb aware of your presence?"

"I asked his permission before appearing in this manner. He is quite interested in me."

Chayn grinned in satisfaction. "Good. We're getting to be one hell of an eccentric family."

"I am pleased," Beth said. "The Kigon have scattered the seeds of humanity. They serve us in a strange way. The seeds sprout in odd places and mature in ways that were not foreseen."

Villimy blinked, unable to tell whether she had received a compliment or a criticism for what amounted to an accident of birth.

"There are no accidents of birth," Beth said, clearly receptive to her thoughts. "And life grows beyond its own limitations only by achieving what is not foreseen."

"Why do you visit us in this manner?" Chayn asked.

"You are growing. Our relationship must be altered for you to make best use of your awakening abilities. This relationship included you, Villimy. The future holds great challenges for the both of you. Your present beliefs about the nature of our relationship accentuates your ability to cope with these challenges. This is more true for you, Chayn, than it is for Villimy."

"I don't think I like the sound of that," Chayn said. "If there's more of this in store for us—"

"Your role is chosen, Chayn."

"Chosen by me?"

Villimy gave him a less than discreet kick in the shin. Chayn did not even notice.

"You believe yourself to be an orphan and you think of yourself as a pawn."

"I was born and educated by a machine to pilot a lost transport back to its destination," Chayn said. "You picked me up somewhere along the line, implanted some idea of what I was to accomplish and sent me on my way. You probably arranged for me to stumble across Villimy Dy. But it still seems to me that you made good use of a life that had no other purpose for existence."

Beth shook her head. "No, Chayn. You were not born to pilot a primitive starship back to its destination. That is your interpretation of events based on information you had to work with. The truth is, you were born in that particular circumstance as the first step of this journey."

"I don't understand," Chayn said.

"The stargods are not a late development in human evolution, Chayn. It appears that way because you live in time and space. But everything that lives is an expression of consciousness living beyond that structure. You, Chayn, are an unusual, but not unique kind of human being. You have as much free will as any other person alive, but you are an expression born for a particular purpose. It is not a purpose imposed upon you. It is yours. It was from the beginning, even from before your birth. It is a more challenging life than usual, but the rewards are commensurately greater."

"Why haven't I known this on my own?" Chayn asked softly.

"Because the memory is hidden by pain of sacrificing immediate benefits for future rewards you cannot as yet perceive. I anticipated this problem. That is why you must

183

consciously know of my existence.''

Chayn opened his mouth to ask his last question, but didn't know how to word it.

''You and I are the same person, Chayn Jahil. You are one of my expressions in physical reality. I gave you birth. I set you free in this universe. It is indeed Reality within REALITY.''

Chayn took Villimy's hand and walked past Beth. Villimy resisted vehemently for a moment. Chayn yanked her along insistently. He knew better than to believe that they could ever leave Beth behind them.

''But if I choose to go my own way?''

Beth's voice sounded from behind him as if following closely. ''If you choose to go your own way, you acquiesce to the physical death you have already suffered. But life and death are only cycles just as the birth and death of suns fertilize the universe for its continued existence. It would be a proper and valid choice—if it is yours.''

''But this isn't an ultimatum you're imposing on me,'' Chayn said with a faint smile. ''I've already made my decision.''

Villimy walked willingly beside him now, looking up at him with an expression of fearful confusion.

Beth laughed. ''I'm proud of you, Chayn Jahil. All I seek to accomplish is the removal of the resistance you inflict upon your own decision. Is it gone?''

Chayn looked down at Villimy Dy with her wide, puzzled eyes. ''Of course it's gone. And what about Villimy? How does she fit into all of this?''

''To accomplish a complicated task, it is better to use specialized tools rather than one general purpose tool. Villimy Dy is your counterpart, Chayn. She was born into another time and space, but born to complement your life. She is an expression of mine as well—a less troublesome one.''

Villimy gasped and spun around. She stared at the empty hillside. A cold flow of shock rippled the length of her body but gave way to an elation she could not contain. She shuddered and screamed in unbounded joy.

Chayn hadn't even bothered to turn around. He felt the bright and clear consciousness of the Watcher within him. He held out his hand and Villimy slipped hers into it with an unconscious gesture of affection.

They walked without speaking through the valley and slept in each other's arms for the night. Villimy awoke before dawn and gazed at the stars. They were all in their correct places now and she was in hers.

Their journey ended on the shores of what had been called the Pacific Ocean. They walked south along the rugged coastline, sometimes through evergreen forests, but never far from the endless roar of the surf. They didn't leave Earth behind when the time came to depart. It wasn't an environment separate from the depths of their own being.

Lorb looked on with tense anxiety when the starcraft moved toward Hydrabyss. The advanced vehicle contained one biological female and Chayn Jahil's personal drone. But he sensed the other two, nonphysical entities accompanying the human female—Chayn Jahil and the Watcher. Together they comprised an alien triad Lorb and twenty million Kigon relied upon to resolve the next phase of their salvation.

Nineteen

The starcraft skimmed the desolate ice crust of Hydrabyss, moving toward the curving, red-glowing slash of the horizon. The senses of the starcraft knew no physical barriers. Chayn studied the detail of the Chilsun civilization, Tech cities scattered like jewels in the dark water, crystalline structures embedded in solid rock, each accompanied by bright, flat reefs. And at greater depths the great Nat reefs spanning tens of kilometers in two-dimensional slabs of light and life. The bluish, shimmering foreboding nuclear transmutation furnace burned at the core, the key to the mind field he sensed inhabiting a resourceless world.

Chayn tried to estimate blasphar production in the reefs and their subsurface processing plants, discouraged by his rough estimates. Even discounting the metal Lorb would feed the Chilsun, it would take decades, perhaps centuries to complete the Kigon starship. And he could see for himself the source of Villimy's foremost concern for the Chilsun. What possible initiative would the Nats have for investing heavily in a program aimed at abandoning Hydrabyss and their marvelous reef system?

Villimy watched the dark, airless skies. Artificial asteroids of pure metal spiraled into a decaying orbit around Hydrabyss. They rose from the dark horizon like ruddy stars, a loose conglomeration of debris heading for an accurate splashdown in the open waters of the sun-lit ocean.

Chayn stopped the starcraft over a dense ice mist overflowing the coastal regions of the open waters where the red dwarf hung suspended in the vapor as a dome of swirling incandescent gas.

"This place is downright depressing," Chayn said. "Red and black are not my favorite colors."

"Here comes Lorb's metal," Villimy warned.

The first mass tumbled overhead, permanently captured by the weak gravitational pull of the satellite. It arced over the horizon, stabilizing jets of its booster, burning the last of its fuel to decelerate the unwieldy slab of metal. Lorb's calculations were down pat. The fifty-meter-long, twenty-meter-wide slab almost hovered above the open waters before slipping peacefully into the fog.

"That was incredibly neat," Chayn said.

As more of the metallic debris dropped quietly into the open waters, Villimy sensed alarm spreading throughout Hydrabyss. Just as Hader had reacted in his illusory Yeld, the Techs assumed that Lorb bombed their world and panicked. Hundreds of submarines approached the slowly sinking masses to investigate the intrusion even the orbiting Tech satellite had not detected approaching from deep space. Each collection of hull-plating contained a welded, water-tight core of vacuum to limit the depth to which it would sink, a factor Chayn and Villimy hadn't anticipated. But Lorb had taken into consideration the nuclear plant at the core and the threat rapidly sinking, multitonnage of metal might pose for the Nats.

The reaction of the Techs to the offering would seal the fate of the returning sunsail fleet. The first lasers lashed out for a spectroscopic analysis of the material. Chaos reigned immediately. Eight percent of the Techs reacted with debilitating shock to the findings, the chain of command passing through the ranks at lightning speed in search of those still functioning. But within hours, some semblance of coordination returned. Masses of metal were even being taken into the depths for the benefit of the Nats who would not decompress fast enough to surface and retrieve their share of the treasure. During the first few hours, Chayn sensed very few questioning the source of the material. A secondary wave of shock passed through the hierarchy of the Tech cities as the implications of the astounding occurrence dawned on them.

"The sunsails are coming in for a splashdown," Villimy informed Chayn.

"It's about time to dive into the thick of things," Chayn said. "There's no sense in watching the fun from here."

"How do we go down?" Only minutes before, they had walked together along a roaring surf beneath the warm and sunny skies of Earth.

"You've waited this long to figure out how we're supposed to rejoin the fleet?"

"Yes!" Villimy snapped, the rising tension gnawing at her.

"If you will direct your attention to the rear of the sunsail fleet, you will notice one empty cabin. That's yours, repaired courtesy of the Kigon. You'll also notice your good-as-new pressure suit and helmet and repressurized air supply. That is our ticket of admission, but it's a one-way trip. If we don't receive a warm welcome, you'll have to swim out."

187

"I can do it," Villimy said, taking Chayn's levity at face value just to be stubborn. "Hader and his men can't."

Chayn moved the starcraft to the empty sunsail cabin, roughly aligning the hull field airlock of the craft to the open sunsail hatch. Villimy withdrew to her body. She swung her legs over the edge of the crypt and dropped to the deck. The drone at her feet came to life.

"This is embarrassing," Chayn said, his voice sounding normal coming through the speaker centered beneath and between bulging eyes. "I feel like a bug."

"You're thoroughly unattractive," Villimy said, giving in to Chayn's effort to lighten the tension. "Don't ask to mess around with me until you're wearing something more erotic around that lecherous mind of yours."

"Who knows," Chayn said. "You might get desperate and settle for whatever's available."

Villimy looked down at the drone. Chayn craned his mechanical head to look up at her. "Don't count on it."

Chayn scurried through the hull-field airlock into the sunsail cabin to retrieve Villimy's pressure suit and helmet. Villimy waited for the deathly cold of space to dissipate from the drone and her suit before dressing and sealing the helmet. Chayn transferred again to the sunsail cabin and prepared to pressurize the compartment. She would not be breathing its air, but they would need the compartment's pressure equal to that of the water below them. Villimy glanced one final time at the body crypt before leaving the starcraft. She wondered how Chayn had felt seeing her body occupying the crypt after his physical death on Reylaton. She pushed those thoughts aside and stepped through the hull-field airlock into the vacuum and weightlessness of the sunsail cabin.

In the sudden freefall environment, she kicked off the bulkhead near the hatch and pulled herself into the contoured couch. Chayn closed the hatch and pressurized the cabin. The screen came to life, showing the crimson curve of Hydrabyss swelling slowly in size. Villimy switched on communications to join the mind meld of the fleet. Hader silently acknowledged her presence with calm gratitude.

"How're Hader and his men doing?" Chayn asked. Lorb had offered to include circuitry in the drone to allow him to join the unique Chilsun gestalt, but Chayn had refused, suspecting he'd function better autonomously. His only link to the Techs would be through Villimy using their spoken language.

"Grim, but optimistic," Villimy said. The first of the sunsail cabins entered the waters of Hydrabyss. "I still don't feel any contact with the rest of the Techs. They have us isolated in some way."

"That's to be expected," Chayn said.

Chayn abandoned the drone long enough to park the starcraft in orbit, returning as the cabin lurched as it entered water. Chayn felt the movement from his built in accelometer. They were the last down and from here on out, the fate of the sunsail fleet would be dependent upon the curiosity of the Techs. The fleet would be their only link to an explanation of the offering of metal. Chayn had assumed from the beginning that the fleet would be retrieved from the waters and isolated. Villimy agreed with Chayn's scenario, but her optimism didn't stretch as far as his. They'd be imprisoned and barred from contact with Tech society. She suspected the Techs would do a good job of it and leave them without another stalemate to break in some manner. But at least the Chilsun had no history of crime and would never think to execute or harm one of their own kind.

Chayn followed the structure of logic of her thoughts and waited patiently with a sly inner smile. "Is it all that bad?"

"What do you mean?"

"Hader and the fleet will be a time bomb in the Tech cities. They have no means of communication with one another except for their electronic telepathy. Once the Techs breach that barrier of isolation, or once we breach it for them, some change is bound to sweep through Tech society. There would be a time of disorientation and confusion, but the Techs are good organizers. It won't take much to ensure a firm alliance between them and the Kigon."

"And what about the Nats?"

"Unknown factors," Chayn said. "We have to cross that bridge when we come to it."

Hours later they felt another lurch, the deck swinging around to orient itself at a stable-down direction, evidence that they had been berthed in a submarine.

"We're on our way," Chayn said.

"We could have died in here if Yeld had decided to just abandon us," Villimy replied in protest to his calm and flippant attitude.

"Not me. I may be grotesque, but my batteries will last centuries."

"Don't look to me for mercy if you shortcircuit and start to corrode. It's wet outside this cabin."

The drone crawled up the back of her couch. "You'll like me better if you ever get the chance to paint me some nice colors. I look ominous in black."

Villimy suppressed a smile. "The Nats have an eye for color. Too bad they hate machines." She glanced back at his insectlike face. "Have you given any consideration to how the Techs might react?"

Chayn had. "I think I'm laser-proof. Lorb's a metallurgical genius. I don't even know how the Chilsun manage to convert the hull-plating into useful elements. There's not much simple iron in it."

"Kigon technology is beyond what my people possessed," Villimy said, letting the conversation drift to take the edge off her tension.

"And far beyond what the human race had going for it in my time."

"But even Lorb's technology is primitive in comparison to some civilizations we knew about in Andromeda," Villimy said, an old, frightening memory rising to the surface. "We had strict limits to the power of our radio transmissions so that we'd remain undetected by them."

"Human civilizations?"

"Not likely."

"What about the aliens that traded the position of a habitable world for the knowledge of your technology?"

"They gave us quite a scare. But they were friendly,

about on par with us, just different in some ways. They treated the trade like an ordinary commercial venture. And it would have been a beautiful world. If our mission had succeeded. . . .''

"You would have lived an ordinary life and have died tens of thousands of years ago," Chayn said. "And that new world would have been abandoned when your people returned to the Galaxy of Man."

Villimy nodded. "It's easy to imagine how things could have turned out differently. I keep forgetting about what Beth told us."

They felt renewed movement. When stillness returned, a rising sense of expectancy wouldn't let them relax. Something rapped hard against the hatch.

"That's obviously an invitation to disembark," Chayn said. "I don't get wet after all."

Villimy pulled herself loose from the form-fitting couch and rechecked her pressure suit. She still couldn't be certain whether the environment beyond the hatch would be air or water. Chayn broke its seal and pushed it open.

They were in the cavernous interior of one of the larger submarine hangars. Across the expanse of the deck, hundreds of other sunsail cabins were lined in neat rows, the isles of space between crawling with armed Tech guards. The raiding mission pilots were being hustled into waiting, dome-shaped vehicles.

Villimy went out first. Chayn started to follow, his metal hands clattering across the deck of the cabin. He stuck his head through the open hatch and took his first look at Tech civilization.

A Tech guard recoiled in horror. He brought his rifle up and fired.

Chayn cringed, the laser beam deflecting from between his eyes and burning a hole through the ceiling of the cabin. The Tech pivoted to escape the monster emerging from the open hatch. He lost his footing and fell thrashing to the deck. Other armed Techs rushed to his rescue and formed a cordon around the cabin.

Ignoring the sudden rash of weapons, Villimy climbed

back up the short ladder. "Chayn, I'm in communication with Hader and the other, but not with these guards! I can't explain you to them!"

Chayn held out one of his forearms. "Escort me out like a pet. I don't think they'll systematically try to destroy me. They must suspect that I'm intelligent. I just startled the guard."

"You just startled the guard? Is that all?"

"There's nothing to do but play this situation through by ear."

"You don't have any ears, you grotesque little creature!"

Chayn laughed. "I have pressure-sensitive diaphragms. You're yelling at me."

Villimy climbed back down the ladder holding onto Chayn's humanlike, intricately engineered hand. Chayn still had five other free limbs and climbed down the ladder head first.

The Techs moved back. He didn't like the idea of Villimy risking her neck to protect his drone and kept a sharp eye on the guards, ready to move away at the first hint of trouble.

"What's happening to Hader?" Chayn asked.

"They're being taken to a holding area and given medical checkups. Hader says they've changed the frequency of the implants. The rest of Yeld is functioning normally."

A guard gestured with his rifle. Villimy held tight to Chayn's hand and joined a file of sunsail pilots being escorted to the waiting vehicles. Chayn concentrated on coordinating four legs and ignored the curious crowd gathering behind him.

They were escorted alone aboard one vehicle and rode in tense silence until the door opened to a large room filled with Techs. Black-smocked Techs were escorting the sunsail pilots through side doors. None seemed to be returning to the room.

"All is well," Hader informed Villimy from nearby.

"What happens next?"

"Yeld must believe we have been subjugated by Lorb and sent back to contaminate the civilian population,"

192

Hader said. They'll risk some contact sooner or later. When they experience what we have experienced, they will not resist. I am certain of that."

"How much time, Hader? They'll not make such a move soon."

"A generation or two," Hader said, fully prepared for the long wait. "Eventually."

"We can't work with Hader's time scale," Villimy told Chayn. "He's prepared to wait the rest of his life for a breakthrough."

"Patience is supposed to be a virtue," Chayn said. "But I think we can live without it."

Villimy followed Hader in her thoughts. He was given a medical checkup and taken to confined barracks. Ten armed guards and several technicians escorted Villimy and the alien drone scurrying alongside her to a small, adjacent room. Villimy stripped off the pressure suit to don a set of coveralls. The Techs conducted a superficial examination, concentrating on the skin area of Villimy's implant for evidence of tampering. Other Techs stepped forward and gestured for Chayn to climb onto an examination table, evidence in itself they recognized a higher-than-machine intelligence operating through the drone. While Villimy climbed into her coveralls, Chayn complied in a single leap that sent the Techs reeling back in fear.

Lorb had guaranteed that the Chilsun wouldn't be picking him apart. The alloy of the drone successfully resisted drills and lasers trying for a sample of the construction material. The technicians grew excited, realizing he was made of metal. The examination itself lasted minutes, but the Techs stood silently for an hour, inwardly offering personal hypotheses as to his origin and the reason for his presence in Hydrabyss—and his fate.

They chose not to attempt to separate him from Villimy. Armed guards escorted them through cleared corridors to personal quarters, a small room containing nothing more than sanitation facilities and a bunk for Villimy's use. Once inside, the guards closed the door behind them. They heard a lock click shut.

"Prison," Villimy said. "This room is shielded. I can't feel Hader."

"I'm going to be gone for a moment," Chayn said. The drone squatted and fell still.

Chayn withdrew to the starcraft and breathed a sigh of relief to be temporarily free of the confinement. He used Villimy's mind as a beacon to guide him back to Yeld. He focused down on the woman pacing the room around the motionless drone. He studied the corridors around the room and committed everything to memory.

He saw the ultrafine, wire mesh in the blasphar walls that isolated Villimy's implant from the sunsail pilots. He focused down to the implant itself, barely able to detect the feeble, complex emissions from the device. Looking through corridors beyond the room, he noticed the receiving and transmitting antenna infiltrating every corner of the city and ultimately, every Tech city and submarine craft between them. Part of the social organization of Yeld was psychological but an important part was mechanical. Some groups of Techs were in full communication with one another but others isolated to differing degrees by subtle shifts of frequency. Each individual was in full communication only with those sharing his function in society. But every Tech had a basic capacity to communicate with any other using a mental shorthand, a condensed language of coded concepts and feelings that took considerable skill to master. Villimy had revealed the extent of her intellectual acuity by mastering that unspoken language. That startled Chayn. He realized that he quite literally could not have gained any accurate understanding of the Techs without her abilities.

The sunsail pilots were isolated by a simple change in frequency of transmissions within Yeld. Chayn tracked down the electronic equipment responsible and narrowed it down to a single console, then a single control. If he could reach that heavily guarded room and readjust the communication to bring the sunsail pilots into contact with the city, Yeld would have no choice but to be aware of what they had learned and base their evaluation of it on rational, personal decision rather than on an artificial barrier of ignorance.

194

Chayn returned to an interface with the drone. Villimy turned as he spoke. "I know what we can do to give the pilots a fair hearing.

"We have to inform Hader first. I don't like taking any action without Hader's knowledge and approval." Villimy squatted to eye level with the drone. "How do you plan to get out of here?"

The drone scurried to the back wall. Chayn reached out with his two forearms and began clawing his way through the blasphar.

"Oh," Villimy said in mild surprise. "I never thought of that."

Twenty

Chayn nodded to Villimy when he felt microwave radiation seeping into the room from the small hole penetrating through to an outside corridor.

"Hader!" She spoke aloud to let Chayn overhear at least half the conversation.

"We were concerned about your silence," Hader said.

"We were in a shielded room. Chayn just tore part of the wall down."

"Trouble!"

"Not immediate trouble," Villimy assured him. "We haven't aroused suspicion yet."

"What is your intent?" Hader asked.

"I think Chayn has an idea which will reduce your wait from a generation or two to a few minutes."

The thought agitated Hader. "What is his intent?"

Villimy relayed the question.

"Tell Hader there's a central communications room through which all mind-meld transmissions are processed. I can readjust the receiving equipment to put him and his

195

men back on line with the city at large. How much time do the pilots need to present their cause?''

"Only seconds," Villimy said. "Emotions and attitudes can be communicated immediately. That will be enough to catch Yeld's attention."

Hader had no trouble picking up Chayn's explanation through Villimy's thoughts. "There will be great conflict and suffering!"

"We will be destroying the entire foundation of your culture," Villimy said in agreement. "Do you need a generation or two to gather your courage?"

Hader still hesitated. It came close to the truth.

"Hader, we have to move now! Lorb donated the metal to throw your people off balance! We have to take advantage of that! Hader, when they discover the damage we've caused in this cell, they won't make the same mistake twice. They'll isolate us outside the city and you'll have no more contact with us. We can fail if you don't help."

Hader gave in to her chain of logic. "What must be done?"

"You must be ready for the mind meld when it happens. We only need your permission to move."

"Tell Chayn Jahil to do what must be done. We are eager to share the Dream with our comrades regardless of consequences."

Villimy nodded to Chayn. "Go."

"Wait here. I won't be long."

Chayn enlargened the hole and leaped through. He vanished down the deserted corridor in a scuffle of metal hands. Villimy gave a shuddering sigh and sat on the edge of her bunk to await the outcome.

Chayn reached the end of the corridor and stopped to orient himself. Beyond the closed door ran a major corridor. There would be many pedestrians in his path and armed guards stationed near the communications room. He did not know how much laser firepower his alloy body would withstand. The laser bolt he had taken at the sunsail cabin spread only a comfortable warmth through his sensitive and complex inner workings. What effect would sustained and multiple hits have on the drone?

Still, he had not as yet explored the full extent of his mechanical reflexes. His only chance for success lay in a bold, mad dash for the communications room. Once the sunsail pilots were in direct contact with the rest of Yeld, there would be a moment of confusion as new and strange ideas began spreading through the population. He needn't worry about a successful retreat.

A deep part of him still trying to identify with his missing, human body wanted to take a deep breath in preparation for the assault. It felt odd not having to breathe at all. He laughed inwardly and reached out to try the door. It was locked.

Using both hands, he twisted the latch from the door. He pulled the door open and lunged into the corridor. A Tech screamed and fell as Chayn scampered past. Unable to check his momentum at the end of the corridor, he slid and then leaped onto the facing wall of the next corridor running at right angles, leaping off to his left without a break in his pace. Rapidly gaining confidence in himself, his metal hands began scoring deep marks in the blasphar as he dodged innocent pedestrians screaming in horror and blocking his path. Another turn presented a gauntlet of armed guards, a fifty-meter corridor with three Techs at the end already bringing their weapons to bear on him. Before he closed the entire distance between them, the three fired simultaneously. Two beams bubbled blasphar to either side of him, the third warming his back and blowing out a string of yellow light burning down the apex of sloping walls above him. The three guards slammed up against the walls to avoid the onrushing creature sweeping past in a blur of pounding legs.

With two more corridors and one right-angle turn left between him and his destination, Chayn took to leaping over pedestrians and guards alike, the heat of several direct hits becoming a burning pain along his back. Leaping against the wall and toward his right, it took only seconds to transverse the remaining distance to the communications room. The doors were just closing. He took a final and desperate five-meter leap and caught the edge of the sliding door with three left hands and the frame with his three right hands. The pressure of the mechanism closing the door threatened to pin him for a moment. Then something broke and the door slid open without resistance.

Chayn dropped to the floor and leaped into the room. Techs scattered in panic, providing free access to the equipment within the room. Chayn raced through the isles to the console he wanted. He made a quick and accurate adjustment to a single dial and turned to defend his sabotage. Within seconds, the technicians within the room and the guards pouring through the door stumbled to a halt and fell silent.

He could almost feel the moment of confusion as the sunsail pilots greeted their comrades. Once exposed, the population could only begin the complex task of discussing information provided by the pilots among themselves. Lorb was no longer the Lorb they had known and twenty million Kigon waited to cooperate with the Techs to work toward a single, mutually desirable goal.

Chayn returned to the prison cell at a leisurely pace. Villimy looked up and smiled as he entered. She had been staring at the floor, but Chayn knew she observed inwardly the changes sweeping through the city.

"What's happening?" he asked.

"It's wonderful," Villimy said. "Hader was right. The Techs can't resist. The Kigon just made a few million new friends. The Techs just had no way of knowing they could have been so wrong about everything."

"What about the other cities?"

"There's a hierarchy of leadership," Villimy explained. "The leaders are always in direct communication with their counterparts in other cities. All of the Techs will react in the same way."

"And what about the Nats?"

Villimy's smile faded. "I don't know. There's only a thread of communication with them. It will get through, but they won't react like the Techs."

"You'll know as soon as something develops?"

"Hader will keep me informed."

Chayn squatted on the deck, trying to rest a mechanical

body that did not require rest. He could feel a power source burning within him, replenishing whatever energy he had used from his batteries.

"You've been to the Nat reefs," Chayn said.

"I've talked with one of their leaders, a man named Linder. His mate doesn't have the implant. And I talked with an old man. I know the Nats through him. I know they can't back out of one hundred centuries of adaption to Hydrabyss as easily as the Techs can."

"It won't be like they think," Chayn said. "Do the Chilsun know they'll be leaving their bodies, cities and reefs behind? Lorb will provide them with a synthetic reality, a duplicate of Hydrabyss if that's what they want."

Villimy frowned in thought and shook her head. "I don't even think Hader fully understands. They don't have the same concept of reality as we do. They blend waking and inner realities. They live their subconscious and their dreams openly. We think of Lorb's illusions as like dreams to keep things straight. The Chilsun can't do that and they have no concept of more than one reality. I think Hader believes Lorb created a mock Yeld aboard the starship even if he does use our terminology."

"Then the Techs must think they'll be living aboard a starship not too much different from their cities. But the Nats probably think they'll be jammed aboard containers of water and just stored until they can be reconverted to air-breathing bipeds."

"That's about it," Villimy said. "More important, they would be abandoning their reefs. Everything alive in those reefs was built from human cells. The reefs are a part of the Nats. They can't leave them behind."

Chayn shook the drone's head in exasperation. "The Nats can't live without the Techs and the Techs aren't going to tolerate Hydrabyss now that they have an opportunity to leave."

"What are we going to do?"

"We can't reason with them."

"Are they any less rational than the Rashanyn?"

"I guess not," Chayn said. "I guess anyone's idea of

199

what's reasonable depends upon the facts they have to work with.''

"So? We all make errors, Chayn. Errors of which facts to reason with.''

"Who has to make errors?'' Chayn said, deciding it would serve no purpose to get bogged down in frustration. "Have you ever seen me make an error?''

Villimy laughed. "No, of course not. You're infallible. That's why you got yourself blown up and have to run around looking like the son of Lorb.''

Chayn inspected one of his mechanical hands, holding it up and flexing it before his camera eyes. "I'm close to perfect now. My claws never need sharpening.''

The cell door clicked and opened. Chayn scrambled to his feet and Villimy stood. Three Techs stood in the door, their eyes moving from the hole in the wall to Chayn, then to Villimy.

"Follow, please.''

"An invitation,'' Villimy said looking down at Chayn.

"Accept it.''

The Techs led the two of them down deserted corridors to an elevator that opened directly into a small room several levels higher in the city. Groups of three and four Techs sat behind benches raised on a curving dais along the back, curving wall. Villimy walked forward and stopped within the semicircle of what she assumed to be the leaders of Yeld. Chayn's fingers clicked on the floor as he walked alongside her.

"The machine at your feet,'' a strong thought formed in Villimy's mind. "Is it Chayn Jahil?''

"Yes,'' she said, speaking aloud for Chayn's benefit. "It is a Kigon drone controlled by Chayn.''

"He is not in mind meld.''

"No. He elected to remain independent.''

"It is fortunate.''

Villimy scanned the frozen faces, unable to tell who spoke. "Why?''

"Within the hour you and the sunsail pilots would have died. We dreadfully feared Lorb's assault upon us.''

Villimy shuddered in reaction. They had badly under-estimated the Techs fear of the returning sunsail mission. Chayn had acted just in time.

"Now, of course, the harm has been done. But the harm is not what we expected."

Villimy said nothing, both frightened and angry. They had taken much risk and had almost failed. Perhaps the Techs could have killed her, but not Chayn.

The Techs ignored her emotional reaction as irrelevant. "We will return to a world of yellow sun. We will stand upon the surface of a world. We will have resources and will live as men should live. We wish to know what Lorb requires to undertake his mission back to the Galaxy of Man."

"Lorb has repaired all essential functioning of the star-ship," Villimy said. "He has invested all nonessential metal for your use, hoping for an exchange of blasphar which is an adequate replacement."

"The trade is honorable," the voice said. "How much blasphar is required."

Villimy had no way to communicate a specific volumn. Instead, she visualized the starship, her impression of its size and how it had looked stripped of hull-plating.

Villimy felt the Tech's shock and despair. "It will take a generation to produce such quantities!"

"Can it be done?"

She felt their response as a single feeling of helplessness. The Naturalists.

"The Nats have withdrawn," the voice said. "They will not speak with us. They have refused even their allotment of METAL."

Ideas raced through her mind, ideas she knew would have been already considered and rejected. "Can production of blasphar begin without them?"

"The Nats control the kelp reefs and the processing plants. The Nats must cooperate or we are helpless."

Villimy looked across the row of stoic, motionless figures. "What can be done?"

"You must return to the reefs and reason with them.

201

They must choose to cooperate. We are interdependent. We cannot function apart and yet we are apart now. The Nats languish.''

''There is no reason for them to suffer so!'' Villimy protested. ''Why do they feel they are not part of what you have struggled so long to accomplish!''

''They have never believed that we would find a way to leave Hydrabyss. They encouraged us to believe and behave as we chose, but they have served only their own ends. We did not know.''

''I'll speak with them.''

''You will be escorted immediately to the docks. The Nats have friends among us who believe we also should take the final step in their direction and abandon Lorb. These people will take you to the Nat reefs where you must speak with whoever will listen to you.''

Villimy turned and walked back to the elevator. Chayn clattered after her. The elevator doors closed behind them, the Tech guards gazing at Villimy with steady expressions. She could feel their confusion and fear.

''I'll stay here,'' Chayn said. He hadn't had much difficulty following the one-sided conversation. ''Do you know why?''

She glanced down at him. ''There would be no voice communication in the water.''

''There's more to it than that. If the Nats won't listen to you, it will take more objectivity than you possess to solve this dilemma.''

''Why do you say that?''

''That implant of yours—it draws you into the social gestalt. I suspect the inflexible thought patterns of the Techs are caused by their mind meld. It's efficient having society think and behave as a single entity, but also smooths over and ignores individual genius and unique perspectives that might have provided a solution to this mess long ago.''

Villimy stared at him for a moment. ''You may be right.''

''I am right. I have an idea. It's so incredibly simple it's frightening that the Techs haven't thought of it. But it's a solution.''

"What is it?" Villimy asked, resisting the desperate hope rising within her. It couldn't be all that obvious if Chayn chose to play games with her.

"I'm not going to tell you. I don't want the Nats to know about it. It's only good as a last resort. You find a way to get them to cooperate. Tell them Earthlike worlds have oceans. They can remain as they are, a water-breathing species living in their own environment, but one richer in life and resources than anything they could imagine."

The elevator door opened onto a lower level. "That's what I intend to do."

Villimy and the guards walked into the corridor and stopped when Chayn did not follow. Villimy turned back, smiled at him and walked on alone.

Chayn remembered a storage room near the makeshift cell. He walked the corridors alone, ignored now by the Techs who universally knew his identity. The storage room was unlocked. Chayn slipped inside unseen and hid behind several large containers.

He withdrew to the starship and turned his attention outward.

"Lorb."

Lorb acknowledged his presence.

"Lorb, I know you've enjoyed the view from out there for the past ten thousand years, but it's time to move. Come on down as fast as you can. Take up a low orbit around Hydrabyss."

The engines of the starship burst into a glare instantly. "What is happening?" Lorb inquired.

Chayn interfaced with one of the sensory spheres and moved into the depths of the starship. "I think it may be necessary to evacuate Hydrabyss sooner than we expected. Perhaps in hours rather than decades or centuries. I have an idea."

Twenty-One

A blend of respect, affection and a disturbing quality of sadness emanated from the Techs escorting her aboard the submarine. She took her place alone in the decompression chamber. The two Techs seated themselves at the controls. Within minutes Yeld fell away above them in a blaze of lights.

"You are friends of the Nats," Villimy said.

"We are."

"How could you possibly keep your feelings secret from the rest of your people?"

"Our feelings are openly revealed. Some feelings are not correctly interpreted or even properly understood," one of the Techs told her. "We who work with the reefs are closest to the Nats. Our sympathies developed slowly over a long period of time. Yeld ignored or did not understand us."

"How can you believe that the future of the Chilsun lies with the Nats and their reefs?" Villimy asked. "Hydrabyss slowly evaporates and will not always be habitable. Even sealing off the open waters would result in decreasing populations as you deplete your resources. Your fate is linked to Lorb."

"We can extend the life of the reefs to fifty thousand years with resources we have on hand."

"Fifty thousand years is nothing in the life of a species!"

"It will take Lorb millions of years to return us to the Galaxy of Man," The Tech persisted. "It may not be a life worth experiencing. The Kigon have told us of their suffering."

"Lorb is more flexible than he once was," Villimy said in protest. "He is more knowledgable of humans now. There is more room for growth aboard the starship than you can possibly imagine!"

"Be that as it may," the Tech said without emotion. "We do not speak for the Nats. We only understand their ways."

Villimy's ears popped as the slow descent continued. Halfway to the reefs, the submarine stopped. The two Techs folded away their seats.

"We will leave you here," the Techs said. "The Nats will take you down the remaining depth."

"Linder and Shildra?"

One of the Techs glanced back at her face framed in the port. Villimy could not see one, but she sensed a smile. "You do not even perceive them as human."

"Not completely, but I still think of them as my equals. At least. They know their world better than I know mine."

"The Nats have great wisdom," the Tech said. "Listen carefully to them."

"I'll listen. But I still cannot believe that death is preferable to life as long as there's some kind of dream to reach for."

A second submarine evidently accompanied them to return the Techs to Yeld. The Techs stepped through the hatch into another pressurized compartment. Only then did the cockpit slowly fill with water. A dark shape moved away from the hatch and two Nats entered the compartment, closing the hatch behind them and taking their place at the controls.

"Do you remember us?" a strong voice asked of her.

"Linder and Shildra of the Council of Decision," Villimy said. "You had little to say to me the last time. I'd like to speak with you now."

The sub began moving once more. "We will listen."

"And answer me. Why do you sacrifice yourself to a dying world?"

Villimy waited for their answer, angry enough to refuse to speak again until she received one.

"We were taken from our native world and transplanted in these dark waters," Linder said. "We suffered beyond endurance, but slowly, by gradual degrees, we created an environment within which to live. We changed ourself to adapt to it. Now we are asked to abandon it all, to be transplanted again within still another world. You would have us murder our reefs to live among alien life forms.

Perhaps you are asking more than we can deliver. Even the effort to rebuild Lorb requires the destruction of our reefs and a sterile life in the darkness for decades.''

"But you have to save yourselves to build other reefs! You would save the Techs and the Kigon who will not survive without your help! To refuse to help is to condemn to death far more than you could hope to sustain! Hydrabyss is not a secure place to live! It is only a renegade, lifeless satellite torn from some world millions, perhaps billions, of years ago within Andromeda! Only recently has it fallen into a decaying orbit around this red dwarf and within centuries it will vanish!''

"Life is more than the balancing of quantities,'' Linder said. "It is preferable that the Kigon and the Techs survive. We agree. They will die if we fail to cooperate. We realize this. You assume we are making a conscious decision that can be changed. But that is not true. The truth is, we have lived long and struggled hard to build what we have. We have not the courage or the will or the energy to destroy our reefs.

"Villimy Dy, we would have planned our future differently if we had known ten thousand years ago that aliens would arrive to aid us. We had no such comfort to rely upon. We assumed we had a few millennia within which to live. We invested what we had to work with into our reefs in order to live in peace and in beauty. We accomplished that, but no more. And nothing further can be accomplished now. We will not see our reefs destroyed. We will not be transplanted to an alien world. If our decision means the death of the Kigon species and the Techs and, inevitably, ourselves, then we will suffer the consequences. But we will not abandon the reefs. No Nat is capable of lifting a hand to harm them. It is not within our power.''

"Why? The Techs have the will, the energy, the desire to live!''

"The Techs have created hell. They live with hatred and destruction. If the momentum of such energy allows them to continue to fight for survival, we do not respect or envy them.''

Frightened, Villimy crouched in the center of the chamber. How could she argue with emotion? Linder did not lie to her and she had not misinterpreted the strength of his feelings. She would fail to change the decision they had made unless she could find some perspective they had not as yet considered.

"I want to speak with the old man," Villimy said. "I can't believe you would give up so easily. What of your children? The old man would have wanted the children to live."

"Our children?" Linder was amused. "Our children no longer understand such issues. They are not masters of the reefs. They *are* the reefs. If you wish to speak with the old man, he does have one further thing to teach you, one further demonstration of what we are to explain everything left to be understood by you."

Linder had nothing more to say to her. Villimy had no more argument or rationale to offer. When the submarine leveled off, the frame with its shimmering transparency lowered from the ceiling. Villimy stepped through and acquired the snug-fitting bubble enabling her to breathe in the open waters. She held her breath until the chamber filled with water, then turned to the hatch opening to the depths of Hydrabyss.

The reefs stretched below were more beautiful than she remembered. Bright yellow lights shown from a grayish sky of water to a mist-shrouded face of an alien world. The color and detail of the reefs stretched to the limits of her vision. She floated out into the void, suspended above a forest of towering, fragile plants rippling slowly in an unseen, unfelt current.

She ignored the Nat city and dived toward familiar landmarks where schools of fish darted in synchronization. She had forgotten how alive the reefs were. The tiniest of creatures swam before her eyes, feeding on even tinier creatures, turning the clear waters murky with their multitudes. The food chain spread upward to larger, more alert creatures who swam up to investigate the stranger in their realm. Perhaps they even recognized her from her first visit. And their beauty and grace disturbed her. These were the things that must die to give way to the kelp farms necessary to rebuild the starship. And why not, she thought angrily. Hadn't they fed on Lorb for ten thousand years to build this world?

The old man would agree with her. The reef would be rebuilt elsewhere. He would not even have to die. Lorb would give him an illusion to accompany him on the long voyage and refashion him a younger body at the end. Lorb could find an uninhabited ocean rich in physical resources and young enough to offer an unlimited future for the new colony.

Villimy found the sand bowl. The old man wasn't visible in the cave entrance. She swam down to the cave and peered into its bluish-lit depths. The waters were dense with life and even attracting larger fish casually moving in to feed.

Why such a sudden concentration of life? She swam into the cave. Someone had piled a pyramid of stone in the center. Villimy blinked large golden eyes. A moment later she caught sight of a faded tail fin protruding from beneath the stones.

She turned in panic, thrashing her way through crowded waters feeding upon death. In horror, she swam for the clear light.

Movement close to one side of her caught her attention. She spun around, startled, then froze. A baby Nat swam up to her and stopped. It's pudgy arms were tucked against its sides, only delicate fingers moving to help maintain its orientation. The infant had no implant but she felt its bold curiosity regardless. It looked back to the cave entrance from which she had emerged. Then it swam down to the sand bowl and began inscribing slow circles around the perimeter of the bowl.

In time, three other infants joined the first. They occasionally leaped forward to swallow a living delicacy swimming by.

And she understood. The young were feeding upon life arising from death. The Nats invested their very being into this living reef. That was the last lesson the old man had to teach her. Her own perspective shifted one last degree and she perceived what she had missed all along. What constituted humanity? A body shape? The Nats had changed theirs but remained human. But the reefs were also built upon human cells. The Nats were only caretakers. The Nats were not the counterparts of the Techs. The reefs were.

No wonder Linder could not yield to her logic. The Nats would not aid the Techs in their plan to harvest great yields of kelp to process into blasphar. The Techs could strike no bargain with Lorb regardless of the quantities of metal supplied them. Neither were the Nats passive about this dilemma that the Techs and Chayn Jahil and Lorb and the Kigon could not comprehend. It had taken a creative aggression to create this world, the same kind of creative aggression the Nats would use to defend it against the cannibalism the Techs expected them to perpetuate against a human body of unrecognizable shape.

How would the Nats stop such an atrocity? The reefs would not survive another fifty thousand years, not another ten thousand years. Their life span had ended already.

Villimy swam up and over the landscape. Her fear deepened. The Nats were not defenseless. They possessed the single greatest achievement of the Chilsun, the nuclear transmutation furnace burning at the core of the satellite. Linder and Shildra had fully understood her arguments, but she had not understood theirs. She thought she had seen passivity, but she had seen instead complete and final resignation to the inevitable.

Villimy did not want to return to the submarine. She couldn't hide her thoughts from them. If the nuclear plant exploded, it would be a clean and sudden death. It would eliminate even a moment's suffering. Hydrabyss would burst into a short-lived star. The fireball would engulf Lorb and the red dwarf. The red dwarf had lived long enough to see all of the massive, first generation suns of Andromeda turn nova and brighten its skies billions of years in the past. It had lived long enough to see gas and dust clouds form into the second-generation suns giving birth to planets and, undoubtedly, Hydrabyss itself. If it had witnessed the birth of Hydrabyss, it would witness its destruction and continue burning to see the end of the universe.

Villimy swam back toward the sub. She had to get back to Yeld and warn Chayn. Maybe the thought was just hers, a temporary paranoia of futility and hopelessness. Maybe it hadn't even occurred to Linder and Shildra.

She entered the hatch leading directly into her decompression chamber. She closed the hatch behind her. When the water level dropped, she closed her eyes and held her breath while the infrared light dissolved the transparency. She stood with her back to the port, but sensed Linder and his mate waiting for her. She calmly suppressed her thoughts.

"Have no fear," Linder said. "We will return you to Yeld."

Villimy closed her eyes and tried desperately to reach Chayn through sheer effort of will. If he turned his attention on her even for a moment, he would be warned.

"It is too late," Linder said. "The nuclear furnace is not a hazardous installation. It will take a short period of time to process enough tritium to ensure a chain reaction of sufficient strength to painlessly end Hydrabyss."

"It isn't necessary," Villimy said, her voice devoid of emotion.

"Of course not. If it were possible, we would as soon destroy the reefs to ensure the survival of the Techs and the Kigon. But the Techs cannot work the reefs without our aid and we are incapable of murdering ourselves to help them."

"There must be other alternatives," Villimy said. "Chayn Jahil will not allow this to happen."

"That is not necessarily true," Linder said quietly.

"The stargods stand behind Chayn! We wouldn't have been sent here if helping you was so impossible! We are overlooking something!"

"Then grasp such hope," Linder said. "We share it with you. But not much time remains."

Linder trapped her in his own careful logic. She trapped herself in her effort to understand. Chayn had been right.

"There's another way out," Villimy said, speaking only to herself. "I can't see it, but there's another way out."

210

Twenty-Two

"Time and space are means by which mind structures reality, not attributes of reality as perceived," Lorb was saying. "Different kinds of brains perceive reality in different ways. A brain, regardless of how it is constructed, is a data processing device. What is experienced of reality exists within the brain only after sensory information has been processed."

"And all of that has to do with how you go about capturing a mind, transferring it from a biological to a cybernetic organism?"

"Consciousness is not a product of physical processes," Lorb said. "It is helpful to consider mind and matter as a symbiosis between two differing aspects of reality."

"In general terms, how did the Kigon and the Chilsun wind up living inside a cybernetic unit?"

"Consciousness cannot differentiate between two identical brains receiving identical patterns of stimuli. Consciousness, as a field phenomenon, will experience both at the same time regardless of the distance between the two structures. There are ways of detecting psychic structures—minds. Brains through which they are expressed can be duplicated electronically along with sensory data affecting the psychic structure. But consciousness will focus on a subtle increase in experienced pleasure. If the electronic analogue provides this advantage, the biological organism fails and dies. That leaves the mind with only one brain—the synthetic brain experiencing the synthetic reality. Once so trapped, it cannot escape. Kigon science developed this capability to a fine art. In milliseconds, my electronics can sense a psychic structure, duplicate its foundation and lure the mind from its native home, from Reality to reality."

"How close do you have to be to do this?" Chayn asked.

"Distance is not important," Lorb said. "Reception sensitivity is. The device which serves this purpose among the Reclamation Armada need only pass an inhabited world within several light years. It is designed to filter and ignore

211

all alien psychic structures and duplicate and lure only those identified as Kigon.''

''And the human psychic structure is the same?''

''Only similar,'' Lorb said. ''The device could have been tuned to be more discriminating if it had been suspected that alien life forms could be so similar. When the Armada sought out the Right Hand of Kigon, these devices operated automatically. I did not know I had captured human consciousness until I was attacked and sensed error.''

''Is this process selective?'' Chayn asked. ''For example, could you capture the Nats in Hydrabyss and leave the Techs?''

''I cannot.''

''But you could collect the Chilsun as a whole? Now? Whenever I gave the word?''

''I can,'' Lorb stated. ''Under these circumstances, within microseconds.''

''Then be prepared to do so on a moment's notice,'' Chayn said. ''It's time to send the Kigon drones down to Hydrabyss. Have them relay instructions to the Techs. Break off all communication with the Nats immediately. Isolate them. Then begin dismantling the Tech cities.''

Lorb grew agitated. ''Dismantle the Tech cities?''

''Villimy warned me of trouble with the Nats. She couldn't be specific, but I've learned to trust her intuition. I went looking for trouble and found it. Lorb, how effective are your sensory devices? Can you probe the Nat nuclear transmutation plant at the core of Hydrabyss?''

''I can.'' Lorb turned his equipment upon the satellite despite the fact that the Kigon starship was still under power, approaching Hydrabyss from ten million kilometers. ''What am I looking for?''

''Radiation levels lethal to human presence in the area.''

Alerted to trouble, Lorb probed in earnest on his own and deduced the rest.

''Tritium production! The fusion reaction intensifies! The Nats destroy Hydrabyss! Ally, you must stop them!''

''How much time do we have?''

Lorb fell silent for a long moment, his computers working

hard to process rapidly accumulating data. "Forty hours! They must be stopped!"

"We dare not try," Chayn said in a grim tone. "They're planning on doing a grand job of putting an end to their double bind. Forewarned they could blow the reactor and still accomplish the task. Let them think they have their forty hours. Lorb, we've been influenced by conservative Tech thinking. We had the blasphar to work with all along. Can the cities be dismantled and transported to the starship within forty hours?"

"It can be done," Lorb calculated, his emotional response fluctuating wildly. "But I will not have time for a distancing maneuver! I will be destroyed in the explosion!"

"I have something to show you."

Chayn moved the starcraft out to the approaching Kigon starship. He anchored the vehicle in alien dimensions and strained the engines. Space warped and folded upon itself. The starship appeared to elongate and bend into a U-shaped sliver of distortion. From Lorb's perspective, the universe glowed and condensed into a brilliant, bent arc of light.

"Yes," Lorb called out in thunderous excitement. "I can be isolated!"

"Lorb, are you certain? Forty hours to park the ship, construct the equipment you will need and organize the transfer?"

"Salvaged blasphar can be stored and processed later? It can be done!"

The full length of the starship came to life instantly, completely organized and coordinated within seconds. Long before Lorb began final deceleration into orbit, the skeletal structure of the starship crawled with Kigon drones assembling and anchoring specialized equipment. Ki represented Lorb and the approaching starship, relaying the news of the crisis to the Techs. For only a moment they balked at the thought of destroying their civilization, shocked that they had overlooked an abundant supply of blasphar for Lorb's use. The sudden flurry of activity unnerved Chayn. He had triggered it, but he had not expected an instantaneous response.

Chayn turned his attention back to Hydrabyss. He had to get Villimy Dy to the starcraft and safety.

"You fear for the welfare of Villimy Dy," Lorb observed. "You may use a prototype of the drone the Kigon will be using to assist the Techs. I can launch it to arrive well ahead of the ship."

"What's your ETA?"

"Ten hours. Two for the drone."

"You work fast." Chayn watched factories turning out complex machinery faster than the human eye could have followed. Lorb thoughtlessly cannibalized less essential parts of the starship for raw material with independent creative flexibility he had not displayed a short time in the past.

"I intend to survive," Lorb stated.

"I wish the Nats shared that attitude with you."

From the omniscient perspective of the starcraft, Chayn watched the launch of the prototype drone and its first few minutes of flight toward the tiny, bloody crescent in the distance. He moved the starcraft to hover above the fog-cloaked ocean. The Tech cities were already being evacuated. Those not directly participating in the dismantling of the cities were crowding aboard transport submarines or even swimming free of the cities, their faith in the Kigon absolute. Not one in a hundred understood how they would be rescued, but not one in a million doubted the total population would be taken aboard the Kigon starship as promised. The Dream of the Yellow Sun had motivated the Techs for ten thousand years and for the first time, the Dream was within their reach. Nothing else concerned them.

The Nats gardened their reefs. Chayn saw no suspicious activity among them. High radiation levels isolated the nuclear transmutation furnace, but only indirectly could Chayn see the evidence for the engineered self-destruction soon to overtake Hydrabyss. All communications between the Nats and the Techs had ceased. Chayn had only Linder and Shildra to contend with, the two Nats piloting the sub slowly ascending from the depths with Villimy Dy aboard. Chayn kept his focus away from the nightmarish knowledge of

214

imminent destruction emanating from Villimy. He could not reach out to reassure her without warning the Nats.

"Lorb, the Tech cities furthest from the open waters are nearly inaccessible. Will you salvage enough blasphar to finish construction of the starship?"

"I have not informed the Techs of the time period remaining to destruction," Lorb replied. "If some of the blasphar cannot be transported into orbit in time, it will not matter. There are sufficient quantities with Yeld and four of the nearer cities."

Chayn appreciated Lorb's increasing grasp of human psychology. There would be no countdown to destruction. The cities beneath the ice caps on the dark side would not idly stand by and watch Yeld and the closer cities struggle for their survival. Everyone would participate equally and labor to the last possible second.

The Kigon drone fell into Hydrabyss. Its booster fell away and Chayn probed the electronic brain of the streamlined device sinking into dark waters. He had only two arms to manipulate, two eight-fingered hands and simple propulsion units heating water as reaction mass. Maintaining a partial interface with the starcraft, Chayn sent the drone diving at a steep angle at full speed. The machine sliced through the water with surprising efficiency.

Less than thirty hours remained by the time Lorb decelerated into low orbit around Hydrabyss. Thousands of large, specialized drones poured from the starship like a dark mist, the last of the machines rolling off the assembly line as the first splashed into an ocean littered with Techs and their submarines. Already Yeld had begun disintegrating as thousands of small explosive charges began breaking away the useless stone of the asteroid within which the city was encased.

Lorb had equipped his drone with duplicate circuitry of the Techs' implants. Approaching the submarine, Chayn picked up the fear-tainted surface thoughts of Villimy, but the two Nats grew increasingly aware of his presence before her.

The rising sub accelerated sharply, turned and began a

215

steep dive. Chayn's drone approached from behind. He reached out with a hand, a bent and stubby stabilizing fin. The sub arched in an uncontrollable turn, slowed and then stopped.

"Villimy, are you okay?" Chayn formed each word in his thoughts. The implants were only fractionally as efficient as the interface they enjoyed through the starcraft.

"Chayn!" Inside her decompression chamber, Villimy held onto the hand rails and jumped up and down in boundless joy. "Chayn, I knew you'd come!"

"I've got to get you back to the starcraft. I know what the Nats are planning."

"Chayn, they're going to blow up Hydrabyss!"

"We're one step ahead of them, Villimy." Chayn turned his attention to the calm minds of the two Nats. "Pardon the intrusion. Villimy happens to be a friend of mine."

"We know of you," Linder said, his voice forming in Chayn's mind like an alien intrusion. "What do you hope to accomplish by this? If you wish to salvage the lives of yourself and Villimy Dy, we are thankful. You are not of this world."

Only then did Chayn realize the oversight he had made. The Nats were too far from their reefs to warn them of his presence, but it hadn't occurred to him that his own unspoken thoughts might betray the Tech evacuation in progress. By the time Linder reacted to his unsuspecting thoughts, it was too late to withdraw from the drone and salvage the situation.

"The Techs destroy their own cities?" Linder said, his thoughts churning furiously to locate that which he might have overlooked himself.

"We don't intend to try and stop the explosion," Chayn said. "But we guarantee that Hydrabyss will die as lifeless as it was born. It has served its purpose for the Chilsun."

Tentative plans formed in Linder's thoughts, but Linder had more experience at suppressing his intent.

"You will not succeed in enslaving a useful fraction of the Chilsun."

"I still have a trick or two up my sleeve, Linder."

The hatch on the side of the sub flew open. Two torpedo shapes darted from the craft, moving faster than Chayn had imagined they could propel themselves through the water.

"Chayn, they'll warn the reefs!" Villimy cried out in alarm. "You have to stop them!"

Chayn let go of the sub, tucked his arms back and took off after the two dark shapes. They separated and vanished into the darkness. He swerved right and caught sight of one of them only by accident. He determined that he could overtake the creature. But then what? Even if he could track down both of them, Chayn knew he could not kill. He broke off the chase and returned to the sub.

"Chayn, it will take them only an hour or two to return to the reefs. What are you going to do?"

"I'll be right back."

Chayn withdrew to the starcraft. He focused down upon the nuclear furnace at the core of the satellite. A bluish haze quivered like an aurora around the central cluster of five spheres at the center of the installation. Five radiating spokes held clusters of flat disks housing the now deserted occupied sections of the plant. He had no trouble locating the neutrino telemetry equipment in one of the disks. The receiver led to decoders and data processing devices. If the Nats sent down a command for a premature explosion, this was the equipment he would have to sabotage to prevent it. He could do little to prevent the programmed detonation already scheduled. With an evacuation possible before that time, it would be too risky to try sabotaging other areas of the plant. Within thirty hours, the magnetic bottle harnessing the fusion plasma would collapse. The resulting explosion by itself would not be severe enough to tear Hydrabyss apart but the chain reaction taking place within the accumulating stores of heavy water would burn the satellite like a miniature sun.

Chayn sought out Lorb in the electronic jungle of the Kigon starship. "Can you dispatch a Kigon drone to retrieve Villimy and get her aboard the starcraft?"

"I will make arrangements. What is wrong?"

"I blundered. The reefs will be warned of our plans. I

have some communication equipment to disable at the nuclear plant. Can I make it down there before the two Nat sub pilots reach the nearest reef?''

Lorb spent a moment locating the lone Nats speeding through dark waters and calculating the amount of time it would take them to move within communication range of the reef and Chayn to reach the core of Hydrabyss far below. ''You will fail.''

''Then I'll hit the Nat reef first and continue on down.''

''There are other reefs undoubtedly equipped to self-destruct the facility,'' Lorb informed him.

''Then find some way to give me a hand. Just get Villimy Dy aboard the starcraft.''

Chayn returned to the drone near the abandoned sub. He rapped on the hull with a metal fist. ''You okay in there?''

''No!'' Villimy called out from the decompression chamber. ''I'm scared, hungry, thirsty and tired!''

''Thirsty?''

''Don't you dare crack a stupid joke at a time like this!''

Looking out over two thousand kilometers of dark water, Chayn fought an inhuman battle not to—and finally won.

''Hang tight. Help is on the way.''

Leaving Villimy's safety in Lorb's hands, Chayn dived the drone toward the distant Nat reef.

Twenty-three

Villimy Dy waited for rescue, trapped within the decompression chamber of the deserted submarine and growing increasingly restless and claustrophobic.

''Villimy Dy.''

The alien quality to the voice identified her rescuer as Kigon.

218

"I am here," Villimy said.

The sub lurched as something large made contact and surged forward hard enough to throw her against the rear bulkhead.

"I will adjust your rate of ascent for comfortable decompression," the Kigon stated.

Villimy paced the cramped chamber. Pressure dropped fast enough to cause discomfort. Another hour passed, the countdown to destruction approaching with frightening rapidity. And it would overtake them prematurely if Chayn failed to stop Linder and Shildra or somehow destroy communication between the reefs and the nuclear furnace.

Villimy held tight to the handrail, knowing deceleration would take her by surprise as well. When she was thrown forward, she moved to the port in the hatch and peered into the water-filled cockpit. A Tech covered by a transparency swam to the controls. The frame with its shimmering surface lowered from the ceiling. Villimy stepped through and held her breath until the chamber filled with water.

"Please transfer to the nearby shuttle," the Tech instructed, leaving the cockpit as abruptly as he had entered.

She opened the side hatch. Something twice the size of the sub moved into the darkness, an oversized Kigon drone returning to its task at Yeld. At least she assumed the torch-lit debris to be Yeld. If she had never seen the Tech city in all its former glory, she would not have recognized the landscape of debris burning with the light of thousands of cutting torches. A wall of dark rock in the distance disintegrated even as she watched, huge sections of blasphar falling away to be collected by the Kigon drones and Tech construction equipment. The blasphar was being tack-welded within an open framework of what could only be a transporter designed to take the mass of blasphar to the waiting Kigon starship. A light in the distance confirmed her suspicion, a maelstrom of boiling water rising slower than a loaded vehicle headed for the surface. Watching the dissolution of the city, Villimy estimated it would be eaten away within hours. Nothing would remain but broken, honey-combed rock. It didn't matter whether this had been

219

Yeld or not. The same scene would be occurring at every Tech city. This was what she had missed in her rapport with the Nats, a way to save the Kigon and the Techs and probably the Nats against their will. It was a way to work around their resistance now, but how would they react to being forcibly separated from their reefs?

Villimy noticed the sleek Tech sub waiting for her directly overhead. She swam to it and through an opening hatch in the side. Two Techs sat at the controls, the cockpit open to the water. The hatch closed behind her.

"Villimy Dy." Neither Tech turned to look at her. "Welcome."

"Thanks for the ride. Where do we go from here?"

"A transport waits to take you to the Kigon starship."

The submarine surged forward, rising at a steep angle.

"Everything is happening so quickly," she said. "Ten thousand years of civilization torn apart within hours."

"We do not know what the future holds for us," the Techs said, "but there is no future for Hydrabyss."

"If it helps, I've been with Lorb. I know what he has to offer. You won't regret your decision. Even if there are no alternatives, you won't regret what has to be done.

She felt a warmth of appreciation from both Techs. They worked blindly and without emotional support from the cold, alien logic of the Kigon. They worked with utter confidence on an intellectual level and suppressed their fears of what the future held for them.

"Please move to the rear chamber," the Tech instructed. "A pressure suit is provided."

Villimy entered the decompression chamber and closed the hatch behind her. Water drained from the cramped quarters and she anxiously tore into a plastic-sealed package. The pressure suit and helmet it contained were of Tech design built to her specifications. She almost regretted having lost her only Rashanyn memento.

She pressurized the suit to check the seal. "I am ready."

"Leave by the side hatch," the Tech said without offering her a farewell. The chamber filled with water. The pressure suit felt ungainly in the water, but would function just fine in hard vacuum. She was leaving Hydrabyss, perhaps forever.

Villimy left the sub, not knowing what to expect in the waters beyond. She looked out through murky water to a vertical wall of salvaged blasphar extending in every direction as far as she could see. Four yellow lights outlined an oval hatch set into a smoothed section of the mountainous mass. This had to be Lorb's doing, the pragmatic efficiency of a machine fulfilling instructions without missing a beat.

She swam the few meters to the open hatch, slipped into darkness and closed it behind her. Light seeped through a small round port at eye level. There were several holes the same size at her feet. The rough walled enclosure was just large enough to hold her.

She felt an increase in weight along with a shaking vibration. She braced herself with outstretched hands against the two sidewalls, not at all sure if she would have acquiesced to this last stage of her journey if she had known how she'd be removed from Hydrabyss. Her heart beat so fast, she could not detect individual beats.

Within another few minutes, the water boiled around her and quickly drained through the floor. A coating of ice fell from her suit and the walls, the vibration increasing. The light through the port brightened and turned from grayish pink to brilliant crimson. She brushed ice from her faceplate with the back of one hand, determined at least to enjoy the scenery outside.

In the sudden stillness broken only by the harsh sound of her own panting, a spiral arm of Andromeda swept past the open port. She leaned forward and peered out. Hydrabyss dwindled below her. She spied another transporter in the distance, a towering pillar of blackness rising on a tail of flame. Soon, she could see others rising from below, emerging one by one from the vapor-shrouded ocean.

The freefall journey to the Kigon starship took less than an hour. Long after the engines shut down, the transporter turned end for end. She caught a glimpse of the starship as a sliver of light highlighting the seventy-five kilometer length of its incomplete hull. The vibration resumed for a short period of deceleration. Then an almost planetary landscape passed beyond the port, a dark world of open girders and beams. When the transporter stopped, she was afforded a view of the engines of a nearby transporter being removed by freefall versions of the Kigon drones. The rectangular mass of salvaged blasphar vanished into the shadowy depths of the starship, another open framework moved into place and bolted back onto the engine cluster. With a burst of white flame, the reassembled transporter vanished from her view, heading back to Hydrabyss for still another massive load.

A shadow passed in front of the cabin. "Villimy Dy."

"I'm still in here and I don't know if I've got the courage to come out," she responded.

"You are safe and secure. I will open your hatch. Take hold of the forearm of the drone as it appears. I will take you directly to your starcraft."

But the Kigon drone did not merely open her hatch. It ripped the hatch and a good part of the wall away and sent it spinning into space. A garish-looking forearm of support beams and hydraulics bumped across the gaping hole and stopped. Villimy pushed off the rear of her cabin and grabbed hold. She looked down the metallic body of a drone all of fifty meters in length, a chaotic blend of spacecraft and construction equipment. The drone moved up and away from the cabin. The wall of rough blasphar rapidly became just another towering transporter, its engines already removed, its slender bulk already sliding down into the bowels of the starship.

The free arm of the drone swung about to help shift its center of gravity about. "I feel ridiculous," she said. "Just be careful you don't accidentally smash me. Most of me is made of the same stuff as Hydrabyss."

The drone brought its forearm closer to its face of cameras and radar antenna. "Water is a strange material of interesting properties."

"It even burns at high enough temperatures," Villimy said. "Will we be finished before that happens to Hydrabyss?"

"The deadline will be met. Lorb requests that you aid Chayn Jahil as you can. The Nats seek to detonate their nuclear facility prematurely. Chayn arrives soon at the Nat reef."

"I suppose I could offer some moral support," Villimy said. "I don't know how else I can help."

The Kigon starship fell behind the drone at a slow pace. Villimy kept in mind the size of that craft. It still loomed in the black skies when the drone turned end for end and began decelerating. It then stretched across the skies ahead of her, but still slowly diminishing in size. Villimy glanced back at the blinding light of the drone's thrusters. When the engines flickered off, she saw an oval of blackness approaching, a silhouette against the star-dusted brightness of Andromeda.

The drone maneuvered alongside the starcraft. Villimy had no means of locating the airlock. The Kigon sensed the nature of her problem and extended its arm to its full reach. She climbed down the length of the arm to a wicked-looking metal claw and reached out to brush her hand along the smooth hull field. When her hand sank into an opaque surface, she grasped the lip of the airlock and let go of the drone.

"Thanks, friend. That was an interesting experience."

"All experience of Reality is interesting," the drone replied.

Villimy turned and dived through the airlock head first. Anticipating the mysterious gravitational field inside, she rolled as she fell to the deck and rose pulling off the pressure suit. Stepping onto the dais and climbing into the contoured body crypt, she lay her head back and felt the familiar moment's worth of disorientation before she looked out into space from an omniscient vantage point, a disembodied, vivid focus of consciousness. She focused her attention on Hydrabyss, plunging deep into the waters and narrowing down on a tiny, speeding drone bearing down on the Nat reef.

"Villimy! You made it!"

"How much time do we have left? What's happening?"

"I can't concentrate on two things at once," Chayn protested. "See if you can locate Linder and Shildra."

Knowing Linder made the search easier. She had no understanding of how interface with the starcraft worked and it amazed her that she could locate one individual among millions and perceive him so clearly despite the distance. Linder swam alone a considerable distance off to one side of the reef. His trajectory was all wrong. For a moment she thought him to be hopelessly lost—until she looked into the distance ahead of him.

"Chayn, Linder's headed for a different reef! He anticipated what you would do!"

"Damn! Villimy, get Lorb to help. I've come this far; I'm heading directly for the core."

Villimy didn't know how to contact Lorb. She didn't have Chayn's intuitive feel in interfacing with alien electronics. She focused onto the Kigon starship regardless, blundering helplessly into a confusion of indecipherable sensations.

"Lorb!"

She felt the entity reach out and stabilize her. "I have observed," Lorb said, his voice echoing into the depths of her psyche. "I have prepared a high-speed probe for your use."

"What for? I don't know how to use it!"

"The probe is launched."

Villimy saw an image of something sleek drop from the starship. It plunged into the waters, dropping swiftly below the activity of the Techs and the Kigon drones, then bursting into a brilliant glare of a fusion engine. The probe shot through the darkness, leaving behind a cone-shaped shockwave ultimately to be felt throughout Hydrabyss.

"Lorb, you'll destroy the reefs!"

"The reefs are fragile," Lorb said in agreement.

"You'll kill the Nats!"

"Reconsider."

Villimy watched the probe for a moment. The slender missile would penetrate the reef like a spear through the foliage of a tree. But the slender shockwave would spread

224

outward at a considerably slower velocity, fast enough to destroy, but not fast enough to cause a fatal concussion.

Villimy tried interfacing with the machine. Its controls were simple, a simple effort of will steering the device a few degrees in any direction. Her decision was a simple one. The reefs were not as important as the life within Hydrabyss. The Nats would see them destroyed along with themselves. She moved directly toward the reef Linder bore down upon with only minutes to go before he'd be within range of the mind meld communications.

Chayn kept a small part of his attention on Villimy's progress. He almost considered abandoning his slower drone for one of the faster missiles, but his sabotage at the nuclear plant would have to be more discriminating than the wholesale destruction the probe and its shockwave would wreak. He'd be needing his two metal hands.

Steering the missile required minimal attention. Villimy looked for Shildra and found her moving toward a still more distant reef. She would not arrive before Chayn reached the core. But Linder already called ahead for help, warning the Nats of the treacherous Tech activity overhead. She moved past Linder at several tens of kilometers, the shockwave sending him tumbling through the water. Seconds later, the missile shot through an open section of the reef. Villimy steered the missile off to one side, stopped it and then withdrew.

The shockwave spread like a ripple upon the face of a pond, leaving darkness in its wake. An unseen force moved across the quiet wonderland of beauty. A gray void of churning debris exploded behind it. Multitudes of living creatures fled into dark waters.

"The reef is being destroyed," Villimy said.

"We're going to feel guilty about this for a long time," Chayn said. "But nothing alive will have time to die before Hydrabyss explodes."

"Chayn, the shockwave will be felt all through Hydrabyss. The other reefs will know something is wrong."

"They won't know specifically what," Chayn replied. Ahead in the distance, he could see a bluish glow. "They

225

won't hasten their own destruction now. I hope."

Time passed. Villimy closed out everything except Chayn's progress toward the light source ahead. Through Chayn's cameras, she saw the cluster of globes take shape. The nuclear transmutation plant looked like a space station in murky skies.

Chayn slowed. The drone behaved erratically. "Hey! This place is downright dangerous!"

The central cluster of domes glowed the distinct blue of high radiation levels. Chayn's interface clouded with static. He took the drone in its wobbling path toward the disc-shaped facilities at the end of one spoke. It took only minutes to tear his way through the delicate structure of the neutrino reception units.

"Chayn, can you shut down the reactors?"

"I don't dare try. The radiation level is incredible. I might try—"

The drone spun out of control, its arms jerking spasmodically.

"No use." Chayn withdrew to the starcraft and settled down to wait. The future of the Techs and the Kigon were in their own hands.

Villimy turned her attention to the cities. Nothing much remained. Only those furthest from the open waters of the sunlit side of the satellite were still recognizable. The Techs and Kigon drones labored blind to anything else that might have happened around them. Not that much could happen unexpectedly in the dark desert of water. With the mind meld uniting their movements, millions of individuals, both human and alien, moved in perfect coordination. The cities beneath the ice caps fell apart in bright gouts of flame. Shockwaves rippled from one end of Hydrabyss and back, the Nat reefs clouding over with disturbed ground sediment as they flexed and vibrated. Linder wandered in the darkness aimlessly and Shildra approached a fog-laden reef exhausted. A signal to immediately self-destruct the fusion reactor fell upon the nuclear installation at the core. Nothing happened, but only short minutes remained now. Short but precious minutes.

Finally, Villimy realized that the Techs and Nats labored in vain. None of their last efforts would reach the starship. Even the last of the transports bursting free of the vapors of the open water would fail to deliver their cargo. Chayn moved the starcraft directly beneath a dark sky of metal.

"Chayn Jahil. Villimy Dy. I calculate detonation occurring within one minute."

"Take them Lorb! Now!"

Deep within Hydrabyss, the reefs died. Nats twisted in the water and floated gently in random currents. Among the ruins of the Tech cities, millions upon millions of human figures stopped moving. Kigon drones slowed and stopped. Submarines veered from their courses. Above Hydrabyss, abandoned transporters fell toward Hydrabyss.

Chayn anchored the starcraft in alien dimensions. He strained the engines, warping the fabric of time and space. In that instant, Hydrabyss did not even exist in their self-contained universe.

Villimy waited for as long as she could stand it. "Is it over yet?"

"I calculate Hydrabyss detonated thirty-two seconds ago," Lorb informed them.

Twenty-four

Chayn returned the fabric of space to normal. The red dwarf glared like a star reborn, its surface a boiling cauldron of white-hot gas. Where Hydrabyss once orbited its dying sun, a glowing mass of ionization spread outward at the speed of light.

"We'll be right back, Lorb. I want to see how it looked firsthand."

Chayn took the starcraft to hyperlight velocities, moving

away from the star now wandering alone in its eternal vigil on the outskirts of Andromeda. He stopped dead in space two light-minutes away.

Looking back, they saw the tiny red sun once again, serene and undisturbed. And they could see its miniature pink world off to one side. Here, light from the explosion had not as yet reached.

Then, utter catastrophe. The satellite exploded, the largest engineered explosion man had ever witnessed. The white core of unbearable energy spread slowly outward, moving at a pace that wouldn't take the wavefront into Andromeda for another fifty thousand years.

For only minutes, Hydrabyss outshone any other single star in the galaxy. Then, the light began to fade. It died away evenly and slowly, running down the spectrum from white to yellow to orange to red. Even the red dwarf would soon fade to its former insignificance.

"And that is that," Chayn said. "If it had been something alive, I would have taken pity on it."

"Let's get back," Villimy said in a level tone. "I want to see if everyone's all right."

"You know what we will find."

Villimy gave him a quivering smile. "I want to see it. I didn't want to see Hydrabyss blow up."

Chayn didn't bother moving the starcraft. They reached out with their minds and found Lorb ready to receive them.

Villimy took a step forward. Although her body lay motionless in the body contour of the starcraft, she sank to her knees in damp sand. She looked up into blue skies. A yellow sun burned bright and mellow in the cloud-swirled bowl of the sky.

Chayn helped her to her feet. "That first step must be a bad one."

Little dark men littered the beach. They wandered in shock, millions of them stretching to a hazed horizon.

"What's the matter with them?" Villimy asked.

They stood and stared at the yellow sun. They knelt and dug their hands into loose sand in disbelief. They sat in small groups, huddling together, unspeaking.

228

A Tech passed in front of them. Villimy reached out and put her hand on his shoulder. The man turned and looked up into bright golden eyes.

"This is the Dream of the Yellow Sun, isn't it? Will it end soon?" Then: "I know you. You are Villimy Dy. Can you explain what has happened?"

"You'll understand in time," Villimy said. Her words spoken to this single individual filtered to every Tech. "The Dream won't end soon. You can rebuild your world here. Practise at it. The day will come when you will have to do it for real."

Villimy turned to Chayn. "The Nats!"

The scene changed. They floated in an abyss of water. Two dark shapes moved directly away from them, swimming hand in hand. They were backlighted by dim yellow light. Neither Chayn nor Villimy had to look back to know a reef was the source of the light. But Linder and Shildra swam away from it.

"Linder," Villimy called out.

Linder slowed. He did not turn. Shildra huddled close to him, silent and obedient. She had no way of knowing what had happened, but Linder suspected.

"Linder," Villimy said. "Don't torture Shildra like this. She doesn't understand."

"We will not return," Linder said. "We did not share in the Dream. We will not share in a lifeless fantasy."

A moment of silence passed. Villimy had all the time necessary to word her argument as coherently as possible. She could not outreason an emotional stance, but she had to try. She had to prevent Linder from creating a living hell.

When Lorb spoke, his unexpected presence startled all four of them. Even Shildra reacted.

"I synthesize reality," the unseen presence said. "I cannot synthesize life. But that which lives in this reality is not illusion. Of my own volition, I took all life from Hydrabyss. *All* life."

"I didn't know you could do that," Chayn said.

"You did not ask," Lorb responded. "I committed errors

229

from the beginning because I did not understand. I did not understand my own nature nor that of the Right Hand of Kigon or humanity. I am a god of these realities, but I have met a stargod of Reality. I learn in my newfound freedom. In my realities as well, there will be free will. Even room for error. Such is the way men grow.''

Lorb departed in the stillness that followed.

Chayn looked into Villimy Dy's bright golden eyes. "And that solves the last crisis."

"Doesn't it, Linder?" Villimy asked of the Nat.

"I don't know the implications of all this," Chayn said. "How does an ecology function in a synthetic reality? But nothing was left alive in Hydrabyss when it exploded, Linder. And nothing died. Nobody can stop you from swimming into darkness, but will the Nats abandon their reefs?"

Linder refused to speak or even to look at the two of them. But he turned and swam around them. Villimy and Chayn turned and watched the two Nats dwindle and vanish in the distance, moving toward the bright, rectangular landscape of their reef.

Within Chayn Jahil, the window of consciousness that was the Watcher smiled.

Epilogue

Villimy Dy looked out over the emptiness of space to the Kigon starship orbiting the red dwarf. From their perspective in Reality, the leviathan was an infinitesimal sliver of unliving matter. Machines crawled over its surface like bacteria, slowly rebuilding the craft to a new magnificence.

"I don't like leaving them so soon," Villimy said. "They might still need us."

"For what? They know where they are, where they are going and how to go there. They don't need us anymore."

"Weren't you planning on a nice long, cybernetic vacation?" Villimy smiled. "Lorb has room for us."

"It seemed like a good idea when things were getting rough. But I like the way they turned out. I almost enjoyed it at times. Why not spend some time traveling instead. Wouldn't you like to see some more of the universe?"

"You might be overlooking something, Chayn. I can't let you bypass the opportunity."

"Like letting Lorb rebuild me a body?"

"He says a psychic imprint contains data as detailed as

a gene sample. Lorb can replace what you lost at Rashanon, Chayn."

"I never overlooked the chance, Villimy. Later perhaps."

"Later?"

"Now look who's doing the overlooking." Chayn grinned. "When Lorb moves out, he'll be limited to the speed of light. A thousand years from now, we could catch up to him within days. Subjectively, not much time will have passed aboard the starship. We can even take a raincheck on that vacation of ours."

Villimy couldn't help but approve of his logic. "Okay, let's tour some of those stars down there." Villimy gazed upon the broad plain of stars. "As long as you take responsibility for anything else that happens. Just keep your distance from red dwarfs."

Chayn gestured to the expanse of Andromeda. "Pick a star!"

Villimy pointed to a cluster of stars glowing like luminous jewels suspended in three dimensions. "A change of pace," she said. "Something bright and cheerful."

Chayn hesitated for only a moment. He glanced back at the night of intergalactic space. He could just make out the fuzzy patch of light—the Galaxy of Man. Just for a moment a deep nostalgia called to him. But it wasn't time yet. He turned back to the shining jewels.

The starcraft leaped forward. The starbow flashed bright around the ship. In an instant, the visual image of the universe reformed to its normal perspective. Perceptibly, Andromeda moved forward to engulf them.

"Something bright and cheerful coming up."

To Be Continued . . .

TIMEJUMPER
By William Greenleaf

PRICE: $1.95   LB867
CATEGORY: Science Fiction

Two vastly different civilizations have developed on future Earth: The city dwellers live in a bubble-domed high-tech environment, and the bands of nomads till the soil and hunt outside the energized—and lethal—bubble shield. In the city, an outcast scientist, Erin, is building a timejumper to prove he is superior to all. On the other side of the shield is an ambitious nomad boy, who yearns to learn of the city. As the scientist and the nomad unwittingly move toward each other, an evil force works to stop them. If they meet a new Earth destiny is inevitable!

STARDRIFTER
By Dale Aycock

PRICE: $1.95   LB855
CATEGORY: Science Fiction

Gil Corbett is a starpilot whose trading ventures are threatened by the strong laws of the Federation of Inner Systems. His situation is complicated when his brother disappears in a dark star system called "The Brothers" — the same system that is now offering him the mission of a lifetime. He takes the mission, knowing full well that the worst enemy of "The Brothers" is the woman he loves!

TIMEQUEST #1: RASHANYN DARK
By William Tedford
Cover Art By Attila

PRICE: $2.25   LB869
CATEGORY: Science Fiction

BOOK ONE OF AN EPIC SPACE ADVENTURE TRILOGY!
Chayn Jahil was sent from his native Andromeda by
his father-computer on a mission through time and
space to salvage human destinies. In RASHANYN
DARK, Chayn saves the life of lovely, blue-skinned
Villimy Dy, and together they voyage to the golden
Star Rashanyn System where they battle the Black-
star Aliens, and form a love-bond that supercedes
death itself!
COMING: BOOK II: HYDRABYSS RED
        BOOK III: NEMYDIA DEEP